A PROUDER MUSIC

A Prouder Music

JEAN RENNIE

WILLIAM KIMBER · LONDON

First published in 1988 by
WILLIAM KIMBER & CO. LIMITED
100 Jermyn Street, London, SW1Y 6EE

© Jean Rennie, 1988
ISBN 0-7183-0676-7

Typeset by Printit-Now, Upton-upon-Severn
and printed and bound in Great Britain by
Biddles Limited, Guildford and King's Lynn.

Contents

. . . . Now may my life beat out upon this shore,
A prouder music than the wind and waves can compass in
      their haughtiest mood.
I need no world more spacious than the region here:
The foam-embroidered firth, a purple path
For argosies that still on pinions speed,
Or fiery-hearted, cleave with iron limbs
And bows precipitous the pliant sea:
The sloping shores that fringe the velvet tides
With heavy bullion and with golden lace
Of restless pebble woven and fine spun sand.
The villages that sleep the winter through,
And, wakening with the Spring, keep festival
All summer and all autumn: this grey town
That pipes the morning up before the lark
With shrieking steam, and from a hundred stalks
Lacquers the sooty sky; where hammers clang
On iron hulls, and cranes in harbour creak
Rattle and swing, whole cargoes on their necks: where
Men sweat gold – that others hoard or spend –
And lurk like vermin in their narrow streets:
This old grey town, this firth, the further strands
Spangled with hamlets, and the wooded steeps
Whose rocky tops behind each other press,
Fantastically carved like antique helms
High-hung in heaven's cloudy armoury,
Is world enough for me . . .

From 'A Ballad in Blank Verse' by John Davidson.
Greenock Schoolmaster Poet. 1857—1909.

This poem is the cause, and the basis of this book.
            J.R.

Acknowledgements

I should like to acknowledge my indebtedness to the late Mr George Blake, Mr John Donald, the British Museum Libraries, the Librarians of the Greenock and Paisley Libraries, the Registrar-General of Shipping in Cardiff, the Editor and staff of the *Greenock Telegraph,* the National Maritime Museum at Greenwich, Margaret Steen, Mr Gabriel Setoun and finally –

In Dedication
To My Grandfather
who loved me very dearly

PROLOGUE

GREENOCK 1847

Like a glittering magnet, the Annual Fair in Market Street drew not only the local populace, the rowdy small boys, the farmers from the surrounding countryside, and sailors from the foreign ships at anchor in the bay. It trapped the refugees from starving Ireland, who had been pouring into the west coast ports of Scotland and England during the last two or three years, to escape from the Great Hunger of their own land. They laboured, they fought, they drank. They said Mass, and called invocations to their Gods. They sang and danced and loved; they mourned for Ireland and cursed the day they left her. But they stayed.

The surging crowds jostled and shoved in the glare of the gas jets and naphtha flares, and the din of the hooters on painted roundabouts jangled discordantly with the music of fiddles and concertinas, the screams and laughter of excited girls, and the shouts and ribald singing of the town drunks.

A small boy, ragged and pinched-looking, clutched the hand of the girl beside him as she talked to him. Half her mind was with the cluster of noisy, chattering girls nearby who were watching the merry-go-rounds, thrilled by the swaying crowds and the raucous shouts of the mob. She stopped talking as she felt the clutching of the hand on her skirt.

'Bridie! don't leave me! I'll work in service with you . . . Don't leave me!'

'Joe, I must. You'll be all right in the church with Father Manahan. Look, here's some money . . . ' She gave him a shilling, nearly all her week's wages.

She ran round by the blazing lights of the merry-go-round, her eyes glittering with tears. In all her 17 years she had known nothing but work and poverty, until she came to Greenock and was sent by her priest to service in the west end. This was a different world altogether. It hurt her bitterly that these people seemed to have so much, while her own family, and thousands of others, were starving to death. Her wages were £6 a year, paid quarterly. She sent £1 home as soon as she was paid. But money couldn't buy the food that wasn't there, and the money didn't always arrive anyway. And then came the news, through Father Manahan, that the little croft had been burned down and mother, father and little Joe had been turned out onto the roads to die. By the time she got to Ireland, Robert Mulligan and his wife Anne were buried, and Joe was living, a small, quiet, fiery-headed ghost, in the Presbytery.

She brought him back to Greenock with her. They landed at the Old Quay with hundreds of other refugees, in the late evening of a June day. The next two nights, Joe had slept in the church hall on mattresses with other boys.

But the Annual Fair and Market came to town, and it was impossible for the west end ladies to keep their cheap, plentiful Irish slaveys away from the bright lights, and the only bit of excitement they had ever had in their lives.

So Joe stood there with his fists clenched in the pockets of his ragged trousers, and watched as she joined her friends. She turned and shouted something to him, but no word reached him. The girls gazed rapturously at the wild horses galloping round, and scampered away to the other displays.

A young man in rough, foreign, seaman's clothes, caught the flashing eye of Bridget as she passed; he had seen her turn when she called to young Joe. Their glances met and held. He turned to follow her as she ran, laughing, round the booths filled with gaudy trash, lifting her skirts to clamber over the shafts of the painted caravans.

He laughed too, when he caught her, for no reason except youth and excitement and the eternal challenge of the female to the male. His arms held her and she looked up at him, her face glowing with the wonder of some undiscovered feeling that seemed to melt her very bones.

In spite of the rough seaman's clothes, there was about him an air of confident authority. He stood six feet tall, with almost black hair and dark, steady eyes, and an unmistakable look of Spanish nobility.

He could walk with her, home?

*

Joe Mulligan stood and watched, petrified. He saw, dimly, the two figures clasped together, and he knew... He had seen mating before, of animals as well as humans, and he knew in that instant that his lovely sister was lost to him. He was wise beyond his years, and something in the tilt of her head, the glamour of the night, and the fiery glow all round him, told him that she would not come back for him.

He turned and ran. Ran along the riverside. Ran and ran till he dropped beside a bush with exhaustion. He slept till morning, and in the soft June air he looked back at the grey town, and then went on, keeping close to the shore, and walked . . .

He walked, over the next few days, down the coast-line, until he reached a farm, just over the hillside, in Ayrshire, near the straggling little village of Largs.

He never saw his sister Bridie again.

*

The way 'home' lay along the soft gloaming of quiet streets, to heather-covered slopes where the dignified mansions stood. She led him over the springy turf of the shelter of the Lyle Hill, in her mind the possible consequences of her late home-coming, in her heart exhilaration and excitement, and in her body a devouring passion that matched his own. She was innocent, but not ignorant.

Since she had arrived in Greenock in the cold damp of a Scottish winter, she had known nothing but long hours of hard work, an occasional meeting with her compatriots at Mass on Sunday, and the constant worry of the news from Ireland. The thrill of the cheap Fair, the touch of the boy's hand on hers, like a shaft of sunlight in a dark cellar, gave a glow to the flashing beauty of her eyes, a lilt to her voice, and a dance to her feet.

They came to the warm turf and bracken on the steep hill that overlooks the small bay at Cardwell. And it was here, on a June night fading into a June morning, that the bogs of Ireland and the vineyards of Spain were joined.

PART ONE

The Bog and the Vine

I

The cry of a new-born infant; the bark of a scavenging dog: sounds familiar enough among the dockside slums. The sounds came from a derelict wooden shed that served as a sleeping place for tramps and beggars, for promiscuous copulating and as a playground for small boys. On this bitter night in March 1848, it had become a rough, unprepared maternity ward.

The girl lay exhausted on a pile of sacks, and in the dim light of stray moonbeams struggling through a hole in the roof, her face was grey with accumulated dirt, pain, weariness and hunger. She had seen birth and death before: there was no mystery for her in this birth. She bit through the cord that bound the child to her and tied it with a string torn from her grubby petticoat, which she then wrapped round the baby. She gathered up the bundles of old newspapers and filthy sacks that had served as a bed for her labour. She would throw it all in the river, where she had intended to throw the child too.

All through the months of waiting, she had determined she would throw the child in the river, as soon as she could move, she said. She didn't want it: she could see no reason for its existence. She couldn't even remember what its father looked like, and the rapture of that June night was forgotten in the tears and misery of the bitter March winds. There was no place for her with a child dragging about her, so as soon as she could move, she said, she would throw the child in the river.

But the feeling of the soft, warm flesh of her daughter, new and beating under her hands, was a revelation that she had never expected. The child cried again, a weak, hopeless cry, and then it slept. Especially after that cry, she could not kill. There was only one way; she must abandon it, and leave it to the great heart of the townspeople, and if it died, then that was the end of it. So she told herself, as she pressed the small warm body close in to her. Her tears this time were pain of a different kind: a pain she had never known before, the pain that is remembered when the birth pangs are forgotten.

She cradled the baby in young, strong arms, and on the edge of sleep, she thought that she ought to have looked for young Joe. But where to look for a nine-year-old among the dark streets, through all the last winter? And she was too ashamed. Some day Joe would come back.

Before it was light, she woke. The infant was still asleep. She took off her jacket and wrapped it over the grey flannel petticoat round the child, laid her on the pile of sacks, and crept quietly out of the shed. Her slight figure was soon swallowed up in the icy mist that hung over the waterside.

A prowling dog, chasing rats, pawed the wrappings and made snarling jumps at the motionless bundle, until a woman who lived in a hovel nearby came into the shed and threw a brick at him. The dog cowered, but went on barking, and the woman scuffled over to the dark corner where he stood snarling. She kicked the dog away, and bent over the bundle.

The baby gave a feeble cry, and the woman waited. If she left the child, it would surely die, and that would be the best thing for it. Grumbling, and cursing, and still aiming kicks at the dog, she picked up the infant and took it into her own filthy hovel and washed it, and then, for several weeks, she lavished love and milk on it in enormous doses. Then she grew tired of it, and left it on another doorstep.

For the next seven months the child was passed from one doorstep to another – fed on watery milk or slops, or suckled at a whisky-sodden breast. On a raw misty day in autumn, the woman who carried the child on her arm wrapped in a shawl, came by the harbour at the Customs House Quay. As she stood there, she saw a ship a-sailing, at her prow the effigy of a woman naked to the waist, painted in bright, obscene colours. The ship's name, painted on the bows, was *ISABELLA*. This much the woman could read.

'Ah well, I suppose you'd better have a name of some kind. That will do as well as any other – seeing that nobody knows where you came from.'

The baby gazed up at her, her eyes wide in the ingrained dirt of her face. She looked resigned – as though she had heard it all before. Under the dirt the skin was clear, the perfect features free of the scabs and sores so common among the children of the dockside slums. She lifted her small grubby hand and thumped the thin breast, as the shawl was gathered firmly round her and the woman made her way wearily home.

Later that night, she wrapped the child in clean clothes and a ragged bit of blanket so that her tiny face and bright eyes were just visible. She walked quickly through dark alleys westward, to the streets where the tenements looked a little more respectable. She came to a quiet street of dull, grey stone buildings near the West Burn. There was no one about, and there were only the usual night noises, cats howling, the occasional clatter of broken bottles, some drunken cursing in the depth of dark corners – and angry snoring. She looked round hurriedly and went into one of the closes. She held the child tightly for a moment – she had fed her on a mash of biscuits and watery milk, and she should sleep till early morning when, before six o'clock, men would be turning out to work.

Inside the blanket was pinned a scrap of paper with one word scrawled across it. In crude, illiterate characters, it spelt 'Isabel'.

'There, my wee pet – I hope to God somebody will be good to you!'

She kissed the cheeks, rosy in slumber, and the softly-closed eyelids, and laid her gently in a corner, with her face to the wall and the shawl well over her head. Then the woman turned away, and went out into the night.

Thus, and thus, was this child of the river begotten, born and raised. The Irish colleen drifted – the Spanish seaman sailed back to his own life – and they were never heard of more.

Isabel took the best from both – she was the first fruit of both. She was conceived, if not in love, at least in high passion and all the splendour of clean, unspoilt youth. She thrived. Against all the laws of hygiene, dietetics and psychology, she lived, and thrived, and grew in stature and beauty.

Rats prowled by – mice scampered near the corner – but Isabel slept as though she were in a pink, satin-lined cot. Towards morning, she wriggled a little.

*

The first chill streaks of early dawn filtered through the rain-heavy clouds of a sharp October morning – before any lark knew that day had come. The tall, blackened chimneys of the iron-foundries belched smoke and soot, and steam whistles shrieked a warning to lazy sleepers. Robbie Munro clattered down the stone stairs three at a time – pulling on a greasy jacket, an equally greasy cap and a muffler all at the same time. The door had banged behind him, and his words were lost in the din of his hobnailed boots striking sparks from cold stone.

'Sure as God – I'll get the bag the day. If I just' (one more corner turned) 'get down as far as the Square, I'll be – God Almighty! – what's that?'

His foot kicked the bundle at the entrance. He would have rushed on, but the bundle gave an indignant squawk – and the boy stopped short, and bent over it.

'God help us! It's a wee bairn! What'll I do with it?'

He tore back up the narrow stairs, panting with excitement – and when he reached his own landing, he burst into the house with a deafening clatter. His words tumbled over each other, in the rough vernacular of his own people.

'Maw! Maw! There's a wee baby – a wee bairn doon at the foot of the stair. It's wrapped up in a shawl and it's lying there – it's just lying there – and it's greetin'! Maw! what'll we do with it? I'll be late for my work!'

'Mercy on us, son! What's the matter? A baby? What kind of baby? What are you talking about?'

'Come down and see. It's lying there. Hurry up – or someone else'll get it.'

'What do I want with a baby? I've enough bother with you and Willie. Oh well – I suppose I'd better come down and see. You get away to your work.'

Robbie clattered down the stairs again – later than ever because of Isabel. He raced along the Vennel, to the yard at the Victoria Harbour, and wriggled through a hole in the wall that gave on to the river, mingling with the hundreds of shuffling figures in the now nearly day-lit yard.

His thoughts were jumbled: 'Hope the foreman hasn't reached our shop yet . . . maybe I'll be in before him . . . that wee bairn . . . I hope my mother keeps it . . . I wonder what it is?'

He felt his face flushing as the implication of the last thought struck. At thirteen, you were just beginning to find out things. But this baby couldn't be like other babies, could it? They didn't usually come this way?

He reached the carpenters' shop, and peered round the door furtively.

'Come on in, Rob. He hasn't been round yet. Get over to your bench now – hurry!'

He grabbed a saw – and spent the morning with his thoughts on the little moving bundle in the corner. He learned very little about carpentry that morning.

When the echo of Robbie's thundering feet had died away, Millie Munro went quietly down the stairs and looked at the small, still bundle. She bent and picked it up, and gently eased the wrappings off as she walked slowly back up the stairs. She saw the scrap of paper, but she had never learned to read or write. She kept it, till Robbie or Willie should come home. Willie went out a little earlier than Rob to help at the nearest farm, in the Inverkip Road.

When he came back, about eight o'clock, he would go the Parish School for the morning, and then in the afternoon, he worked in the sheds, shovelling coal for the boilers in the great, dark, ugly sugar works near his home. Robbie could read and write a little, but Willie seemed to be learning more easily – it seemed to come more naturally to him.

Willie had just turned ten, and could only vaguely remember his father. Millie had lost her man, Donald, at sea. His ship had gone down with all hands, in a storm, and the owners had given her the astronomical sum of twenty pounds, which was presumably to feed and clothe her and the two boys, Robert, who was seven and Willie just four, for the rest of their lives. She hoarded it carefully, spent it frugally, and went on with her work. She took in washing again for the ladies of the West End. She scrubbed heavy clothes on her washing-board, boiled sheets and white linens in the boiler in the wash-house on the green, and sun-bleached them on the one patch of luxuriant grass that even stray dogs and cats seemed to recognise as a hallowed place. She crimped and goffered the maids' caps and starched their aprons. She pressed the gentlemen's dress shirts with her special polishing iron. And she kept her home, the wee kitchen at the top of the stairs, where they lived and slept and ate, spotless, aired and fresh – and brought up her two boys clean, and honest, and fearless. She was a tall, striking woman, neat and tidy rather than good-looking.

She looked at the child in her arms, and when she reached the kitchen, she took the wrappings off.

'A wee lassie!' she breathed; and just for one wild moment she cradled the child's head against her neck, in a gesture of possessiveness. The little one started whimpering, and Millie hurriedly replaced the ancient shift, making little sounds of disgust as she did so.

'Poor wee thing; you're not even clean, or bathed, and I'm sure you're hungry. I wish I knew what to do with you. *I* can't keep you. Now I wonder . . .'

She pondered for a moment, and the child, lulled by the comfort and security of her firm arms, and the warmth of the glowing fire, slept again.

'That's it . . . I'll go and see Flora McGarvie. I've got enough to do with Rob and Willie. Flora will be taken with the wee thing. There, there, my bonnie. Come away now, and we'll see Flora.'

She took her shawl, which hung on the kitchen door, and wrapped it round herself and the child, letting the weight of the baby rest on the folded shawl by her left arm. She opened her door, which gave straight on to the landing, where there was a lavatory on the left, used by the three families on that floor, and straight across lived Flora McGarvie and her husband, John. Millie tip-toed across and knocked on the door; then she pushed it open, and called into the small, dark lobby.

'Flora! Are you there, Flora? It's me, Millie.'

'Come away in, Millie; I've just finished the bed. Come away in . . .' She stopped short, and drew in her breath sharply.

'Millie! God's sake, Millie, what's that you've got?'

'It's a baby – a wee lassie. Didn't you hear Rob this morning? He found it at the close when he went to work.'

Flora stretched out her arms – and Millie saw the naked hunger in her gesture.

'Give her to me!' she whispered.

Flora was small and soft and clean, with the faded, once-fresh air of the Highlands about her. A tired little scrap of a woman, worn out with her attempts at motherhood; the still-born child – or the brief hour of a tiny life and its inevitable death – or the miscarriages that had spaced, at intervals, eight years of marriage. And now she was holding a real, living infant – and for a timeless moment, it did not matter whose it was or where it came from.

She moved over to the fire and sat down, with the baby on her knee – just holding it – just looking at it.

'What will we do with it?' said Millie, when Flora had settled in a low chair. 'There's this wee bit of paper, but I can't read it. Maybe Willie can read it when he comes home from school. Can you read it, Flora?'

'No, but John can. He'll read it when he comes home at dinner-time.'

She cradled the child in her arms, and her heart cried inside her for the dark beauty of the girl she would become. She could not look up at Millie. Deeply and fiercely she wanted this child, and she was afraid to show, too much, her need.

'Do you think we should take her to the police, Flora?'

Flora clutched the wee one closer, and looked at Millie in terror.

'The police? No! Millie! I want to keep her. They'll take her away from me.'

'What about John? Will he let you keep her?'

Flora's face smiled. Her whole face smiled. She said quietly: 'Aye. Oh aye! He'll let me keep her all right! Seeing we can't keep one of our own.' She sighed. 'Yes, we'll keep her – if they'll let us.'

'You'll have to tell the police, Flora,' Millie said gently. 'You can't just take a baby – like that – without some kind of . . . some kind of . . . law, or something. But *they'll* not want her, don't you worry. Another bairn on the parish? Not likely. But you'll need to make it all square and above-board, like. Anyway, see what John says, at dinner-time. I must go now – I've to go and get some washing. I'll come and see you after dinner-time. I'll away, Flora. Bye-bye.'

Flora nodded, wordlessly, all her attention on the child in her arms. She was fairly well cared for, at, Flora guessed, seven months old, even if she was very dirty in the soft folds of arms and legs and buttocks.

She lay now placidly in Flora's arms, gazing up at her as if fully conscious of the upheaval she was causing.

She held Flora's deep blue eyes with her own, brown,

wideawake, and almost, aware. She gave a deep sigh, and
then, as if feeling that life had been far too tranquil for
the last hour or so, she screeched. She howled and cried
and struggled to sit up in Flora's enveloping arms.
Instinct, not experience, came to Flora's rescue then.

She unwrapped the clothing on the child, and holding
her so that she looked over her left shoulder, she worked
quickly and quietly, moving about nimbly with soft
murmurings that gradually calmed the child's crying. The
whimpering faded to an occasional, contented hiccup,
the brown eyes focussed on the objects nearest, and the
small hand beat haphazardly on Flora's shoulders, as
though she knew her journeyings were over.

Isabel had come home.

II

When the whistles blew at twelve o'clock, Robbie and his
workmates clattered out of the yards, and ran most of the
way home.

One by one they separated, going in different
directions round the multitudinous corners. Coming at
last to his own 'close' he glanced instinctively at the
corner where the child had lain this morning, and with
renewed energy, scampered up the stairs and flung the
kitchen door open.

'Maw! Where is it? Where's the baby?'

'Sit down and take your dinner, and be quiet. The
baby's all right. I took her to Mrs McGarvie.'

'Mrs McGarvie?' The boy's tone was incredulous. 'But –
but – she doesn't know anything about babies – she can't
look after it. Anyway – it was *mine*. I saw it first. Did you

say . . . is it a wee lassie?'

'Aye, it's a wee lassie. And sit down and take your cap off – here's your soup. Mrs McGarvie will look after it – maybe better than anybody.' Her voice was quiet, and significant.

'How do you mean?'

'Never mind. Take your soup.'

'Well, can I go and see it . . . it . . . her?'

'Yes, you can go across to Flora's when you've had your dinner. Now, where's Willie got to?'

'Isn't he home from school yet?'

'No, and I want him to read this paper.'

'What is it?'

'This bit of paper that was pinned to the baby's shawl. I can't read it.'

'Let me see it. I can read a wee bit.'

Millie passed the scrap of paper to Robbie. He looked at it, and something – he was too young to know what – stabbed through his body. Pain – no, not pain – a quick sort of tremor that made his heart jump – and which ended in a flush that covered his face and neck. The scrap of paper, although he was no great scholar, having spent most of his schooldays up the burns, fishing, still told him all he wanted to know. He said the name in a kind of whisper:

'Isabel –'

'Is that what it is? Yes, we thought it might be a name of some kind for her. Is that all it says?'

'Aye, that's all.'

'Isabel. My, it's a bit high class, isn't it?' Millie laughed. 'There now. There's Willie. Come on, son – what's kept you so late? Haven't you been to school?'

'Aye. Where's my dinner?'

'And what did you learn today, Willie?'

'Oh, sums.'

'Is that all?'

'No, he was telling us something about history.'

'What's that?'

'Battles and Kings.'

'Maw! Can I go and see the bairn now?'

Willie looked up from his soup. 'What bairn?'

'A wee baby that was left in the close this morning. Didn't you see it when you went to school? You went out just before Rob.'

'No, I never saw anything. Where is it now?'

'*Mother!* Can I go now?'

'Yes – away you go. Wait a minute. I'll come with you.'

Halfway to the door, Robbie turned back, and strode to the sink. The cold water tap and soap did little to take the grime off his hands, but he seemed satisfied, and rubbed them on the towel that hung below the dresser.

'Come *on*, Rob – I've got a lot of washing to do yet.'

'All right; I'm ready now.'

'Can I come too?' Willie spluttered through a mouthful of soup and bread.

Rob turned at the door, and almost snarled.

'No! Not just now. Come on, Maw!'

'Gracious! You'd think you'd never seen a child before! What's up with you, Rob?'

Millie knocked when they reached Flora's door, and the boy scuffled his feet, and looked sheepish.

'I . . . I don't know. I just thought I'd like to see it . . . her, I mean.'

'Well, oh, there you are, Flora. Robbie wants to see the baby.'

'Come in, come away in.' Flora opened the door into the lobby, and whispered, 'John's got her. He's just fair delighted with her.' Then in a louder tone: 'Come away in, Millie. John, here's Millie and Rob. They want to see the baby.'

John McGarvie sat in the low chair by the fire, and held the baby, who had been bathed and was now dressed in a plain, long white flannel nightgown and a white knitted shawl. He looked up, and they all saw the glow in his face, before he pretended an indifference he was far from feeling.

'Och, she's just a wee bit bairn. Our Bella. It was you that found her, eh, Robbie?'

'Aye.'

Bella – for so they called her, and so she remained for the rest of her long life – bounced up and down on John's knee, on her bottom, and leered up at Robbie. She stretched out a pudgy hand to him, and caught his little finger, and crowed with glee. She tried to put the finger in her mouth, but Robbie snatched it away.

'It's dirty,' he muttered. 'It's not good for her.'

Bella was not in the least perturbed. She shoved her own hand in her mouth, and gurgled.

'Isn't she bonny? Isn't she a braw wee lassie?'

'Yes, she is that; a bonny wee thing. What will you do, John?' asked Millie.

'I'm going down to the police – but it'll be all right. I'll just need to have her registered and we'll adopt her, you know, all right and proper.'

'Poor wee thing – and she can't tell us where she's been, or who she is – maybe we'll never know.'

He stood up and handed the wee one to Flora.

'Here ye are, wife. I'll need to get away to my work, but I'll call in at the police station first and ask them to send a doctor, just tae make sure she's all right. Just a kind of formality . . . you know how I mean.'

Flora took the child, – and then she saw Robbie's face.

'Would you like to hold her, Robbie?'

The boy flushed, and turned away, muttering. 'No. I'm greasy, and dirty.'

Flora smiled. 'The shawl will wash. Here you are, Robbie. You found her. She's really yours!'

The boy hesitated. 'Well . . .'

'Go on – she won't break.'

He flung his cap on his head, rubbed the palms of his hands down his trousers and awkwardly held out his arms.

She was quite indifferent as to who held her at any given time. She crowed and gurgled and her eyes were wide and beautiful as she looked at Robbie. He felt as though he were on a stage – or stuck up on a table for everybody to see. It was as if his heart were laid bare. He could not speak. His eyes were wet . . . He could scarcely see anything – except the small, perfect face resting on his arm.

It was a moment that stayed with him all his life – a picture held as if on canvas.

He braved the threat of ridicule, or scorn; he discounted the possible threat of harm to the child from his dirty working clothes, and his none too-clean hands and face – and bent his head low, to place a soft kiss on the warm little forehead. Then, without a word, his face scarlet, he handed her back to Flora, stumbled out of the door, went thundering down the stairs, and ran all the way to the harbour.

John went out after Robbie had clattered away and walked thoughtfully down the street. Instead of going along to the harbour, to Scott's yard where he was a plater, he walked slowly to the Town Hall. His work in the yard that day would have to take second place.

He was a skilled tradesman, when he worked, but on those occasions when Flora's hopes of a living child were dashed again, he would 'knock off' to go into one of the spirit stores that were springing up all along the main street, as well as in some hidden alleys.

Although he would never admit it, scarcely even to himself, he often wondered if it could be his fault that his children always died. When he had drunk a lot more than usual, he would set off home, anger rising in him, against his wife – against ships of all sorts, shapes and sizes, against his own failure – and determined to give Flora a good beating – see if that would make her keep a bairn alive, by God! But when he got home, he usually burst in on the bright little kitchen, and throwing himself into the low basket chair by the fire, his anger would melt, and he would break into maudlin tears, that were somehow all the more real for their alcoholic origin. And in the comfort of their closed-in bed, they could always hope – they were still young.

As John had anticipated, there were no difficulties put in the way of his adopting an abandoned female child, parentage and date of birth unknown – approximately March this year. The formalities were few, and hurriedly performed. A doctor, appointed by the Town Council, called that afternoon and made a fairly comprehensive examination of the female infant, paying particular attention to the condition of her buttocks; it being his theory, firmly held in the teeth of much opposition, that most of the ills of the human race were laid in babyhood, starting with raw and chafed buttocks. In which belief the poor man was probably quite right before his time. Bella was uncomfortably red and raw around the folds of her thighs, but she was liberally smothered in vaseline, with soft muslin below her pure white nappy. It was obvious that she would never again have a sore bottom, and that nothing but loving care awaited her in the future.

So that night, bathed and dressed this time in a frilly white nightgown, Bella lay with sweet-smelling blankets over her. A few friends and neighbours gathered in the evening when work was done, to drink tea and eat cold ham and bread and butter, and rich 'bun' with some precious short-bread hoarded for the New Year.

To drink tea – with just a nip of the 'hard stuff' for the men – to wet the baby's head. Willie was there, but he looked at the baby and fidgeted to be away again. He didn't like it.

Robbie had to tell, over and over again, his story of the finding of the baby, but soon they were all satisfied, and talk drifted into topics of the town, to the work in the yards, the new roads being built out to the west, the railway, and . . . the future. For now, for Flora and John, there *was* a future. A future sleeping soundly in spotless splendour in the washing basket.

*

Robbie remembered the stricken look on his mother's face when she heard of the loss of the ship in which Donald had sailed 'chippy' to Canada. He had had it all planned.

He would get there, sign off, and from what he had heard, would soon have a good job, and could send for his wife and sons.

When Robbie was eleven, he had taken out the small tool box his father had left at home, with his older, less used tools in it. It seemed that when he picked up the tools and fondled them, it brought some comfort to his mother's heart. In another year, he started his apprenticeship in the yards.

In the winter they played football on Saturday afternoons. In the evenings, they stood at street corners – or just wandered along the streets. There was nothing else to do.

In the summer, they ran over the fields, and climbed trees; they fished, and paddled in the burns that trickled below the green hills. They walked miles and miles, over the range of hills to Corlic, where a farm nestled secure and lonely at the top. And they never even noticed the glories of their inheritance around them. Only the exile can see them.

But in the next few weeks, Robbie did no running around the streets. He and Willie had always taken turns at carrying coal up from the cellar to the bunker in the kitchen. Now, when Willie should have gone for the coal, Robbie was already on his way down to the cellar, and said he would bring the coal when he came. He took candles, stuck on old tin lids and made himself light to see what he was doing. The flickering naked gas jet in the entrance gave no light down to the cellars. Along one side he shovelled the coal, never more than a hundredweight at a time, and on the other side he had rigged up a bench and had found an old chair on which he could balance a piece of wood for sawing. He kept very quiet about what he was doing so busily down in the cellar, and nobody went in to see. It took him nearly two months, but one night, very late, his mother came down to find him. He was sitting on the floor, his head bent over something that he was sand-papering with slow, tired movements. He was nearly asleep.

'Robbie!' Millie whispered. 'Rob, lad, what are you doing so late? It's nearly ten o'clock. You've to be up at five. What's that you've been making?'

'Oh, just a wee kind of . . . cradle. It's for Bella – only I didn't want anybody to see it till it was done.'

He stood up and lifted the wooden cot that he had made with his own hands, and laid it on the bench. It was heavy and solid; rough and unprofessional – and not altogether symmetrical – but it had loving care in every groove and nail. He touched it gently, and set it rocking.

'My, Robbie, it's a wee rocking cradle! Oh, that's a good boy – but you shouldn't have been working so late. Come on now, lad, and I'll help you with it tomorrow. We'll get it varnished and polished, and it'll be fit for a queen. Come on, now, son. Oh, Rob lad, you're just like your father!'

She held him, for a moment, close to her heart, and then quietly, so as not to disturb the neighbours, they went upstairs together, the boy almost asleep on his feet. Millie helped him to take his clothes off, to his vest, and he tumbled into the bed beside his brother, who was fast asleep.

Millie had made herself a small, narrow bed from an old couch thrown out by one of her ladies. It slid easily under the set-in bed during the day, and as Millie was always last in bed, and first up, it was never really seen at all.

Quietly, she tucked the boys in. By the glow of the fire she prepared for bed, and lay for a while awake. She saw, perhaps, in the gesture – or symbol – of the cot for a strange child, something of the future.

But she was being fanciful. A baby, a small baby of eight months or so, and her Robbie – a young man, nearly. He was a good boy. It was the kind of thing his father would have done – a kindly deed – the only gift that he could give – the work of his own hands. Yes, he was a good boy.

*

Flora opened the door to Millie's knock the next morning.

'Oh, Millie – come away in – I've just made a cup of tea – and I've fed the wee one – have you come to see her? She's just lovely. Come away in.'

'No, Flora – you come and see what I've got for you. Come on across – just for a minute.'

Wiping her hands on her apron, and looking puzzled, Flora followed Millie in, and shut the door. Millie pulled the cot out from under the curtained bed, puffing a little with the exertion.

'There! There you are, Flora. I'm just going to varnish it. Robbie made it, for Bella.'

'Millie! Isn't that just grand? And Robbie made it? Oh my, oh my. He's fair taken wi' oor wee Bella. I can see no harm will come to her while Rob's round by.'

'Aye indeed. He's just like a big brother to her. I can see that. He's worked every night down in the cellar. I didn't know what he was doing.'

'I'm just delighted, Millie – and John will be, too. Now, come and have a cup of tea, and I must see how Bella is.'

Back in Flora's house, they were met by the contented crowing of Bella, kicking her legs and waving her arms in glee. Millie made fond noises at her, while Flora busied herself with cups – and there was a quiet smile on her face as she went about the homely task. The lines that had drawn down her mouth and furrowed her brow had almost disappeared. The calm, serene look in her eyes had never been there before, since Millie had known her.

'She was a wee bit restless last night, and the night before – it's her teeth, I think' – said Flora, as she handed Millie her tea and sat down beside her at the table.

'Flora,' said Millie, rather hesitantly, 'how is it you know so much about babies when you . . . er . . .'

'You mean when I've never had any of my own? Well, we were a big family, you know, before we left the

Highlands, and I was always about with children – always had to mind *somebody's* baby. Maybe it's just . . . I don't know . . . we *want* her to grow up well and strong and nice. I think that's half the battle. She's a good baby too, you know – she's very easy to look after.'

Millie rose, and put her cup over on the dresser. 'Well, thanks, Flora; I enjoyed that. I'll away and do the cradle, and let Robbie bring it in tonight, or tomorrow. I'll away now, Flora. Bye-bye.'

Rob that evening, made his daily visit to Bella, this time proudly bearing the cradle.

'There. So she'll sleep good,' he said.

III

'She'll have to have a proper birthday, like anybody else,' Flora was saying. 'She's about a year old now, although we've only had her for five months. Did that doctor not say when she was born, near enough?'

'He only said approximately in March,' John answered; 'and they have no record of any births not accounted for. The Town Council asked some of the midwives, but nobody seemed to remember anyone having a baby about that time, except normal births, and the babies still with their families. It must have been some poor lassie – deserted – maybe she didn't even belong to the town at all – maybe she came from one of the boats – or from Glasgow – or one of the Irish; you never know.'

'Do you not think there *is* a wee touch of the Irish about her, John?'

John looked at the chubby, grubby little figure crawling happily around the floor in the wild delight of finding odd corners for herself.

'M'hm. You're maybe right, wifie. She's got a kind of foreign look about her too. Black hair and dark eyes. I just wonder who her father and mother were.'

'Well, anyway,' persisted Flora, 'what about a birthday for her? A date, I mean, that will have to be her birthday?'

'Aye – aye, lass – I was thinking of that. Well now, do you see, there's the Irish Saint's Day in March – on the 17th – St Patrick's Day. We couldn't do better than that, could we?'

'St Patrick? – John! We don't want her made a Papist!'

John laughed. '*That* won't make her a Papist, lassie – and she won't learn any Catholic ways in *this* house; but I'm sure as I stand here, that she's got a bit of the Irish in her, so we'll make it the 17th March. I'll put a pound in the bank for her – if we're still working, I'll try to make it more – but you never know with the yards . . .'

His voice trailed away, and he turned to the fire to light his pipe.

Just now, the town was prosperous; there was work in the yards, and the sugar-houses blasted smoke and sparks out of their tall chimneys. Iron hammered on iron hulls, and hordes of black-faced, grease-covered men poured out of the yards and foundries. It had never occurred to them to wonder at the whims of a world that could tire of their ships, their sugar and their wool. But none knew better than the townsfolk how swift could be the descent from decent, honest living wages that never exceeded twenty-five shillings a week – to harsh, terrible, hungry poverty – on nothing.

They did not then – nor do they yet – know their own strength.

All along the narrow streets were the small insanitary cottages, that had been sufficient for the fishing population of three hundred years before. But with the sudden and prolonged invasion of the dispossessed people of the Highlands, after the tragic rebellion of '45, and a century later the influx of the decent farming people of the Ayrshire and Lanarkshire Lowlands, lured by the promise of the riches to be got from the opening up of the river, the shipbuilding, and the new steam-packet boats needing engines, and engineers, the town was stretched to its limits and beyond. People slept in barns, alleyways, old sheds, and in the rotting hulks of old sailing ships in dry docks.

Then there were the new mansions gradually spreading out along the river, among the trees and meadows . . . the houses where the ship-owners lived, and the rich successful tradesmen.

So the big grey stone tenements were hastily flung up, with little of comfort, but built solidly, and some standing today, two hundred years later. Solid, but with some thought for sanitation. One water-closet, for two or three families was at least a step in the right direction, and God knows, there was plenty of water hereabouts!

Here, in these tenements, in the small cottages, now housing two or three families, here lived the men who built the ships, who manned the ships, who stoked the ships – never the men who *owned* the ships.

There was to be another century passed before these men or their heirs saw these facts, and even then, they did not fully grasp them. Nor have they, yet.

John, like Flora, had come from the Highlands, and, rooted deep inside him, the legacy of a persecuted people, in spite of persecution, was the sure independence of the man who commanded his own life, and kept his own fireside.

He watched the antics of the child, and shared in Flora's preparations for putting her to bed. She still slept in the wooden cradle that Robbie had made for her, but it would soon be too small: she needed room to kick and wave her pudgy arms. She would never be a creature of dark and narrow paths.

Bella crawling, stumbling along holding on to chairs, Bella toddling, walking, Bella skipping along beside Flora, clutching her long skirts when she went to the shops; these were pictures that made up the story of four years,

and then an event happened which changed the whole of
Bella's life, and perhaps the lives of those about her.

Flora discovered, and waited till she was quite sure
before she announced it, that she was pregnant!

IV

Where the narrow tributary Cart joins its parent Clyde,
just above the Victoria Harbour, stood one of the solid,
grey stone Protestant churches that were nearly as
numerous as the public houses in the town. For
governments, kings and queens, presidents and dictators
may come and go, the real ruler of Scotland is the Kirk,
the Established Church of Scotland. And although the age
of intolerance, inquisition and plunder was past, there
has always been a mixed religious population in Greenock,
drawn occasionally to clashes and feuds, and on feast or
holy days, to sticks-and-stones fighting; much blood is
spilled and many harsh words are said, and many are the
sore heads in the morning. But many, many are the good
neighbours among the women of any faith.

Rambling over the hillside, there is, or there was, for
you'd be hard put to it to find it now, an old Roman road,
that straggled past fields and farms, round banks of lush
heather and golden whin, past grim wooded valleys, and
running beside the railway, for seven miles of meandering
beauty, to the inland village of Kilmacolm. The church,
near where the little river rippled under a bridge, is there
now: and it is well that we should know which one,
because the people who lived there – those whom Flora
and John symbolize – are not all gone to their rest. Of
their children and grand-children, there are still some

who remember the almost cloistered calm of the big church: the terrible days of flood and disaster, and the martial hymns, sung in loud voices, when a country went to war. Well, the church was the one that lay just under the hill, below the Roman road; the church that was called, perhaps, St James's.

Round at the side of the church on this warm sunny evening in July 1852, the vestry door was open, and from inside came the sound of voices, in sure, confident tones: voices of men who walked in the ways of God, who served their Church, their congregation, and their minister with faith and loyalty, and only occasionally slipped from grace. The elders, the office-bearers, the men whom John McGarvie was now to meet, and he felt himself completely unfit for the ordeal, although he had been proud of himself when he left home.

The change in John had been gradual, over these four years, although the impetus for the change had been sudden and positive: it had happened the moment he had taken Bella in his arms that cold morning in October, nearly four years before.

Deep down, he had always been a good man, even if not deeply religious, and when he and Flora had left the Highland croft, he had had dreams: of a home and family, a good job and savings, enough to take him back to the Highlands some day. The home was a fairly simple matter. The new tenements had single apartments in plenty, the kitchen, with its 'set-in' bed, where they lived and ate and slept. He got jobs, while there was work, but he could not know security. But the family that he had hoped for eluded him, and his inability to father a live child from whatever cause, had sapped his confidence, and made him as he was when Bella came, a shuffling, seedy, pitiable figure, with neither care nor hope for the future.

The ill wind that had blown a Spanish vessel into the safe harbour of Western Approaches, had blown some good into the lives of the inconspicuous little couple, who had been slowly but surely coming to grief, and probable tragedy.

It had scarcely seemed to John and Flora that their lives
had been any different from what they had been before.
Indeed, it was only the actual, physical fact of the
growing child that convinced them that those years had
actually passed. Somehow, in centring all their anxious
loving care on the child, they had gained a tranquillity
that had woven itself into their feelings for each other.

Modern psychiatry might have explained this
development but not even modern psychiatry could
have found such a successful cure for the ills that were
slowly destroying them. Flora had become calmer, less
inclined to brood and weep. John, in gaining physical
strength, found also a moral strength that urged him on to
the pinnacle of Scottish achievement: Respectability.

This was what had brought him, in decent suit and shirt
with collar and tie instead of his usual muffler, to the
gravel path outside the church – with butterflies in his
stomach. His new cap and new boots gave him acute
discomfort, but the thought of what this interview might
mean, to Flora and Bella – and not least to the coming
child – took some of the sting out of his pain.

Dragging himself, subconsciously, out of the rut that
had almost engulfed him had been one thing; to make this
positive effort to better his position had been quite
another, and not at all so easy.

But the force that is in every parent, to a greater or less
degree, especially in the Scot, which insists that its
children will have a better chance than they did, sprang
to life again when Flora had made her announcement.

A few weeks before, an advertisement had appeared in
the local weekly newspaper – a respectable family man
was required, to be the church officer – the beadle – of a
Protestant church in a busy, east-end parish. Free
housing, heat and light was to be provided, with a salary
of six pounds a year. John thought long and earnestly of
the possibilities in this prospect. It would mean, he
thought, a chance to save: he was strong and well, so the
work of cleaning the church and stoking boilers would

not worry him, and Flora was a good worker too. It would be good if he could stay long enough to save, and get away from the sluggish, smoky town back to where, across the moors of heather, the winds of God blow sweet. His father's little croft, with sheep and a few cows, had been mercifully one of the few spared in the burnings by the hereditary dukes. He left his heart in the Highlands – and it would be a long road back. So long – so long for John – that he never did get back . . .

He answered the advertisement, for he could read and write, passably well, and he was chosen for an interview, with four other men, equally deserving, equally respectable, and probably with a less harried past than John's had been.

Gathering all his courage, and smothering the butterflies, he knocked at the door of the vestry punctually at seven o'clock – and was bidden to enter.

'Ah, come away in. You'll be Mr McGarvie?'

'Yes, sir, John McGarvie.'

'Aye. Will you sit here, Mr McGarvie, and we'll hear what you have to say – sit here, beside Mr Foster, our senior elder. Mr Allan – Mr Morris – Mr McLean – and myself. I'm James Smith. Mr Burns – no relation of the poet, I'm afraid – ha, ha!' (This was his standing joke whenever anyone was introduced to Mr Robert Burns). He laughed, and John dutifully smiled.

The room was a small annexe to the church hall proper. In here, the choir practised, and small committee meetings were held. It led into a narrow passage in which was the minister's vestry, and the door into the church, used only by the minister and his direct subordinates.

The church was built on a slope, and the wide stone passage at the back door led into the hall, and across this were the two rooms where John and his family were to live for more years than they dreamed of – then.

All this, however, John did not see till later; for the moment he was intent on the faces of the men seated round him.

They questioned him; they probed into his past life

and they asked where he worked. They asked about his
family – his father and mother, and his wife. And then
there was a small silence, and from far away, he heard Mr
Foster say –

'I think this is the minister now – yes, here he is. Will
you be upstanding, Mr McGarvie, to meet his Reverence?'

Into the hall came a young man – a handsome, virile
man with strong features, and a mop of rough sandy hair
on the well-shaped head. He was tall, about two inches
taller than John, and when John looked up, he saw a calm
face that welcomed him with a smile. Deep blue eyes –
the eyes that sailors have – gazed down at the meek,
eager face of John, taking in, in one glance, the whole,
open character of the man.

His eyes caught and held John's as the voice of the
elder made the introduction:

'And now, Mr McGarvie, we must introduce you to our
minister, the Reverend James Christopher: late of Her
Majesty's Navy.'

A strong, smooth, cool hand took the rough, working
hand, in a clasp that said, mutely:

'This is the man – this is my Friend – till death us do
part!'

He said, in a Scottish voice, that still had the refinement
of Cambridge University overtones:

'Well met, Mr McGarvie. I am hoping to find a man for
the church who will be glad to work with me. There is a
lot to be done – and so little time. If my elders are
satisfied, and you would like to come, I would just say –'
he turned to James Smith – 'I like Mr McGarvie best of the
men we have seen, Mr Smith. I must leave the choice in
your capable hands, but I wanted you to know my views.
I will leave you now; as you know, I am going to be
married tomorrow, and I have many people to see. Take
your time, gentlemen. We will meet next Sunday, and
you can tell me your choice. Goodnight, Mr McGarvie –
goodnight, and God be with you all.'

They asked John more questions, and he told them,
rather hesitantly, about Bella.

'And you took this child – you don't know where from
or who her parents were or anything about her? You
took her, and adopted her, and you're bringing her up as
your own?'

Smith was very forthright in his manner. John nodded
briefly.

'An act of Christian charity,' said Mr Robert Burns.

'Indeed yes.'

'I don't know,' said the man Allan. 'For all you know,
she might be the child of thieves or murderers.'

'It will depend on the child's upbringing what she will
become. She won't know what her parents were.'

'Ah, but heredity, John, heredity – and the Second
Commandment: "the iniquities of the fathers upon the
children".'

'Oh, be quiet, Jimmy! We are elders in a Christian
Protestant Church, and we have a shining example of true
Christianity in our minister – God bless him! And I say,
with Bob Burns, it *was* an act of Christian charity, and I'm
inclined to agree with the minister that Mr McGarvie is
the man for us. However, just to give us a chance to
discuss it, would you excuse us for a moment, Mr
McGarvie? Perhaps you would care to sit in the vestry
for a wee while, seeing the minister's away? And we will
discuss the whole thing. In here, Mr McGarvie – we won't
keep you long.'

He was left in the vestry, and sat down on a black
horsehair armchair that was anything but comfortable.
The fireplace was empty, and the shabby carpet on the
floor, with the dark furnishings, gave a dreary, unlived-in
look to the place. An oak bureau, with books and papers,
and a mahogany table, on which lay a very large Bible,
completed the furnishings.

It was only about five minutes passed when the door
opened, and John jumped to his feet. Bob Burns looked
in, and beckoned.

'Will you step in by, Mr McGarvie?'

They went back together into the small hall and Smith,
now taking the minister's chair, motioned John to a seat

facing him.

'Mr McGarvie, we have discussed your position, and also, we had applications from other men who – you will not mind if I say it – were perhaps better recommended than you. I may tell you, Mr McGarvie, that we are not unanimous about this appointment – but then, we were not unanimous about any of them! But we have the biggest majority for this, having only one vote against it. The thing that tipped the balance in your favour –' John's heart seemed to come up and choke him – 'was the fact that our minister liked you. We are very pleased to offer you the position of Beadle for St James's Church in this parish, with accommodation which is spacious and fresh, as you will see, and a wage of six pounds per annum to be paid monthly. Free coal and gas, of course, and your duties will be outlined in detail when we meet next week. Are you willing to accept this, Mr McGarvie?'

John's voice was small and almost inaudible, as he answered.

'It's very kind. I'm very glad you're satisfied. I'll be taking the job . . . but I didn't think you would decide just now, and I was going to talk it over with my wife.'

'Do you think she will like it?' asked Allan.

'Yes, I think she will,' answered John with some spirit, 'because she wants the best for her children – and this is good and solid. I would like to come here.'

Smith stood up and held out his hand. One by one they shook hands with him – even Allan, though he did so with a faint grudge. Even if they were never active enemies, it was to be a long time before either of them gave the other an inch, towards friendship.

'Goodnight, goodnight. We will write to you.'

Afterwards, he couldn't remember leaving the church. He took the low road along the town, past the Square along the narrow confines of Cathcart Street and then, when he reached his own corner at West Burn Street, he turned, instead, down towards the river again. He felt he had to sort out his thoughts before he saw Flora. Children ran barefoot, screaming and laughing – in the endless fun that children of all shades and degrees can find in just running. They would play in the streets till sometimes nearly midnight – and they would grow up on a diet of porridge, mince and good soups, with discipline in the form of a skelpit backside – or a cuff over the ear – to be the strong, skilled workers of the dear river, destined for the scrap heap, or the plains of South Africa – and their sons for the fields of France. Very few of them would be washed before they went to bed. Many of them would wear the garments under their trousers or pinafores until they dropped off. But very few of them would ever see the inside of a prison – or a home for delinquents – or a divorce court.

John's thoughts were jumbled as he walked along in the direction of the new Albert Harbour and came to the edge of the river. He sat on an iron bollard and lit his pipe. His gaze was fixed on the Argyllshire hills, and far beyond.

'I could maybe get a holiday, and take Flora and Bella and, well, when the wee one comes – if ever it does. Supposing this is just another false alarm? But I liked that minister. I wonder how Flora will like him . . . and he's getting married tomorrow – well, I wish him the best . . . it will be a help to have no rent to pay. That's the curse of living, the cursed rent, years and years of it. I wonder if folk will still be paying rent for our house in a hundred years' time? Ah, things will be different in a hundred years!'

He rose, and strolled the length of the harbour. Dusk was beginning to fall, and the silence of the summer air moved his heart more than any amount of sermonizing could have done.

He murmured, half-joking to himself:

'Aye . . . my heart's in the Highlands, my heart isna' here. Och, John – ye daft thing! Get away home!'

*

They moved into the church in September, and the Munro family helped with the 'flitting' with a small handcart. The young ones ran to explore the two big rooms across the church hall. A small dark lobby lay between them, with two cavities meant for 'set-in-beds'. Flora refused to sleep in them – they had neither light nor air. So the first thing they had to get was a big brass bedstead, to take pride of place along the wall facing the door.

Bella's cot stood at the foot of the big bed. Later, when she grew up, she would move into the other bigger room. John's big grandfather chair stood at the side of the fire, near the door that led up the spiral staircase to the church vestry; the church itself was built on the solid rock that ended in green fields round the farm at the top of the hill.

The child remembered all her life, those two pieces of furniture in the big kitchen – the brass bedstead with a clean white bedspread over it, and John's big chair, with its cushions. They had no easy chairs – such luxuries were unknown in their lives.

'You'll come and see us often, won't you, Millie?'

'Goodness – yes, of course I will. You'll soon get used to the new neighbours, and the new shops. I'll be coming to wash for you, one of these days. And – Flora –' She stopped, and hesitated.

'What is it, Millie?'

'Flora, watch yourself. Take care of that wee new baby. It will be a wonderful thing to have one of your own, but –' Again she hesitated.

'I know what you're thinking, Millie – but don't worry. Bella is as much our own as if I'd carried her. I feel almost as if I *did* have her. No, Millie. She'll always be our bonnie wee Bella. But she's going to get a better chance than we got. We'll send her to school proper, and bring her up nice, and maybe in a few years we'll go back to the highlands. It depends . . .'

V

Flora's first, completed pregnancy was difficult, but at last she emerged the proud, if a trifle shaken, mother of a tiny, beautiful daughter.

Bella was at school, absorbing in the methodical, thoughtful way in which she did everything, the fact that C.A.T. spelt cat, and that two and two made four . . . These were mysteries enough, but when she got home one snowy January day from the school just across the road, to find that she had a 'sister' – her joy reached its climax. She burst into tears – because she was too full for laughter!

A gusty, cold, wet winter gave place, once more, to a cool, light spring, and the summer sun, occasional, and often rain-spattered, brightened the close-packed town.

The long, pleasant sweep of the tree-lined Esplanade, with the new mansions being built on its south side, tempted the Sunday walkers, young, and old, in their Sunday best. And none prouder than John McGarvie and his wife, Flora, as they walked along the side of the river with the new infant, Jenny, sleeping soundly in an ancient, basket-weave pram. Just fourteen months later, Flora produced a boy, with very little difficulty. They called him Andrew.

Little Jenny was a joy to everybody – and she began to know it. Flora's second pregnancy had made impossible, again, John's hope of taking his little family to the Highlands for a holiday.

Holidays were a luxury he could not afford yet. Work was slackening off – imperceptibly, and not too dangerously, as yet. Two weeks without pay was bad enough, but he might not have a job when he came back, and his little family was too important for him to take any risk.

His church duties absorbed the other half of his devotion. The once-gloomy vestry now had heavy red velvet curtains at the windows, and a dull gold carpet with a pattern of red roses. A white lace cloth covered the side-table, on which stood a brass flower-pot holder with a spreading aspidistra, lovingly cared for, and in winter a bright fire burned in the clean and shining hearth. In summer a beaded fire-screen gave a note of lightness to the black grate and the dark brown wood of the surrounds and mantelshelf. The old black horsehair chair had a brilliant Spanish shawl draped over it, and a glass-covered stand of wax flowers and fruit gave a final note of Victorian elegance to the room. On top of the writing desk, there was a picture, in an elaborate frame, of the minister's wedding.

Schooldays, snowy winter days, and celebrations, like holidays, and New Year time, filled the next few years of Bella's life, and the duties of the Church, as she pattered about helping Flora and John. She would miss big, loyal Robbie, for he had always been there to play with her, and her other playmates were poor substitutes. She began to notice Willie, who avoided her as much as possible. He came with his mother on visits, but he was always glad to get away. He quite positively did not like Bella.

*

Robbie was twenty-one now, too old to play games of horses with small girls. At the back of his mind, he felt a vague searching. He wished he had not spent so much time running wild over the hills.

The Mechanics Institute provided evening classes for the purpose of 'improving the health, expanding the mind, refining the taste, and elevating the character of the people', and to 'provide for young tradesmen and others a knowledge of grammar, composition and mathematics, naval architecture, drawing etc., so necessary to make them proficient in their respective professions.' And who could put it better?

Robbie thought these classes would help him in the future. His energy and doggedness kept him going. He now had no time for sporty friends, for games with girls, or for social evenings. He worked in the shipyard; he brought his money home to his mother, and he spent long evenings over his books, struggling, with intense concentration, to teach himself.

Millie Munro watched her son as he packed clothes into a seaman's bag. His three years of study had fined him down. He was a journeyman carpenter, and he was going to sea.

It had all happened before – Millie knew the feeling. She seemed to hear the voice of her dead Donald in the gruff speech of Rob.

'Will you – will you be away long, Rob?'

'About two years I think, mother.'

He moved about, not looking at her. He spoke again.

'You'll be all right with Willie. He'll be eighteen soon. He can look after you till I get back. He seems to be getting on all right with the coal lorries.'

She nodded.

'I'll send you some money regular, through the shipping office . . . you'll not need to wash so much.'

'I can wash for a while yet, Robbie. Where will you be going?'

'First to America, then South America, and then, maybe, China. But I'll be back.'

'Rob . . .' She stopped.

'What is it, mother?'

'Is it, is it some girl? Or what's making you leave

home?'

He turned away, and spoke angrily. 'No! It's no girl!
I'm not caring for girls.'

Dear God! Could *nothing* give him relief from the agony
that had been slowly devouring him these last eight
years? The depth of it – the black despair of it – this
thing, that only *he* knew . . . It was to be shunned – to be
fought and conquered – but bring it out into the light of
day, he could not. The mother he adored, in the gruff,
undemonstrative way of the Scot – even she could not
help him here. For he could never tell her. He must carry
his pain – alone.

He had to join his ship in Glasgow, so he walked to the
station and waited for his train.

He did not go to say goodbye to the McGarvies.

It was best not to.

VI

Next to his family, John's friendship with the minister
was the greatest thing in his life. Although he dominated,
naturally, his wife and children, it was with a kindly, if
severe and righteous rule. But he also needed to serve,
and it was his humble pleasure to serve the Reverend
James Christopher almost to the point of worship. There
was nothing he would not have done for him – and his
church.

He kept the boiler fire going, shovelling coal and
climbing stairs, cleaning brasses and windows. Every
Sunday morning, he moved the heavy wooden seats,
which had iron legs and iron supports, into square
formation for the afternoon Sunday School.

Bella loved to see him dressed in his long, black frock-
coat, and his very high, stand-up collar, with his shirt-
cuffs showing below his black coat-sleeves. He would go
and see that the bell-ringer had the correct time, so that
he would stop ringing the bell at exactly eleven o'clock.
Bella hopped about, getting in everybody's way, with
her chitter-chatter and bounciness. Her Sunday dress was
a dark brown serge, with a velvet sailor collar. The dress
reached down nearly to her ankles, and was buttoned at
the back: it had several tucks in the skirt, and down the
front of the bodice. The tucks would let down as she
grew – for a Sunday dress had to last for many winters.
She wore dark kid gloves, with a button at the wrist. She
loved going to church with her mother and father – and
she was so very proud of him.

When John had put the hall ready for the afternoon
Sunday School, and come in and finished his dressing, he
would give Bella a little silver threepenny-piece for the
collection, and then he would see that he had in his inside
jacket-pocket, easily accessible without any rustling of
paper, a goodish supply of peppermints – in their
peculiarly Scottish form of pan-drops. Then he would go
slowly, methodically through the hall to the little passage
and take Bella, solemn in her Sunday hat, with her black
hair in sedate ringlets, into the pew behind the minister's
wife.

Sitting there, Bella felt her happiness was too much –
she was almost at bursting point. But her happiest
moment was to come – the moment that carried her from
one Sunday to the next – a moment that lived in her
memory through all the Sundays of her long life. It was a
kind of anchor, a solid thing carved out of time and
majesty.

The bells stopped ringing. The little murmurs and
coughs from the congregation faded – the last comers
shuffled guiltily into their pews; the choir settled in its
seats, and from the organ, the last chords of Handel's
beautiful 'Largo' floated softly over the hushed church,
with a touch of infinite calm.

In the vestry John was helping the minister into his robe. This was not part of his routine duties – but it was a labour of love.

'Good congregation, John?'

'Aye – very good, James, as always. You'll be ready now, sir?'

'Yes; on you go, John.'

Now . . . now . . . would come her moment.

The door opposite the vestry opened, and John came in, carrying on his left arm the large Bible, that he would take up to the pulpit.

Bella knew every movement, and lived it greedily, with bursting heart. John walked with slow dignity across the choir stalls and up the wooden steps leading to the pulpit. Reverently, solemnly, he laid the Bible on the lectern, and came down the steps again.

He stood at the bottom, and waited for his minister. The Reverend James Christopher walked across as John had done, and up the steps. John could reach the door of the pulpit from the floor, and when he had seen the minister sit down, he would stretch up and shut the pulpit door with a tiny click. It looked as if he were almost casual and nonchalant about it – and then he walked back through the choir, and out of the door.

Bella wriggled in her seat – and waited. So well she knew just what would follow.

John went outside and round to the front of the church, and shut the big doors from the outside. Then he went along the passage and came into the church, and sat in the pew beside Bella, as the congregation was singing the first hymn. This was the wonderful part of the day: that, out of all the people in the church, only her father was allowed to come in late!

Then, when the service was over, and just before the benediction, John would quietly leave his seat and go round and open the doors again. Bella thought it was a great pity that he never heard this benediction, because the Reverend Christopher's words always seemed so full of meaning:

'Now unto Him Who is able to keep us from falling, to present us spotless before His Presence with exceeding joy, to the only wise God Who is our Saviour, we ascribe everlasting Power, Dominion and Glory, now and for evermore, Amen.'

*

When the question of the christening of the new baby, Andrew, came up, as Jenny had been christened much earlier, the minister asked:

'Where was our little Bella christened, John?'

John suddenly looked at Flora, and then at Bella – and then back to the minister. His face was red, almost as though with shame.

'Oh, Flora! Jimmy! – We never thought about it, you see – how she came to us, we . . . we just never thought about it!'

'I see. Well, do you not think we should accept her into the House of God?'

'Is it no' – it's a wee bit late, surely?' Flora asked.

'It is never too late to come to God, Flora,' said the minister, quietly and sincerely.

'I don't know what to think,' Flora was hesitant. 'What would folks say?'

'There's only one way to settle it,' said John. 'Do *you* think, sir, that she should be christened – even now – she's eight years old?'

'I do, John. I doubt, from what you told me of her arrival, that she had been christened before.'

'Aye, it's not likely, poor wee thing that she was then. Well, for the child's sake, then – not in the church, among the congregation.'

'*In* the church certainly, John. But if you wish, after the morning service. And we can christen her on the same day as your boy. Andrew, isn't it, John?'

'Aye, Andrew – for my father, ye ken.' His thoughts wavered for a moment, as he remembered the lowly crofter, and his humble, honest toil in the hills with his sheep. His heart ached a little. Would he ever see the far mountains again, or talk with the kind, hard-headed father, or breathe the sharp, clean air of the glens instead of the foulness of the noisy yards and foundries and the narrow mean streets?

The minister was with the family in the kitchen, where Bella and Jenny were playing happily on the floor, Bella building with coloured bricks – which Jenny just as promptly knocked down again with a podgy hand. Then she cried when the coloured heap lay scattered on the floor while Bella patiently built them up again, talking admonishingly to the child as she did so.

The grown-ups drank tea, and talked quietly, and the day of the christening was decided.

'I will talk to her at the time,' said the minister, 'and explain what I am going to do. Then she won't be frightened.'

But far from being frightened, Bella was delighted, and not in the least disappointed when she was told that she would be christened after the service and not, like Andrew, with all the congregation there. She never really liked the limelight – never liked being singled out and pointed to.

When the Sunday came, she was subdued and submissive, and inwardly excited. Willie Munro sat beside her in the pew, and she adored Willie. It meant nothing to her that Robbie was missing from the other side of him. She went through her usual emotions when her father made his rounds of the church, and carried the big bible up to the pulpit. And when, towards the end of the service, Millie came in with Andrew, followed by Flora in her best hat and costume, she listened intently to every move and sound of the christening. And she loved the way the congregation sat to sing the hymn, instead of standing. It was a queer kind of chant – instead of the martial verses she was used to.

The Lord bless thee and keep thee.
The Lord make His face shine upon
thee and be gracious unto thee. The
Lord lift up His countenance upon
thee – and give thee peace.
Amen. Amen. A-a-a-a-men.

She saw the little flick of water on Andrew's face, and
John standing white-faced beside his wife. Willie, on the
seat beside Bella, fidgeted impatiently.

He didn't really like Bella, he didn't like the church
and he didn't like this new baby and he wanted his
mother and his dinner. He was eighteen, and he was
interested in older girls than Bella – although he thought
young Jenny was not so bad. He didn't know, yet, why
he didn't like Bella. But Bella loved every moment he was
beside her. She couldn't imagine that he didn't like her.

The benediction was said, the organ burst forth into the
Trumpet Voluntary, and the congregation filed out.

When they had gone, John went and shut the big front
doors, and there were only one or two of the elders left.
Millie went down through the minister's door, with
Andrew, to see to young Jenny, and look after the dinner,
for they were all to have dinner together that day – the
two families, whose lives had been so long intertwined
and were to be so much closer in the future. Willie saw
his chance, and darted swiftly after her. *He* wasn't going
to wait to see Bella christened!

John came forward to the pew, and took Bella's hand,
and led her gently into the choir space below the pulpit.
On a pedestal covered with a white cloth, stood a huge
silver bowl, inside which there was a crystal dish,
containing water.

Bella came forward, shy now, and a little fearful. Flora
put her arm round her, and made her sit down beside her.

The minister sat on the other side of Bella, and spoke gently and softly to her.

'Bella, do you know what this is going to be?'

'Yes,' she whispered.

'Do you understand why this was not done when you were a baby, like Andrew, or Jenny?'

'No, I don't know.' She looked up at him, puzzled.

'Well, your mother and father will tell you about that, very soon, but now I must tell you what this is for. Will you listen very attentively, Bella, and tell me if you don't understand?'

Her big brown eyes looked up at him, her face expressing her wonderment at the solemnity of the occasion.Whatever it was, it seemed to concern her alone, and she thought that this was much better than the way they had held the baby, with the whole congregation looking on. She nodded, and kept her head down.

'Bella, this is a little ceremony, where a little child is acknowledged in the presence of the minister and the people, as a Christian. You are too young to understand that there are, in this world, many different religions and many different gods. In this country, we have accepted the Christian faith, and our Heavenly Father, who loves us all, as our God. You have been brought to us, to the simple beliefs of the Scottish Protestant Church, in the care of Our Lord Jesus Christ. That is what this is for, Bella, just to – '

Bella cut in. She had been following very closely.

'To let God know that I'm *here*?' she said.

The minister smiled, very gently.

'Yes, indeed, Bella, that is exactly it. He knew that you were here on earth, of course, but He likes to be told that you are in His Church, when we ask Him to receive you.'

Bella smiled and nodded again.

'Will you stand beside me, Bella?'

She came and stood close to him, and he put his left arm round her shoulder. He dipped his fingers in the cold water, and laid his hand very gently on her forehead. His hand was cold and wet, her head was at an uncomfortable angle, and some of the water trickled down her face and neck. But, she thought – if this is the way I have to tell God I'm here, it doesn't matter!

The minister said: 'Our Heavenly Father, we ask that this child may be brought to Thy Holy Table, as ordained by Thine only Son, our Saviour, Jesus Christ, in communion with Thy saints in glory everlasting. We ask this blessing especially in the case of our daughter Isabel who was left, a waif, from we know not where, in the care of her loving foster-parents, here present with us this day. May she grow in love and kindness of heart, honouring her father and her mother, and keeping Thy Commandments. In accordance with the rights placed upon me by the Established Church of Scotland, I baptize thee, Isabel McGarvie, in the name of the Father, the Son and the Holy Ghost . . . I baptize thee, obeying the command of our Saviour, who said – "Suffer little children to come unto Me." The Lord bless thee and keep thee. The Lord make His face shine upon thee, and give thee peace.'

As he came to the end of the grandeur of the words, the organ played the three Amens. Mr Dutton, the blind organist, had insisted on staying behind to give this touch of majesty to the occasion.

Bella's father – her real father – was descended from those who had no doubt burned many a heretic. And Bella's mother, the dark-eyed Irish colleen, had said many a confession – and paid her poor coppers for a candle for forgiveness, many poor pennies which added up to build papal palaces for pomp and priesthood.

But this child of their passion had added, to her store of happiness, the joy she felt this day in being baptized into the Protestant Church of Scotland; the plainest and simplest form of worshipping whatever God there be.

She had such a happy childhood – her heart was filled with love for everybody (especially Willie Munro), her playmates, the two children, and her mother and father, as she knew them, and his kindly discipline. She loved the spacious, if not over-comfortable surroundings she lived in, where there was room to run and jump and play and, as well, to help in the church duties. Her life was filled with the joy of just living. Even chilblains in the winter soon went, when Flora treated them with melted mutton fat.

She was twelve when she discovered the squalor, the degradation, and the beauty, that lay at her feet.

VII

AMERICAN INTERLUDE 1858 – 1863

There was a long dark lane that led from the docks on to a brilliant street. Rob had never seen such brilliance, and such hurrying, seemingly aimless, crowds. The ship had come into New York harbour at night, and the young ones of the crew were eager to be ashore on their first night in this fabulous, famous city.

Snow had been falling, and the cold was intense. A full moon scudded across a black sky, where cold stars glittered, so close, it seemed, one could almost touch them. Babble of voices, shouts from saloon bars, and itinerant musicians outside, begging for dimes.

This busy, bustling world was new to Rob, although they had called at other busy ports during his two years at sea, and something of the vigour and surging life of the country, its insides grumbling even then with the stirrings of a savage civil war, called to the youth and ambition in him. With his mates he went into one of the saloons, and soon they were absorbed in the crowd round the bar and at the tables, where gambling was in full swing, unharried by the shouting, milling hullabaloo of the serious drinkers. It seemed to be a house well used to seamen, and there were all kinds of nationalities in the mixed crowd.

Rob sat down at a table, with a foaming tankard of ale, and quietly watched the scene. The talk, in jumbled phrases here and there, was of the opening westlands, the railways, and the opportunities in this vast, sprawling cosmopolitan continent. It seemed there was wealth for the taking – the grass is always greener on the other side of the road – and anybody who didn't make a fortune was a fool.

One of the firemen from the ship joined him in his contemplation of the scene, carrying a bottle of whisky and a glass.

'Are you having a drop of scotch, Rob?' he asked.

'No – I like this beer, Jimmy.'

'What are you thinking about?'

'Oh – I'm just listening to the talk. It seems there's a fine country here. It's big enough anyway.'

'D'you mean you think you'll stay here?'

Rob drank some beer slowly. Then he spoke again.

'I'm not sure. I think I might . . . I'm just wondering. This is only the edge of it. We haven't even seen anything yet. Could I get work here?'

'You mean could *we* get work here,' said Jimmy Miller.

'But you'll want to go back home, surely?'

'No, I don't.'

'Wasn't there a lass – you were getting married, weren't you?'

'That was *her* idea – it was never mine.'

'Oh.'

There was a silence while they drank. Then Jimmy spoke again.

'Ah well, that's enough whisky for me. Are you for a drop from the bottle, Rob?'

'Aye, well, maybe just a drop. Then we'll get back.

How long have we got in port, Jimmy?'

'Captain ordered steam for Sunday, early like.'

'Gives us four days.'

'If you'll jump ship, so will I.'

'It'd be fine to have somebody with you, if you were thinking of starting life in a new country. We'll sleep on it, and see how it looks in daylight. Come on, Jimmy.'

The two boys made their way back to the docks, and went on board. They found the crew in the foc'sle drinking cocoa, and the hot sweet drink warmed them.

Robbie had not grown very tall – his father had been a small man, and, in fact, Millie Munro had been two inches taller than her husband. He and Jimmy Miller were complete contrasts, Jimmy standing 6ft 2ins in his socks, fair, almost red-haired, and handsome, and Rob only 5ft 8ins. Later, when they had been a long time in the country together, Jimmy dressed, whatever his circumstances, like a millionaire. Rob always looked like a rag-and-bone man. But they formed an attachment that night that lasted through hell and high water, through time and mud and blood, even through the icy snows of Klondike, and through to the gates of death.

'Find anything worth having, chippy?'

'Wasn't looking for anything. Only a drink.'

'Bet I find something tomorrow night.'

'Bet you find more than you bargain for, bosun.'

'Ach! You young ones don't know how to look for it. I'll find something, and I won't be aboard till steam up.'

'You're welcome,' said Rob. 'There's plenty about – Jimmy and me just had a drink.'

One by one, the men crawled into their bunks, and it was only then, in the quiet of the night, that Robbie fully realised the cramped, unhealthy atmosphere of the narrow place that held eight grown men.

Even in the intense cold of the winter in New York Harbour, the foc'sle was hot and suffocating. Robbie felt it even more now, since he had breathed the exhilaration in the keen icy air of New York. He got out of his bunk quietly, and pulled on his thick seaman's jersey. The smoking oil lamp, hanging from the low ceiling, gave enough light, and he carried his boots outside and up the main iron stairs to the deck, where he slipped them on.

He went to the side where he could see the line of the harbour, and it was only a few moments before another figure came and joined him. Without turning round, Robbie knew who it was.

They stood in silence for a while. Robbie lit a pipe, and Jimmy chewed tobacco.

The lights of the city had scarcely dimmed. The life of the city, even at two o'clock in the morning, throbbed and hummed in front of them.

'Hey, what are you two doin'?'

Jimmy turned. The nightwatchman was behind them holding a lantern high over his head.

'All right, Taffy – we couldn't sleep – just looking at the lights.'

'It's a fine country, they tell me,' said Rob.

Taffy spat contemptuously into the harbour.

''Tis a fine country – for women – and dogs,' he replied scathingly.

Jimmy laughed – 'Not for men, eh?'

Taffy shook his head.

'Well we're going to try it,' said Robbie –

'We'll *make* it good, for *us* anyway.'

Jimmy put his hand on Robbie's shoulder.

'Made up your mind, Rob?'

'Aye. Taffy just put the finishing touch on it.'

'We'll tackle it together, eh?'

'If you like, Jimmy.'

'Shake on that then, Rob – and we'll be off tomorrow.'

They shook hands, Taffy watching them in silence, with his lantern now dangling at his side. There was something here that he didn't quite understand. It was something more than just two rough seamen jumping ship. He gave it up, and turned to move away, growling at them as he did.

'Huh! Should be in bed asleep. Some folk don't know when they're lucky – tramping about in the middle of the night . . .'

Rob and Jimmy went back to their bunks, but they slept very little, and they were up and about, part of the bustle of the ship, when the nightwatchman had finished his rounds, and had made a huge jug of hot sweet tea. After their breakfast of rough salted porridge, they went together to the first mate.

'So you want your books, eh?'

'That's right, sir,' said Jimmy.

'Think there's a fortune waiting to be picked up in this country eh?'

'Waiting to be worked for,' said Rob.

The mate looked at him.

'Well – I can believe you'll do that, anyway. All right, I'll get your books cleared and get the old man to sign them. You've got some wages to come, I suppose?'

'I haven't got much,' Jimmy said, 'but I can soon make more.'

'You've got a bit, haven't you, chippy?'

'I haven't drawn any for six months. I want to send some to my mother.'

'Right, I'll get it ready for you – come back in an hour.'

They turned to go. The mate called them as they reached the door. 'Wait a minute!'

They turned. 'You're sure about this? What about your folks – your mother?'

'I'll work and send for my mother, and my brother,' said Rob.

Jimmy grinned – a fiendish grin. 'My mother would never be sober long enough to get on a boat. Let her sink or swim – she never bothered about me. I'll send her enough money, when I make some, to keep her in gin, but for me, I'm game to try my luck here.'

The mate nodded. 'All right – come back in an hour.'

There was scant ceremony in the handing over of seamen's discharge books, and a line for the shipping agents for the amount of money due to them. The mate was more concerned about replacing his crew – although this was not difficult. There were always men glad to be at sea again, even glad to be anywhere else than where they were – there was always the riff-raff and the throw-outs, and this great, sick country never had any compunction about throwing out its misfits and its failures.

When they left the shipping offices, they found a small, reasonably clean, downtown eating house. Rob had taken part of his accumulated wages in a banker's draft and partly in silver dollars. Jimmy, the little he had to come, took it in cash, and laughed.

'Easy come, easy go,' said Jimmy.

First thing was lodgings, and second, a job. Lodgings for two respectable Scotsmen were not too hard to come by, and they settled in a fairly decent house, along a quiet street, a good way from the docks. Jobs, too, were not too difficult; both boys were strong and willing, and even at casual labouring they could find something to keep them going.

They stuck together, and the months passed, until, when summer came, they decided to leave the sweating, burning streets of New York and make for the countryside. There was a lot of building going on northwards, near the shores of the Great Lakes, almost into Canada. There were small shipyards along the St Laurence river, and coal boats ferrying across the lakes.

For a short time they parted, Jimmy going on a coal trip down the lakes, and Rob working in a boat yard where the St Laurence divides the States from Canada.

From the yard to the place where he got lodgings, a small, growing township called Bessant, was a three mile walk, morning and evening. The town was spreading northwards, eastwards, and southwards, but the lake was a boundary to the west, and there was a vast stretch of vacant and unclaimed land, for the nation was not yet land-hungry, and many thousands had gone westwards, over the long trail to the sunny lands on the Pacific coast. Many thousands died on the way, and their stories are still being told.

Rob walked by the lake alone on a Sunday, and tried to stifle the picture of his homeland in the pine-trimmed fringes of the lake. For many months now, his resolve had been strengthening: his long absence from the people he knew, from the family and those he loved, had not dimmed his feelings for the girl who was growing up, still thinking of him, when she did at all, as her big brother Robbie.

But walking over the rough land near his lodgings he planned, and schemed, and it seemed his plan was not too impossible of fulfilment. The small town of Bessant boasted a council and a Sheriff, with a lawyer and two doctors, and even a dentist. It had three or four churches of different denominations and a school. It was a clean, wholesome, respectable little place, with opportunities for growth and expansion on a wide scale, but as yet lying dormant.

Rob kept his plan to himself until Jimmy came back from his trip.

'Rob! It's good to see you again. Come on out and have a drink on me.'

'All right – I'm glad you're back – just one drink, I want you to come for a walk with me. I've got an idea, and I want to show you something.'

'Something in the female line?'

'No, you idiot. Come on – I'll show you.'

'Well – all right – maybe you're not the only one with ideas.'

'Oh? What have you got in mind?'

'I'll tell you – first a drink. I've been shovelling coal for a month – I'm dry.'

They walked along the roughly made road that was the main street, and made their way to the saloon.

When they were settled at a table, Robbie with eagerness in his usually calm, slow-moving hands, brought out a piece of paper and spread it on the table, moving his pint tankard and Jimmy's whisky bottle.

'I'll start, because I think I've got something real good,'

he said. 'Now look, this is a rough map of the district. You see, up here, there's the boat building yard where I'm working and all along this lake side shore, it's all empty, and then there's this wee town – well, it's hardly a town, but it will get bigger. I've been walking a lot while you've been away, and I'm going to talk to the local magistrate and council, or whatever they have here, like a corporation – or estate agents or anybody who knows. I'm going to buy a bit of land, now, while it's going, because you mark my words, it will get valuable in a few years – and I'm going to build a house.'

'A house?' echoed Jimmy.

'Yes, a house, and then I'm going to live in it and then I'll build another one, and live in that and sell the first one.'

Jimmy breathed a deep long breath.

'Well, I'm damned! But by God, you're right, Rob! Here – that calls for another drink. Have a drop of the cratur, Rob.'

'Aye well, just a drop . . . I'm glad you think it's a good idea.'

Jimmy went to the bar, and pushed his way in. The hum of conversation rose and fell around him. His mind, intent on his own idea, and now on Robbie's, did not trouble to isolate the sounds – it was all a jumble of words and phrases. It was not until some months afterwards that he recalled four words that must have settled in his subconsciousness as he waited for his drinks.

The little town was not really very progressive. Neither was it backward or stagnant. Peaceful, contented, lazy, were perhaps the only words that would describe it. The only saloon in the town was run in a respectable manner by an immigrant Italian, and it was more of a club house, and eating house, where the men of the district could meet without the carping, inhibiting presence of their women-folk. The town was not on any stage-coach, or railway route, and its population, then about 800, were mostly of professional status, some from the nearby boatyards, some railway officials and shareholders, the owner of a small growing grocery store, one or two – a little outlying – fruit farms, and some owners, and owner- captains, of the boats that plied across the length and breadth of the great lakes, and up the St Laurence river to the sea.

So when Jimmy was waiting for his drinks, the chatter of the men was not the wild, lawless braggadocio of the westlands, or the waggoners, but the newsy, gossipy chatter of men who read about these things in the papers, or heard of them from travellers. Four words came distinctly to Jimmy's ears, but he didn't consciously hold them then. They were, thrown in during the conversation – 'Bonanza Creek,' 'Gold' and 'Klondike'. Words that were to ring the world in less than two decades, but Jimmy went back to Robbie with his drinks, full of their individual plans for the future: for a future that would hold both their plans – for their friendship had become imperceptibly very real to both of them.

'Now then,' said Jimmy. 'I've been doing a bit of thinking too. You know I've been away on a boat?' Robbie nodded. 'Well, I had a few days ashore at a wee place over on the other side of the lake. The engines got locked and we had to wait for some parts, from Detroit or somewhere. Anyway, I was mooching about this God-forsaken place, and I went back to the ship for my dinner. There was this old woman talking to the mate. She wanted to get a big bag over to her daughter, or somebody, 25 miles away, down the lake, and not on any railway track.'

He drank deeply and passed the bottle to Rob.

'Here – have another drink. Well, anyway, this old dear was fair upset and in a bother. She didn't know how she was going to get the bag to her daughter, and it was 25 miles away, and her wanting it by tomorrow. So the mate says to me, he says, "Miller – can you ride a horse?" Now me, you know me, been on boats ever since I could walk, but my old grandfather went out with a baker's van, and I used to feed the old nag sometimes and ride up on top of the van with him, so I knew how to handle the reins anyway.

'Drink up, Rob, and I'll get another bottle. God! this cheap rye whisky rots your guts! Well, anyway, to get back to what I was saying – I said yes I could handle a horse, so the old woman was that thankful – oh dear! There wasn't enough gold in the world to pay for the kindness I'd be doing her. So the mate said I could go, and the ship wouldn't be ready before I got back – the old lady told me where to go, and then she took me to a farm, just by, and she gave me this great farm horse.

'God! That was a journey I'll never forget, I'm telling you, Rob! I started off about six o'clock in the morning – the old horse had never had a saddle on it, and I'd never ridden a horse, so we were well matched! Anyway, I got to the place all right and gave the lass the bag.'

He stopped to refresh himself again, and the level of whisky in the bottle grew noticeably lower, the saloon began to empty, lights were dimmed, but Jimmy and Robbie sat there building their future.

'So I began thinking, after I got back, if she needed a bag taken to a place that wasn't easy to get at and she could give me five dollars for it, it's likely that other folks might need the same – you know, a kind of parcel service. Aye, I know the stage coach takes parcels, but sometimes there's folk not on the stage routes, or maybe they've missed the stage, anything like that. If I had a wee horse and buggy to start with, even in this wee town, I could find people who wanted parcels sent – safe delivery guaranteed! And another thing – ' he pushed his cap to the back of his head, and stabbed at Robbie's waistcoat with his finger, 'when this town grows a bit, it will be quite a step from one end of it to the other. So I'm going to get a smart turn-out and get folks to ride on my waggon, to visit their friends. You'll see, Robbie.'

By the time they had finished another bottle, the night was far advanced, and they were both very, very drunk. They staggered, falling and spluttering, all the way to Rob's lodgings, singing some bonnie Scots songs in raucous, tuneless, excruciating tones, so that even the cats turned tail and ran as they made their wavering way along the street.

Jimmy, slightly more steady than Rob, got them both safely into Rob's room, while he kept demanding truculently, where the hell did he think they were going. Jimmy took Rob's boots off, and one of his own, but that was as far as he could go. They slept on the floor, side by side, and woke next morning as fresh as the lark, with only a slight wonderment about how they had got home.

Jimmy started a business that in 60 years his son sold to one of the great car hire companies for five million dollars. To tell of the long battle he had with organised transport, and with the carriage trade, would be a romance on its own. To see his horse-drawn 'brakes' cutting in and out of traffic, getting parcels and passengers to and from one end of a town to the other quicker than the other fellow: to see, later, his motor coaches doing the same thing, was something the generation that lived with him would never forget, nor ever see again. For Jimmy and Robbie, their friendship lasted, although their ways divided at times, and their greatest adventure was still to come.

Robbie got the piece of land he wanted, a long stretch, big enough to build two houses on. Working at nights, as long as it was light, on Saturday afternoons and Sundays, with his own hands he built a two-storey house, and finished it in a year. With every brick, in every corner, as it grew, he saw a figure, mainly imaginary, for he could not really know how she was growing up, the slim figure of a dark-haired, dark-eyed girl, who smiled at him, as if approvingly; he was building it for Bella, but he could tell nobody about her. And yet, Jimmy knew something. For it was just about two years after they had arrived in America, that Jimmy announced he was going to be married.

'You know Louisa – she's the engineer's daughter on that boat I go on in the summer time.'

'Well! That's fine, Jimmy – I'm very glad to hear it.'

Jimmy looked at him for a moment and then said, a

little hesitantly, 'What about you, Rob? Have you got a lass at home?'

'What makes you ask that?'

'Well, you've never bothered about the girls here, and there's some beauties – I just thought maybe . . .'

'There's plenty of girls, everywhere, Jim – and I can take them or leave them. There was a few in New York – I'm no angel, Jimmy.'

'No, I didn't mean that – there's always those kind of women – and sometimes we need them – but I meant a girl, your own, I mean. You should get married. It's best for a man to have a family.'

'I'm willing to take care of any girl that wants me, Jimmy, but there's only one I'll give my name to.'

'Ah, so there is a girl in Scotland?'

Robbie turned away. Not even Jimmy must know the full truth about the girl in Scotland.

'Well – yes – in a way.'

'All right, Rob, it's none of my business. I just thought it would be good for you – but maybe – oh! I see! That's what you're building the house for! You'll be sending for her?'

'No! Not yet anyway. No! I wouldn't send for her. I'll go and get her . . . when . . . '

'When what? You've got a good job. You've got money saved. You've got a house. Does she not want to come, then?'

'I haven't asked her yet . . . she's too young.'

That was enough – she was so very young – a child – a child of *twelve!*

Letter from Willie Munro to his Brother Robert in America

Greenock. 1st January 1860

Dear Rob,
Mother wants me to say she is glad you've got your new

house finished. It seems a good idea to make them and sell them like that. You'll be a millionaire some day I suppose! I've to tell you that the McGarvies are fine. Bella is growing into a fine girl. She'll be 12 in March. Jenny is a bonnie girl too, and wee Andy is just fine. Mother says you're not to run yourself short of money to send her . . . she's still doing some washing, and I'm on the coal lorries now, so I can help her. I'm going to the Church socials . . some fine lassies, but I like wee Jenny . . . I'll maybe wait for her.

Regards to your friend Jimmy Miller, and a Happy New Year from us all.

From Mother and Willie

Letter from Robert to his Brother Willie in Scotland

Bessant, 3rd April 1860

Dear Mother and Willie,

Don't worry about money. Jimmy is working on the boats, but we are thinking of going to the goldfields. We might be lucky, only Jimmy says he wants to buy some land . . . where there's forests, he thinks the land might be valuable in some years' time. He's getting married soon. I would like Mother to come out and see me some time. I'll send her fare when I get my next house built and sold. We're getting on fine, Jimmy and me. Give my love to the McGarvies.

Your brother Robbie,
and love to Mother

Give my love to the McGarvies. He knew that there was only one McGarvie who meant anything to him. Rob put his pen down. 'I'll go back,' he thought. 'I'll go back when she's eighteen. I can wait another six years. My mother will come out soon, and then I'll go back, when Bella's eighteen.'

VIII

GREENOCK 1860

Laughing and shouting, the children romped out of the
school gates on the last day of the term, the first day of
their summer holidays. Bella skipped along with them,
her black hair blowing in the boisterous wind that was
blowing the last of the summer showers away, and
leaving a day that was July in its mellowest mood.

Adventure was in the air – it was only half past one,
instead of four o'clock, and there was a whole afternoon
to play in and explore. Bella followed with her special
friend Maggie Forbes, where the others led, shouting and
laughing . . . happiness and love had engulfed her,
surrounded and protected her since the day she had
come to Flora and John. She had never seen or heard evil,
or wrong. The poor ragged children she saw at school
puzzled her a little, but Flora had told her that their
mothers didn't keep them nice and that had satisfied her.

Now they ran along unfamiliar streets, along narrow,
dirty alleys, past the railway bridge and down towards
the Vennel. Along one of the streets where small once-
whitewashed cottages stood huddled in sickening
profusion, a crowd was gathered outside one of the but-
and-ben dwellings. Suddenly silenced and curious, the
children ventured near. The crowd, women and
children, and some men, stood glowering and muttering,

but quite powerless. At the open door stood an old man, big and bearded – once a strong and husky lad, who had laboured, too long, in the heat of the iron foundries. Beside him, with her hand in his, stood his wife, smiling and nodding, foolishly, vacantly, at everything and everyone round her.

The old man was trying to plead with a burly official who stood in front of the doorway.

But it was no use. There was to be no mercy. The old man could no longer pay the miserable rent of a shilling a week for the hovel, although, in the years since it had been built, it had been paid for over and over again. But these poor people didn't even know that, then. His wife, grown senile and unaware of anything but her immediate needs, and the person who was so familiar to her, had no idea what was going on. They had never been separated since they had been married over sixty years before. For four years now he had watched his bonnie lassie deteriorate, had watched the light of reason die out of her eyes, and for these years he had kept her fed and clean, and looked after her as if she had been a baby. Their children, all gone and scattered, had never been near them for years. They were alone – but together. His love for her was as deep and true as when she had been a gay, saucy lass of eighteen.

And now – for a shilling a week – they were to be separated.

Now, he could not work, or if he worked he could not look after her. So they were to go to the Poorhouse, in accordance with the iniquitous Poor Law, devised to protect society against such unfortunates. Desperate – his pleading in vain – the old man tried to struggle with the bailiff's man, who cared not whether the old couple lived or died.

The schoolchildren, tiring of the spectacle, tried to pull Bella away, but she stood rooted, and shook off the pulling hands of her playmates. Something weird and uncanny, and stronger than the call of youth or adventure, held her here. She had a feeling that the story was not all told. She waited, and her heart began to thud hard against her chest, and she watched, tensed, the drama before her.

Suddenly, the old man gave a wild, loud shout. It held desperation, terror and despair, ringing out against the still hush in the air. He swung his arm free of the official who impeded him, and thrust his hand deep into the pocket of his jacket, and fumbled there briefly. It was so quick and unexpected that no one had the chance to stop him – or even to guess at what he intended.

Something glittered with a brilliant flash as he withdrew his hand from his pocket . . .

He raised his hand to his throat, and the flashing razor turned red . . . red . . . as his life blood spurted over his clothes – over his wife, and the bailiff's man, and on to the stone pavement.

One look – of bewilderment, or beseeching, he turned on his wife whose hand he still held; and he fell heavily to the ground. The little woman looked puzzled at him and at the crowd – stunned for a second to silence. It seemed to penetrate her feeble mind that something was wrong. The big, proud figure lay at her feet. She started to whimper.

Bella was shocked to immobility. The screams and shouts seemed to come from far away. Something inside her screamed at her to get away, to run, to escape from the horror that seared through her. But she could not move, for several moments.

What happened to the old woman she never knew, for the crowd, now suddenly increased, it seemed from nowhere, turned on the badly frightened official, whose peremptoriness had vanished, and beat him to the ground, as though to avenge the faithful old man who lay in a pool of his own blood, on the cobbled street among the musty tenements, at the door of the only home he had ever known.

Someone, pushing a way through the crowd, shut out for a moment the bloody spectacle, and with the screams of terrified women and the shouts of maddened men ringing in her ears – Bella found her legs moving again.

She turned and ran . . . as little Joe Mulligan had run thirteen years before . . .

She ran without pause or direction. She ran till she could run no more, till her heart was bursting, and the tears streaming down her face.

People looked at her as she passed, momentarily wondering – but a crying girl was nothing unusual, and they passed on, heedless.

She ran till she passed the end of the houses and streets, uphill . . . up . . . to be away from the stench and squalor of the closed-in buildings. Anywhere, anywhere, to be in any place that would not permit such things to happen. She had learned nothing at all, at church, or school, or home, to prepare her for the scene she had just witnessed. All she had been told, like her playmates, was that she must not speak to strange men, when they went walking or playing on the hills or fields or glens; it was hammered into them that a strange man must be a bad man. Many a poor tramp, scratching a meagre living on the roads, must have thought bitterly on the actions of a bevy of young girls, if he had so much as asked them the way. They would inevitably scream and run. He was a strange man, therefore he was a bad man.

But this was the nearest to the seamy side of life that Bella had ever known. Blindly, her steps had taken her uphill, and she found herself climbing the green slopes of the Lyle Hill, above the bay that curled in to the shore, along the bend of the river.

She had been on this hill before – walking with her mother and father and young Jenny, and the baby, Andrew.

But seeing it now, with wide-awake eyes, it was like another world. All round her the grass was lush and green. Wild rose bushes with their fragile pink blossoms spread in disordered profusion, mixed with brambles, ferns, whin, and low clumps of heather.

On the lower slopes, buttercups and daisies looked up with their yellow eyes, and there lay over everything the calm, golden beauty of a soft summer day, and birds wheeled and sang in the sunlight. She sat down near a whin bush and gradually her tears stopped, her legs grew less shaky. Her heartbeats steadied and the pain in her throat, from crying and running, subsided. She drew her knees up to her chin, clasped her hands round them and sank her head on her knees. She was almost afraid to look up. The sight she had just seen was still in the back of her eyes; in the impulses of her brain she still saw the red of blood, and even the shape of the screams made a pattern of nebulous grey that seemed to come and go with a cold insistence under her eyelids.

For a long time she sat like this, not thinking, just letting the thoughts and scenes move through her mind, until the red blur faded and the sounds of tyranny died away. She could not know it, but she had done the best possible for herself in letting it all flow over her – in not trying to battle with panic.

When she could think, her first thought was a grim determination that she must get away, far away, from a place that could let such things be. They must leave this town (for surely this could happen nowhere else?) and go far away, leave the squalor and degradation, the cruelty and misery of poverty and old age.

A long time she sat, first with her head bowed, and then with her eyes lifted to the winging birds.

She would ask her father; she would ask him that very day. Go now, and ask him when they could go away to the Highlands he had so often talked about. Back to the quiet peacefulness of the glens where, even if people were poor, it was a clean, decent, dignified poverty, not a grinding, monstrous thing that could snatch a man in the evening of his life from the mate who had come to him in the fresh bloom of her youth.

This much she had understood. That the two old people were to be separated and this should not be. She could not think of Flora without John. She did not know why they should have to be separated; she was, after all, only twelve. The economics of a country were too much for a child to understand.

She stood up, feeling a little calmer now that she had decided she would ask her father to take them away. She wiped her face with her handkerchief, but now it was grubby, so she used the tail of her petticoat. She was right on the top of the hill and she was facing across the river, northwards.

She had seen it all before. Everyone who lives in the town has seen it all before. But only a few really *see* it. Now Bella really saw it, in all its wild, majestic beauty. Mile upon mile, in front of her and on all sides, the landscape stretched as far as she could see, so breathtaking that she could only gasp and look. It was too much. She had never known such a feeling of splendour in space in an afternoon. The air shim-mered, and the whole world of poetry was flung, it seemed, at her feet.

Over to her right, as far as she could see, the river shone silver-blue, with dancing golden specks where the sun caught the rippling waves. Eddying from the smoky outline of Glasgow in the East, it turned just below her, and across on a stretch of golden sand it seemed to leave a swirl of lace-trimmed velvet. Purple-gold to the north, the high bonnie hills, with the steep frowning glories of the peaks of Ben Lomond jutting blackly into the blue dome of the sky, made a dark crown for the farmlands on the gentler slopes. A wisp of white smoke drifted lazily from a train going up the side of the loch to the Highlands, and ships lay at anchor, or sailed, under steam or canvas, down the Firth to be lost under the horizon.

She turned slowly, as if afraid to lose a single inch of this scene. Behind her, fold upon fold of deep blue mountains made up the formation of five counties and near her, to her right, was a wooded valley below pastureland spreading from a prosperous white farmhouse and, rippling through it, a sparkling of clear water, gurgling down to the sea.

Turning again, she looked eastwards and saw the pulling current of the river, the sandbanks in its centre making the narrow shipping lane, and the buoys marking the safe path for mighty ships. The black rock of Dunbarton cut between the blue-and-silver ribbon and the green fields on the north shore and merged into the grey line that stretched back along the working side of the river – the long grey smoky line that was the ugly, priceless jewel in this perfect setting.

Bella was utterly shaken and bewildered by what she was seeing. How could such beauty live side by side with such ugliness? Surely, living in this should make people good and kind, and loving this land of greatness?

The mind of a child struggled with the complexities of life, and she left her childhood behind her, then, in the gutters running red with sacrificial blood.

But now a new feeling came to her heart. Words were meaningless. Her feelings raced through her in snatches of incoherence . . . breathless, as though they could not stop to explain – nor could she. She could only feel: 'This is what I need, this is the world. I'll never leave here now, never, never, *never!'*

The sun sank behind the hills; but the light stays all night through in early summer in the north, where time stands still on the border of the world. Still the child sat there, as if she could take the whole vista and hold it in her hands, and look and look and she would never have her fill of the changeless, ageless glories.

Long after the lamps had been lit and the last revellers had tottered homewards, and the only people on the streets were the besotted drunks who roamed aimlessly in search of more drink and some wandering souls who had no home to go to, and a few women, when even those who hung out of windows to watch the street scenes and the passers-by, had gone to bed, to wake up to another day of toil and wonder, the child walked back down the hill and along the quiet streets, alone and unharmed, till she saw the dark outline of her church against the night sky.

The gas light shone through the uncurtained window of the big kitchen, where Flora sat at the fire, almost in a state of collapse. John had just come in, after another fruitless search round the streets and asking at doors if anyone had seen Bella. None had, since early afternoon. He had come home for one last look, to see if she was home, then he was going to the police. He looked grey, and tired, and distraught. He was too tired to be angry, but he *was* angry. He sat down and bowed his head. Flora tried to make him drink the hot tea she had made. She felt helpless; she wanted to be out, helping to search for Bella, but she had to think of the two smaller ones, and she could do no more than John had done. No words of hers could help him. Where had they failed? Had their child left them – or had she been taken, somehow, by roving bands of gypsies, or sailors?

And then they heard it, the light, stumbling footsteps, running, falling, scuffing, over the big church hall to the kitchen door, guided by the line of light under the door.

John jumped from his chair and flung the door open.

'Bella! Bella, oh, lassie, what's happened to you? Where have you been?'

She stood for a moment, blinking in the light. Her face was dirty, her eyes were wide, like great black saucers in a smeared, grey face, under her black hair, tousled and matted. Her dress and pinafore were torn and streaked with mud and green splashes from the grass, for her descent of the hills in the gloaming had not been as easy as her terrified rush to its summit, nor was she so sure-footed at midnight as she had been at mid-day. She came in slowly, and Flora's heart missed a beat.

'Dear God,' she thought, 'she's not a child at all. What . . . what's happened to you?' She had said the last four words aloud without knowing it.

Bella came slowly across the wide stretch of linoleum that covered the floor and slid to her knees in front of Flora.

John looked at Flora across the black, tousled head lying in her lap, and then he sat on the fender-stool in front of the hearth and put his arm round her shoulder.

'Bella, lass . . . ' he spoke softly. Although his mind was filled with terror and the fear of what might have happened to her, he could not increase her agony. He could only share it. 'Come, lass, don't cry; you're home now, and safe, thank God. You'll need to get to sleep. And you'll be hungry, lassie?'

She looked up and smiled. 'I'm tired,' she said. 'I've been away up on the Lyle Hill.'

'All the time?'

'Yes, since this afternoon, when we left school. We . . . oh!'

She hid her face in her hands – and then the tears came and she sobbed. Deep, quiet sobbing, while Flora rocked her gently to and fro, and she seemed to want the touch of someone near her – as if she had been too long alone.

Her sobbing grew less laboured, her eyes were closed.

Gently, they took off her clothes and slipped on her warm flannelette nightdress.

'She'll sleep with us, John,' said Flora.

The child lay between the two good people in the big bed and slept, dreamlessly, till morning.

John slept in snatches, but Flora lay awake, fearing for the thing that she thought had happened to her bonnie lassie . . .

They let her sleep – long after John had gone to work and Flora had given the other two children their breakfast and sent them out to play.

When she woke, the firelight was dancing against the ceiling. The kitchen was dark, and even in summer it could be chilly. The table was spread with a white cloth and the place was filled with the appetising smell of hot porridge and frying bacon. She stirred, and sat up. Flora came to the bedside – questions in her eyes.

'You're awake, lassie? Do you feel better?'

'Mama, can we go and live up on the Lyle Hill?'

'Gracious me, Bella – what a funny thing to say!'

'Well, can we?'

Flora shook her head sadly. 'I'm afraid they wouldn't build houses up there for the likes of us. What makes you ask that?'

'Some day I'm going to live up there and I'm never going to leave it, never – never – never . . . '

This was not what Flora had expected. Something had happened to Bella, there was no doubt about that, but it did not seem to be the thing she had dreaded and feared.

'What happened to you yesterday, Bella? You surely didn't get lost?'

'Lost? No. Will you get old, Mama?'

Flora was nearly out of her depth.

'Old? Yes, of course I will. Everybody does. Come on and eat your breakfast, pet.'

'Will I get old, Mama?'

'Oh, Bella! What's all this about? Where did you go yesterday?'

'It was an old man, in a wee funny street near the Vennel. And they tried to take them away, and he was very old, and then he was lying on the ground, and there was blood . . . and then I ran – '

She covered her eyes with her hands and gave a little moan. But it was only momentary. The worst of the shock had gone from her.

Flora had heard all about the heartless eviction of the old couple, and the tragedy. So that was it; Bella had actually seen the whole thing. Feeling a little ashamed of herself for prying, she wanted to ask Bella all about it. But as Bella slid out of bed and began methodically to put on her clothes, there was a stony look in her eyes, a shut-in look, that gave the chldish face a hint of inborn dignity. For a moment she looked almost regal, much older than twelve. She said, quietly:

'They shouldn't separate *any* old people. I'll never let them take Dada away from you.'

Such relief Flora felt, to know that the child had not been set on and raped – she could only think the word inside her, she could never say it aloud. At the worst, Bella had seen the terrible death of an old man and, in a wider sense, she had seen a System in action. She was too young to know about this part of what she had seen. She could only see it in relation to individuals, particularly those she knew.

To the simple, clean mind of Flora, it was much more important that the child was whole, and still innocent.

Something had come out of the shambles that she had witnessed yesterday. Her tight little world had new horizons; there was suffering – injustice, hardship, tyranny – but she had found beauty – beauty that would last for at least as long as it had already endured – beauty that was a haven – this corner of the world, from the heights above the smoky streets.

*

Bella went back to school, but she grew serious. She spent more time at her lessons and she asked questions. But there was no answer for her memory, which demanded, often why this thing had happened.

The business of growing up seemed to have been painlessly completed, for when she was fourteen she left school and, after a year, she went to service.

She learned to wash dishes, cook, make beds, dust drawing-rooms, wash and iron clothes, polish floors, and knit and darn and sew. She helped in the church and she watched the young Jenny grow, and she saw her selfishness, emptiness and deceitfulness, which Bella tried to hide from Flora.

And as Bella grew in years and beauty, she fell more and more deeply in love with Willie Munro – who had eyes only for Jenny. Andrew, the youngest, was like his father, but he ignored Jenny most of the time. He followed Bella like a little lost sheep. He was slow, and truculent, and loyal, and he didn't understand Jenny at all.

Bella watched with almost possessive indignation when the first shovels were dug into her beloved hill. She was then sixteen, and the cycle of unemployment had come round again.

Skilled craftsmen delved and dug for a shilling a day,

and made a road: and where a road was, then came the houses. Bella was feverish with dread and impatience. She wanted a house on the top of the hill, and soon, it seemed there would be no room for *her* house.

The fine road was finished, but it still left the pinnacle of the hill free, and a rough-hewn flight of steps took her up to the very summit where she could still see her own corner of the world. This, she thought, *is* all the world — enough for me . . .

AMERICA: 1864—1868

A nation wrestled within itself, and the North gathered its battalions against the upstart South. Waggons rolled across alien prairies, and men and horses starved and rotted. And scarcely any of it touched the small community of Bessant, except that it grew bigger. Jimmy Miller and Louise moved into one of Rob's newest houses, and in time Louise was to present Jimmy with two fine sons and a daughter.

'A fine country,' the old bo'sun had said on the ship where Rob and Jimmy had met, and America had certainly taken the two Scotsmen to its heart. The social life of the town took them in enthusiastically, and even after Jimmy's wedding, Rob was still a very popular bachelor.

And into Robbie's life there came a woman who might have taken his heart, if it had not been lost to a squawking bundle in a close sixteen years before.

After Jimmy left, Rob discovered the trials of house-keeping, and buying groceries. He began to depend more and more on the girl who attended to his needs in the local store at the end of the street.

Her name was Martha, and she was the daughter of Matthew and Sarah Hallam, the store owners. She had two great, dark, domineering brothers who scowled at Rob when he met them in the street.

It was at a New Year's party, a festival dear to the heart of every Scot, wherever he may be, that he found himself dancing with Martha, and in the hub-bub of music and laughter and shouting, he led her out on to the porch under a full moon in a cloudless sky.

Martha was not generally considered a beautiful girl: in fact, she was rather plain and homely. But there were stars in her eyes when she looked at Rob.

The excitement of the dancing, the nostalgia of the occasion, and the close proximity of the girl beside him, together with his long denial of his natural desires, made him tremble as he swept her fiercely into his arms, and they seemed to melt into one figure in the moonlight. His hand, unpractised, fumbled with her blouse, and over her hips and thighs. And all the while he hated himself for his weakness, knowing that it was only her closeness and softness that disarmed him. She seemed to sense his anger, and not without difficulty she drew away and put her hand on his arms; he stood still, breathing hard and fighting for control.

'Rob,' she whispered softly. 'It's nearly midnight. It's New Year. We must go in and see everybody.'

'Martha! Don't go! For God's sake don't go yet! I – I'm sorry. I didn't mean to – '

'Ssh. You can tell me all you want to tell me tomorrow. We'll be at church. Now we must go in. There's the clock striking, and the bells. Happy New Year, Rob. It's 1865.'

He put his hand on her shoulder, and for a moment he was silent. Inside him his mind was saying, over and over again, 'Happy New Year, Bella. Forgive me.' Then he turned to Martha, and led her back to the hall.

'Happy New Year, Martha, and many may ye see.'

*

He was drawn irresistibly to Martha in the following weeks, but he made no opportunity to see her alone. He went on with his building, and working in the small shipyard. When it came to Easter, there was the traditional Hay Ride, and the girls brought out their gingham and cotton dresses, long skirted and flounced, with their white stockings and black patent leather shoes. The boys wore tight trousers and white shirts, with colourful jackets and straw hats.

Coming home in the late evening, to the music of accordions and whistles and tin drums, every lover and his lass found their own private heaven under the spring moon.

Rob was driving one of the hay-carts, with Martha on the box beside him. They were both very quiet, unlike the hilarious crowd behind them. Rob wanted to say something and he did not know where to start. Among the crowd were Martha's brothers, not too busy with their own girls to keep a wary eye on their sister.

Rob made a start. 'Martha.'

'Yes, Rob?'

'I'm . . . I'm awful fond of you, Martha.'

She looked at him. 'Are you, Rob?'

No, she wasn't going to help him. Whatever he had to say, he would have to find his own words, and his own courage.

'I think I'd better go away.'

'Because you're fond of me?'

'Because it's not right. It's not fair. I can't . . . it's just . . . it's not . . . ' He stopped, completely lost.

'Won't you tell me what's worrying you, Rob? I'm very fond of you too, you know.'

'That's just it! Martha, I wish I could tell you the whole thing, but, even if you cared enough for me, I can't offer you marriage.'

She went cold, numb with foreboding and disappointment. She knew it. She had known it all along. There was someone else in his life, and there was no one, there would never be anyone else, in her life. There was another woman. She hated, for a mad moment, the other woman who had a claim on him: what claim could it be but marriage?

She said a very small 'Oh,' and then she asked . . .

'Are you married, Rob?'

He stared straight in front of him, and flicked the reins on the big brown horse, who took no notice of him whatever, and just went clumping along.

'No, Martha. Believe me, I'm not married.'

'But there is another girl?'

'Yes . . . '

'Why don't you marry her, then? Is *she* married?'

(Oh Heaven! Is she married! The child Bella, now just seventeen, clear in his mind as he had seen her last, a happy, dancing, wholesome eight-year-old!)

Why? Why let this mad feeling for a child cloud his whole life? Why not take the happiness that was waiting for him, the good strong love of Martha Hallam, the prospect of life in this huge, rich country, and the circle of friends that he had built up in the last eight years?

'Rob?'

He came back to reality with a start.

'Oh, Martha, I'm sorry. I was far away.'

'Well, *is* she married?'

'No, she's very young yet.'

'She'll grow out of that,' said Martha, a little tartly.

'Yes, but not for a while, Martha. I *want* to see you again, but I haven't any right. I've got no right to be here with you now. Oh! If I could only tell you, Martha!'

He could not say any more. She was silent. They finished the hayride in sad silence, and he helped her down at the grocery store where she lived.

It was a few weeks after this, when he had a visit from Martha's brothers. He was working on another house, which he had already practically sold. Sawing and planing, his thoughts were back in the dim candle-lit cellar where he had made a rocking cradle for the baby he had found.

'Munro.' A voice came from the ground to Rob on the roof.

He looked down and saw the two men, big, dour and tough.

'Aye. That's me.'

'Want to talk to you. Don't rightly see it's got anything to do with the neighbours though.'

'All right. Come along to my house, over there.'

The three walked in silence round to the house where Rob lived.

Rob opened the door and led the way in. They stood in the kitchen, awkward, filling the place and giving no hint of any kind of social call.

'What do you want with me?'

Bluntly, the elder brother spoke. 'What about our Martha?'

Rob put his hands in his pockets.

'You been around with her a lot. Ain't nobuddy goin' to hurt our Martha.'

'I haven't hurt Martha.'

The younger one spoke up.

'She sets around, cryin' all the time. She tol' us she's real fond of you.'

'I'm glad to hear it. I'm very fond of her.'

'You figure marrying our Martha?'

Rob walked to the door and opened it.

'That's my business, and Martha's.'

But the biggest and darkest of the two brothers, Jake, was not to be so easily got rid of. He slammed the door shut and came and stood towering half a head above Rob.

'We reckon to make it our business, Munro. We don't want to see our Martha like she is, no sir. We like to see her laughing, and dancing the way she used to be. That's what we figgered. So we want to know, what about our Martha?'

Rob took a deep breath.

'I know what you want. You want to force me into a –
what do you call it – a shot-gun wedding? Well, I'll tell
you this, and you can do what you like about it. If you
do, the ceremony will be all you'll get. For as soon as it's
over, I'll leave. Martha will get my name, and a house,
and a very generous allowance, and that's all. She'll
never see me again. If you'll leave us alone, to let Martha
do what *she* wants, I'll care for her and protect her, and
give her everything she wants, as far as I can. A home,
and my company, if she wants it, for as long as she likes.
It's up to you, or rather, it's up to Martha. I'm *very* fond
of her, and I wouldn't hurt her for anything. If you force
this, you'll regret it.'

Even in their blundering, bull-at-a-gate fashion, they
seemed to see the logic of Rob's words. They stood for a
moment, and then the elder, more truculent but less
antagonistic than the younger one, turned and made for
the door.

'C'mon, Matt. Ain't no use any more talk. Martha's got
to settle this herself.'

'Will you tell Martha I'll be over to see her tomorrow
evening?'

'In a hurry, ain't ya?' Jake was scowling.

'Please yourself. I'll come anyway.'

Still scowling, but much more pacified than he
intended to show, Jake beckoned to Matt, and they
stamped out.

Robbie was shaken, humiliated and angry. He knew
that Martha had some cause for expecting him to declare
himself, but he shirked, as he had never before shirked
anything, the task of telling her what he had just told her
brothers.

That Martha was a woman in a thousand, he knew.
And if he had come to this country heart-whole, he
would have counted himself fortunate indeed to win the
love of a girl as dear and sweet and wholesome as she.
But always there, like the first star in a blue velvet sky,
was the bright flashing image of the girl in the old grey
town, as he had seen her last, pert and irrepressible,

important in her Sunday clothes.

But if Martha's brothers could intimidate most people they came up against, they could not frighten Martha. It took a very few choice words from her, when she got the story from them, under intense protest! And the pair of them mooched away, to mind their own business.

In the early afternoon of the next day, she tied on her bonnet, put a white lacy woollen shawl over her shoulders, and drove her own little pony and trap the three miles over rough land to the clearing near the lake where Rob was building.

He was up on a ladder, working on the roof. And now that she was here, she was horrified at her boldness. She could not imagine what impulse had brought her here, after her brothers had told her of their meeting with Rob. She felt humiliated and angry, and the only thing that seemed to matter was to make sure that Rob understood that she had no part in that encounter. And she wanted to talk without the cramping presence of her family.

Rob heard the clip clop of her pony, and came down quickly to meet her on the grass verge beside the partly made road.

'I was coming over to see you tonight, Martha.'

'I know. Jake told me. But I wanted to talk to you, without my folks there. Will you drive with me and we can talk?'

'Sure. Just let me wash my hands and put on a jacket . . . I won't be a minute, Martha.'

Rob took the reins and a little way along the lake shore, he pulled up and let the pony nuzzle the lush grass by the roadside.

'Martha, I – '

'No, Rob, don't. Jake and Matt had no business talking to you like that, and I told them so. I'll do what I please with my life. I'm twenty-three, after all, and this is 1865, not *1765*!'

'What can I say, Martha?' I . . . I do . . . kind of love you, in a way. At least, I wouldn't look at another girl round here. And I can't tell you, yet, about the girl who – well, I just can't tell you, that's all. But if you'll take me, Martha, I'll look after you, as long as I live. But if your brothers force me, as I told them, I'll go away and you'll never see me again. All you'll have is a name and a house, and an empty wedding ring. I shouldn't have let myself get so fond of you, or see you so often. Either that, or I'll go, right away, *now*, and never come back. I've no right to even ask you to think about being with me. I should have let the other fellows have a chance, some other fellow who would marry you, and you would have a home and a family. We couldn't have a family, Martha, you realise that? I know there's dozens of chaps who would want you, and marry you. I should – '

She cut his words short, by putting her fingers on his lips.

'Hush, Rob. Listen to me. This is what we'll do. If . . . if you really want me?'

She looked anxiously at him.

'I haven't any right to want you, my dear, but I do.'

'Then listen. This is what we'll do. We'll slip off some day soon, go to Niagara. I can leave a note to say we didn't want a fussy wedding, so we've eloped. I couldn't let any sort of scandal hurt my folks. It will be just between you and me. Nobody else will know.' She paused. 'I'll be a good wife to you, Rob.'

'Better than I deserve,' he said. 'I'll take care of you, I promise.'

She drew her shawl around her, and shivered a little.

'I'm going back now. Come to church on Sunday, and we can let folks see us talking, and arranging. They can't *prove* that we don't get married. Matt and Jake will know, but they won't tell anybody. I'll see to that.'

He bent his head and kissed her very gently on her lips. Then he flicked the reins and the pony trotted homewards. The ride back was pleasant and quite free from strain. It was as if they knew that life would be good for both of them, and if Martha shed a few tears into her pillow, and blindly hated the girl in Rob's secret life, nobody knew. Rob was here, and soon she would be with him. She felt herself blushing in the darkness, for this was a big step to take. Her upbringing had taught her that this kind of thing was wicked, but she could not lose him. Let her have just a little while with him, then maybe . . .

Far better to throw away her orthodox outlook and keep him by her side, than to insist on marriage, and find herself a deserted maiden, lonely and respectable.

They slipped away for a few days to Niagara Falls, and nobody knew they were not really married. Except, perhaps, Martha's two scowling brothers.

They came to live in Rob's newly completed house, and Rob settled to wait . . . The selfishness of what he had done never even occurred to him.

Bella, always in his thoughts as he had seen her last.

Why? Why let this mad feeling for a *child* cloud his whole life? Why not take the happiness that was there for him – the good, strong love of Martha, and the complete, full life in this great, rich country?

Then he remembered the kiss he had planted on the tiny warm face in the white shawl.

'I'll go back,' he thought for the second time. 'When she's nineteen. Just another two years. I'll go back when she's nineteen.'

X

In early September, 1867, Willie Munro wrote, for his mother, to his brother, Rob.

. . . mother says she'll come and stay with you for a wee while, but I'm staying here. I'm getting on fine on the coal lorries. Mother says I've to tell you that Bella McGarvie is getting married soon. She met a lad on the boat – she went on the Sunday Breaker one day, a sailor on the boat. His name's Jimmy Morrison. I don't know him. I'm going to wait for Jenny – I think I'll ask her if she'll take me, when she's old enough. I like her the best of anybody I've seen. Mother will arrive in New York on 30th September.

Your brother,
Will.

Rob stood with his brother's letter in his hand. Bella . . . *his* Bella . . . getting married? At nineteen. But *he* was going back, to bring her to America! His love, now, was legitimate, and clean and proper.

He was mad – mad with hate against this unknown sailor who had captured his lovely. Had he seduced her? God in Heaven! *That* did not bear thinking about. While, he, Robbie, had left the country, put three thousand miles between them so that he would not be tempted before he asked her for marriage, some lout had taken her beauty, her body –

He worked himself into a frenzy of despair. Why the hell had he not gone back when he had said he would? Then he remembered – there had been the Civil War – much had been happening in the little township: Martha's brothers had married, her mother died. Louise, Jimmy's wife, was thrown by a horse, although she recovered after a long time in bed.

All in all, it had been a time of change and bustle, and it had gone so quickly. While he had never forgotten his vow to go back for her, the urgency had escaped him. He had completely ignored the fact that she would now be desirable to other men.

He waited impatiently for the day his mother should arrive. And now he faced a different problem. Martha. In all his letters home, he had never mentioned her. How was he to explain Martha to his mother?

Martha solved this by telling him she was going back to look after her father.

'You're leaving me, Martha?'

'Not really leaving you, Rob. But your mother will want to see *you*, and there's something about that girl in Scotland. You said three years ago that she was too young. I believed you. I thought perhaps she was seventeen, or even sixteen. But you must have been in love – with a girl of *fourteen!* Robbie! What kind of man are you?'

'What kind of man have you found me, over the last three years, Martha?'

'A good man, Rob. But why – ?'

'I've been – in love – with Bella – since I found her when she was a baby. I didn't know what it was when I first held her – she was only a wee mite – and she tried to chew my dirty finger.'

'Since you *found* her?'

It was a relief at last, to tell her about that dark October morning. And to tell her, now, about the news that had made him mad for an hour.

'She's nineteen. I was going back to get her when she was nineteen. I made up my mind about that, when Jimmy and I first came here. Long before I knew you. Now I've left it too late.'

Her first sensation was one of triumph. The child was getting married – now she and Robbie could be married, and she could have his children.

'Robbie! She's getting married! It's her own decision. That makes you free – she could never have loved you.'

'No, she didn't love *me*. She was always crazy about my brother Willie – and he couldn't stand her! God Almighty, what a mix-up.! And now this – this – rogue has got her. Oh God! What can I do now?'

Martha looked at him, and then slowly she moved over to the door into the hall.

She paused just a moment to say, sadly and quietly, 'Robert, you're a fool.'

For a long time, he looked at where she had been. Something tore through him – was it something he felt for Martha? Standing with his hands resting on the back of the chair, he let his mind go blank – he shut his eyes. Inside him, he could see the wholesome sweetness of the girl who had shared every thought and every moment for the last three years. She had brought him comfort and love; affection, a well-run home, health and strength – and everything but the children he knew she longed for.

But then, sweeping every picture away, he saw a small, tidy figure, in brown dress with velvet collar – a brown hat with ribbon and brown kid gloves – glowing with the inside goodness that she felt so serenely when she went to church.

He was a fool. A fool.

Then he had to *be* a fool.

He knew Martha would go now. They had reached the end. He had nothing to keep him here. He would leave things in Jimmy's hands, and as soon as his mother's visit was over, he would up stakes and be off again – he didn't care where, or how. A young man of thirty-two, with money in his pocket, could go places . . . the whole world was open to him.

XI

The *Jeanie Deans* stood out from Helensburgh, her paddles leaving a wide wake across to Gourock, on a bright Saturday afternoon in May. Four young people picnicking on the Gourock shore, watched her lazily: Maggie Leith, and Eddie, her husband of four months, Bella, and Tommy Wilson, who thought that some day, he might be Bella's husband.

It was an unusually warm afternoon, for May, sunny and clear, the river a calm blue sheath, with the sun making sparkling diamonds with the slight movement of the waves.

Eddie looked across at Tommy, and made a beckoning movement with his head, as he walked slowly to the edge of the water rippling over the stones.

Tommy got up and moved towards him.

'Look – there's the *Jeanie Deans*. She sails tomorrow as well. What d'you say to a sail on her?'

'What? On the Sunday Breaker?'

'Aye.'

'Well, I would like it, and so would Maggie. You ask Bella. She's your lass.'

'I don't think she's anybody's lass yet. I wish she was. But I'll ask her.'

He turned and went over to Bella, who was sitting with her back against a rock.

'Bella? Eddie's just said we should go on the boat tomorrow.'

Maggie looked up.

'Tomorrow? But it's Sunday! You mean – on the Sunday Breaker? Oh my!'

'We'll go, Maggie, so – Bella?'

'Oh! My father would never let me!'

'Don't tell him. Just come.'

'I'll need to put on my Sunday hat!'

'You lassies and your Sunday hats!' Eddie grinned.

The sun again shone brightly on Sunday morning. Bella dressed, with her heart beating fast, feeling sure that her father must know there was something different about her this morning. The lifelong habits of duty and obedience are not easy to break, and when John gave her the silver threepenny piece for the plate, as he did every Sunday, she took it with a feeling of guilt.

She slipped out of the big door, and instead of going up the steps to the church, she turned and walked quickly down towards the river, along the narrow streets till she came to the Albert Harbour.

Chattering with excitement, and a little fear of last-minute interference by angry parents, they clambered up the gangway. There were quite a few people aboard, for it was getting popular with the people who had to work all week; and all the Power of the Kirk had been unable to stop it.

The girls must explore the boat: go and look at the engines – not forgetting the engineers! – and watch the paddles churning up the water. The freedom of the boat, and this glorious Sunday morning, was theirs. This was high adventure indeed. Somebody produced a mouth organ, and music that was certainly not hymn tunes carried lilting and gay across the wide, rich river.

Then they must watch the sailors coiling the ropes so cleverly round and round the capstan: and look at the remote figure of the captain on the bridge. It was all as wonderful and exciting as the boys had said it would be.

Bella walked to the stern to look at the receding Princes Pier. She was glad the boat was only going to Dunoon: she would never go where she could not see Greenock. Tommy followed her, and stood leaning on the rail beside her, pondering on how lovely she was. He was not altogether sure . . . there was plenty of time: Bella was only nineteen, he was twenty-one. He knew that Bella was rather fond of the young Munro lad, Will. He remembered Robbie, who had gone to America. But he thought that Will was not really very interested in Bella. They had all grown up together – had fun, gone to socials and dances in the church hall in the winter, and only recently, there had come the new Magic Lantern shows. Picnics in the summer, and long walks, and an occasional sail on a Saturday afternoon. But this was the first time they had ventured anything so wickedly exciting.

Well, he would see . . . time enough.

He spoke to her just as the ship's bell rang as they were coming in to Dunoon.

'Bella?'

'M'm, what is it, Tommy?'

'Bella, will you come out with me again?'

'I'll not be likely to get *anywhere* after this!'

'Aye . . . I suppose we'll all get into trouble. But it's grand, isn't it?'

'Oh yes, it is. Oh look! We're coming into Dunoon.'

'Aye. We'd better move. There's a sailor coming to get the rope.'

Almost casually, it seemed, the seaman turned the wheel and threw the rope on to Dunoon pier, where it was caught and hauled in, and the heavy loop dropped over the bollard at the edge.

He moved round and faced the two, Tommy with his arm lightly across Bella's shoulders. The seaman was a slight, fairly thin man, but strong-looking, for all his slim build.

A dark beard and moustache gave a heavy grimness to his face, and made him look older than his thirty years. His eyes were large, and clear, without a hint of the cruelty that lay behind them.

'How long have we got here, can you tell me?' Tommy asked.

'About twenty minutes, sir.'

There was a scampering of feet and a burst of loud laughter, and the others dashed along the deck.

'Tommy! Bella! Come on, we're going on to the pier. Come on.'

'No, you go, you and Maggie. I don't want to go off the boat. I'll just sit here and wait.'

Tommy did not see the glance that passed between the sailor and Bella. She was watching him, fascinated, almost hypnotised by his easy skill with the heavy ropes, and a strange thrill ran through her body.

'Bella?'

'No, I'll wait here, you go on.'

'All right.' They ran off laughing and shouting.

Bella felt her legs go weak, and she sat down on the nearest seat. The sailor leaned on the rail and watched her.

'Fine day,' he said.

She choked. 'Oh, g . . . g . . . oh aye . . . it's lovely.'

'Is this the first time you've been for a sail on a

Sunday?'

'Aye.'

There was a short silence. Bella didn't know what to say. Then she ventured, timidly,

'The boat's lovely and clean.'

He gave a dark frown, and when he answered, his voice was harder than it had been before.

'The decks on *my* ship are always scrubbed clean. They'd better be.'

Then he looked at her again. 'Will you be coming next Sunday?'

'Oh no! I'll get into terrible trouble for being here today.'

His eyes twinkled. 'It's a terrible thing to be on the Sunday Breaker, isn't it?'

She laughed. 'I expect it will be quite common in a few years' time. Folks won't think anything of it.'

'Aye, I suppose so. But forbidden fruit always tastes sweetest,' he said, a heavy look at her emphasising the words. With the primeval instinct of the male, he saw through the trappings of her petticoats and stays and drawers. He saw only her soft, white nakedness.

'I'll be on the boat all week, if you come for a sail sometime.'

'I'll maybe get my mother and father to come next Saturday.'

She looked at him rather timidly, as though she knew instinctively that he didn't want her mother and father.

'I've got lodgings in Gourock. I'd like fine to see you some night. We could go for a walk along to the Cloch.'

He looked up at the bridge, and took a step away from the rails, his eyes on her face.

The potency of the sexual pull between them was overpowering. *He* knew the urgency and the power of it: she felt only the unfamiliar trembling in her legs, and the single, biting need of his touch. Her whole body felt the need; strange, and yet as if she knew how it would be. She moved nearer to the coiled ropes.

'Will you?'

'What?'

'Come for a walk with me? I could come on Tuesday night, if you'd meet me. About seven o'clock, at Cardwell Bay?'

'Oh, aye, I'll come.'

She stayed with her friends on the return trip, and only caught his eye when they left the boat at the Albert Harbour. She saw his mouth form the word 'Tuesday', but the sound was lost in the general clangour of ship's noises, laughter, and some jeers from the small crowd that waited for them on the quay.

When he threw the rope to the man on the quay, he ran down the gangway, and stood by her, while she waited for Maggie and Eddie.

Without turning round, he said, 'What's your name?'

'Bella McGarvie.'

'I'm Jimmy Morrison. See you Tuesday.'

The four adventurers left the quay to the cheers and jeers of the small crowd, but the jeers were tinged with good-natured jealousy and admiration for the youngsters' bravery.

XII

Bella's father was angry, silently angry, at Bella's escapade on Sunday. He had seen her empty seat beside Jenny and Andy when he had shut the pulpit door, and his heart jumped. His anger changed to worry and puzzlement when he heard where she had been, and that she had arranged to meet a strange man during the next week.

John had never been an articulate man. His work, his

wife, his children, and his minister, absorbed all his attention and affection. Words belonged to other people, to people like the minister, and the elders, and the men who spoke at meetings, and the Sunday-school teachers. He could say very little, but Bella knew he was angry.

'Who is this fellow you've arranged to meet?'

Bella hung her head. 'A sailor, on the boat.'

'The Sunday Breaker?'

'Yes.'

'That was a bad thing to do, Bella.'

'Yes, I know, father.'

'And this man, where are you going with him?'

'Just a walk along the shore.'

He was silent for a moment.

'Your mother would be better to speak to you.'

He paused again, and looked at her thoughtfully. Then he went on, in a gentler tone, 'You'll no' do that again? This is not the thing to do, for a young lassie to stay away from church.'

'I – I'm very sorry, father.'

'Aye. You'll be a good lass then. I'll speak to your mother.'

Flora was nearly as helpless as John, but Bella, tearful and conscience-stricken, proved easy to talk to.

Flora spoke of the night, a hot summer night, when they thought Bella had been lost. 'You remember that night, Bella?'

'Oh yes. I was away up on the Lyle Hill.' That night of soft velvet twilight after the sudden flash of tragedy in the brilliant sunshine. 'I'll go and live there some day . . . '

'Aye, maybe you will. But we thought, that night, before you got home, that some man – that maybe you'd been set on and . . . and . . . ' she faltered.

'I know what you mean, mother.'

'You *know?* How? Did you – ?'

'Oh, we hear things. We know a lot more than you think. We remembered Mary Johnston. She had a wee baby, and she wasn't married. At first, we didn't know you *could* have a baby unless you were married, but then

we found out that you can. But *I'm* not going to. I'm
going to be like you. You were a long time married
before *I* came, weren't you, mother?'

Flora stared at her.

The years fell away, and she realised that she had
almost forgotten the time before Bella came. The lovely
face beside her faded in a blur as Flora's heart missed a
beat. She knew the time had come to tell Bella, and she
dreaded the telling.

'Are you all right, mother?'

She was rubbing Flora's hands. The moment of
faintness passed.

'Aye. I'm all right, lassie. It's better I tell you now. We
tried to tell you some times, but it was never easy.'

'Tell me what, mother?'

'Put the kettle on, lass, and I'll tell you.'

She thought for a moment. Where was the best place
to start, since no one could ever know Bella's beginning?

'It *was* a long time we were married before you came,
Bella, that's true. Eight years it was, and we thought we
would never manage to have a bairn of our own. Then,
one winter morning, it was, Robbie Munro found you, in
the corner of the close in West Burn street when he went
to work at six o'clock in the morning. And your Auntie
Millie, Robbie's mother, you know, came down and got
you, and brought you to me.'

'Found me? The close in West Burn Street? But
weren't we here, in the church?'

'No. We came here when you were about four or five.
You'll not remember it?'

No, no, she couldn't remember coming here. It seemed
she had always been here, in the big rooms below the
church.

'Oh, the kettle's boiling. I'll make the tea.'

'Sit still, mother. I'll make the tea.'

She took the teapot and warmed it. She moved
quietly between the fireplace and the dresser, although
she was a seething storm inside.

Stunned, and somehow ashamed, she suddenly

remembered what Mary Johnston's baby had been called, and yet knowing that she had no need for shame. She went over in her mind, the years between, that day when she was twelve, when she had discovered her own world, out of black desecration, and yesterday, the day she had met Jim Morrison.

Methodically she made the tea, and took some biscuits from a tin. '*Who* found me, you said?'

'Robbie, Robbie Munro. He used to play with you, and give you rides on his back. He went to America. Millie says he's doing very well. Are you angry, Bella?'

'Angry? Oh no, mother! No! I'm just thinking. What would have happened to us all if he hadn't found me?'

'I know what would have happened to us. Your father would have drunk himself into his grave, and I wouldn't have been long after him. I expect you would have been picked up, by somebody, or else the rats might have got you, if Robbie hadn't seen you!'

Bella shuddered. 'Well, I'm not going to do anything like that. My . . . my *real* mother must have left me like that. But you're always my mother, anyway. Only . . .' she hesitated. 'Jenny? Or Andy? They don't know?'

'No, lass. And they won't know from me, or your father.'

Flora paused. 'Will you be going to meet this man?'

Bella walked over to the kitchen window. The trousers of men, and the skirts and boots of women passing were all she could see of the people from the basement window.

She felt the tingling sensation in her arms again, when she thought of dark, handsome Jim Morrison.

'Yes, I'll meet him. But don't worry, mother. Nothing like that is going to happen to me.'

*

When the Tuesday came, she walked along the west end street. He was waiting for her at Cardwell Bay.

Her brown serge dress, with a short velvet jacket, was her last year's Sunday dress. It trailed on the ground behind her, full-skirted and heavy. Her bonnet was a dark brown, trimmed with a ribbon bow at the back, made from the velvet of the jacket. She wore hand-knitted stockings of fine grey wool, and her boots were black leather, buttoned up to the calves.

'Hallo,' he said. 'I wondered if you would come.'

'I said I would.'

'I thought your father might have said you couldn't come out after being on the boat on Sunday.'

'He was very angry, but he wouldn't stop me, if I wanted to come.'

They walked along the sedate main street of Gourock, on to the shore, and sat down among the rocks, with the waves lapping the pebbles gently below their feet.

'Do you belong to Gourock?' Bella asked him.

'No, I only took the river-boat job for the summer. I come from Lochranza, in Arran. I'm staying in Gourock, because my sister's getting married on Friday.'

'Oh. And then will you be going back to Arran?'

'That depends. Would you like a sail there?'

She shook her head. 'No. I'll never leave here.'

'You sound very sure of that.'

'Aye. I'll never leave Greenock.'

'Never's a long time.'

She nodded.

This girl puzzled him. He usually had a way with women, but this one, seemingly so fiery and eager, still gave the impression of icy strength underneath. And he suddenly realised that never in his life before had he been faced with true virginity. The thought hit him with such force, that he stopped in the act of lighting his pipe and gave her a look of such startled curiosity that she flushed and looked away, watching the sea-gulls drifting on the water, or hovering lazily on still, wide-spread wings.

He had to think.

This one *was* different. This girl was the kind who would meet a boy at church, or Bible class, like the youth who had been with her on the boat on Sunday, and they would go with each other for anything up to three or four years, and would then get married.

But she was *here,* with him, and he knew the struggle going on in her mind. Her prudery, and her upbringing, against the elemental urge of human desires and passions. And she didn't know, yet, what it all meant. Yes, this one was worth a siege. This one was pure ice and fire, untouched and almost ready for awakening. This one he would have for himself.

When he leaned over to kiss her, her eyes, starry-bright, gazed at him with an expression he had never seen before.

This was her first contact with a man who looked at her as a woman, not just a pretty girl to flirt with. This man's experienced touch seemed to let loose the fire inside her. His arms tightened round her, and drew her back to lie in a hollow in the rocks. But he was wary: this must be handled with care and caution: if he frightened her now, he would lose the thrill of taming her.

He made a pretence of scrabbling impatiently at the folds of her long skirt, but the truth was that he had not really recovered completely from a slight feverish attack over Sunday night and Monday, and when she twisted away from him and pushed his hand away he did not make any effort to force or persuade her. Plenty of time . . .

'Oh-ho, my fine lady! It seems you know how to take care of yourself! And I thought you were so innocent. But I'll have you yet, my beauty. I'll have you yet.'

She sat up and straightened her hat and her skirt.

She said, timidly, 'Have I made you angry?'

'Angry? No, but we'd better get you home. It's a long walk.'

'You can't come all the way. I'll manage.'

'I'll come along the town with you: I think that cold I got on Sunday has made me feel a bit tired.'

They walked for a while in silence, along Gourock Road, and into Eldon Street.

'I'll manage from here,' Bella said. 'Will you be leaving Greenock after the summer sailings?'

'I don't know for sure yet. I'll see how I feel after my sister's wedding.'

'Who is she marrying?'

'A captain.'

'Could you be a captain?'

'I've got my master's ticket. I'll likely go deep sea, soon.'

'You mean, right away? Across the sea?'

'Aye, America, or China. Maybe even Australia. It's better than the river boats.'

'I wouldn't leave here for anything!'

'Would you no'? Ah well, we'll see. Will you meet me again next week?'

'I . . . yes, I think so, but – '

He grinned at her. 'Are you frightened?'

Bella stood up straight and looked at him.

'No! I'm not frightened of anybody.'

'Well, meet me next week.'

'Yes, all right.'

He pulled her into the shelter of a shop doorway in Eldon street, and held her close. He kissed her, his bearded face scratching her cheeks and chin, and his caresses chased away every vestige of commonsense, and she believed herself passionately in love.

The careless, innocent flirtations of innumerable picnics, church socials and dances, were a thousand years away. The distant, happy feeling she had cherished all these years for Willie Munro, seemed so absurd that she could feel herself laughing inside.

She and Morrison met often during the summer and autumn, and without knowing her own power, she kept him at bay. Not because she did not want to possess, or be possessed, but because she was grimly determined that no shame or regret should come to the two people who meant more to her than anyone else on earth. She thought she loved this man: she did not know that it was only her body that responded to his caresses. She thought she loved, because this man made her feel that she wanted to strip her body naked for him. Her face grew hot at the thought of it, but think of it she did, and could not stop it.

And because it was only her body, and not her heart, or her mind, she could go rigid and cold in his arms while they lay in the shadow of gorse bushes on the Whin Hill, or stood in the dark corner of the church passage, when he took her home.

There was only one way to win this battle. They all had their price. This one demanded the highest price, and because he would not be cheated of fair game, because he was determined to be the first, he was prepared to pay the price.

'I think we'd better get married, Bella my lass,' he said one night. His hands held her close to his body, pressing her tighter against him: he had endured a whole summer and autumn of unsatisfied lust, and he had to own himself beaten, by a slip of a girl not yet twenty!

'Married? Oh, I think you'd better ask my father.'

He knew that. She was under twenty-one.

'I will that. I'll come and see him tomorrow night. I'll be going now. I didn't think to wed a Greenock lass. Still, I'll make sure nobody else will get you! Goodnight.'

He kissed her again, turned and went down the street.

'Goodnight, Jimmy.' Bella whispered. 'I'll tell my father you'll be coming to see him.'

*

John felt a cold hand touch his heart when Bella told him the next evening that Jimmy Morrison was coming to see him. He had met the dark-haired sailor at a church social, and something evil seemed to be held in the air between them. He guessed why the man wanted to see him, and he was almost sick with fear and foreboding. He went down to his cellar, and started shovelling coal with a kind of furious, unnecessary haste. As always, his anger was

silent: he could not find words to voice his disapproval
or refusal.

Morrison stood half way down the steps in the
shadow thrown by the gaslight, and his voice was gruff
and unfriendly. He knew there was enmity in the little
man who stood grasping his shovel, his face and hands
grimed with coal-dust, and his eyes glaring hate across the
boiler door.

'I'll be asking you, Mr McGarvie. I want your consent
to wed Bella. She's willing, if so be you'd let her.'

John could not, literally could not, speak. He turned
away and thrust his shovel into the coal with an angry
push, and fed it into the blazing boiler.

The younger man's face held hate, too, and he turned
and walked up the stairs again.

'To hell with him!' he muttered to himself. 'To hell
with the lot of them! What do I want with her, anyway...
plenty of women about. To hell with them . . . ' and he
strode angrily along the passage to the door.

She was there. Ah! If only she had not been there at
that moment!

The light of a full moon had burst through the rain
clouds that had been hanging over the town all day, and
lay, a silver path across the darkness of the river. The
moon shone on Bella's face framed in a white shawl, and
she was so lovely. He felt the familiar urgent need of her.

'Damn the old man – I'll have you.'

He swept her into his arms and kissed her fiercely,
and just as abruptly, let her go.

'We'll get wed, my girl. You can tell your father that.
I said I'd have you, and I will.'

He looked hard at her, then turned away and walked
down the street, and into the town.

*

John and Flora argued about it far into the night, before
John would even consider giving his consent.

'He'll not be good to her, that's all I know. There's bad in him.'

'He's been very nice to her, and to us, so far, John. And for-why should he not be good to her? Anyway, Bella's a good girl, and she'll be able to stand up to him, if he wasn't good to her.'

'I'll not willingly see her married to him. She can't get wed without my consent.'

'Well, if you don't, said Flora, 'she might just go and live with him. You know what young people are these days. And it would bring disgrace on us all.'

'I'm thinking wc'll have our share of that in the days to come, wife.' John's tone was quiet and resigned. 'All right, but I'm telling you it's against my better judgement. I'll tell the minister.'

They were married at the end of December. On Hogmanay night: a time for rejoicing.

On her wedding night, the minister came down to the kitchen where Bella stood, shaken and silent, beside Jim. She wore a dark blue dress trimmed with braid round the shoulders and over the bodice. The long skirt was braided at the bottom, and fell in folds over her shoes.

John, unrelenting, stood in his socks and shirt sleeves, defiant even of his minister. This was the only way he could show his disapproval.

The quiet little wedding was over. The few friends were regaled with steak pie and cold ham and tea, with a drop of whisky, and the minister left.

Coldness with a foreboding of doom settled on the small gathering, which had been awkward and forced in its jollity even before this, and it was a relief when Morrison stood up and said they would have to be going. He had found a single kitchen in a tenement in the east end, near the docks.

She came, virginal, to her marriage bed, and knew one night of desire, and ecstasy, and pain.

In another three months she knew him for the brute he

was: scarcely a part of her body was without a bruise, and she saw before her only a fate of misery and despair. But she did not yet know the full measure of his brutality.

VIII

Three nights after her marriage, Bella had seen the passion she had mistaken for love, turn into loathing, and then fear.

It was three days after New Year when she ventured out to the shops. Morrison was working on some ships at Port Glasgow docks, but the land job irked him – he wanted to be at sea. As Bella opened her door, the door opposite opened too. A young woman, carrying a baby in a shawl, stepped out and looked round. Bella tried to cover the bruise on her face with a scarf – but the girl had already recognised her.

'Bella! Oh Bella, I never guessed it was you. Oh Bella love!'

'Maggie! Maggie Leith! Oh, Maggie!'

She could say no more.

'I heard there was a new-married couple here. I'm just going to the shops. Are you coming?'

'Yes, yes, but you go on. I'll catch you up. Maggie . . .' She hesitated.

'Don't worry, love. It might be better in a wee while. You'll get used to him. See, wee Charlie's smiling at you.'

'But, I didn't know you had a baby . . . '

'Oh, Charlie, you mean? Well, we had to get married, you know, Bella. But not, you didn't know very much about that – then. Remember that last picnic we had? The day before we went on the Sunday Breaker? Charlie was

on the way then. Oh! That was . . . you mean it was *him*
you married! That sailor?'

Bella nodded.

'Well, don't let him bully you. You give him as good
as you get. He'll soon learn when he's well off. I'll away
and get my messages. I'll see you in a wee while.'

'Maggie, don't . . . don't let him know you're here,
that you know me.'

'I'll watch that, Bella. Don't worry.'

Somehow, she felt that if he knew about Maggie, one
of her dearest friends, he would make sure that she got
no chance to see her.

He had hit her that morning, for the first time.
Exhausted and repulsed by his attitude, his body and his
words, the vile obscenities that seemed to come as easily
as ordinary speech, she had pleaded for mercy, for pity
– for relief from his repeated demands of his 'rights.'

'No, no. Please, I don't want – '

'Don't want to . . . don't want to . . . ' he sneered,
mimicking her. 'Who the hell do you think you are,
whether you want to or not! You caught me with your
innocent-miss game, and by Christ, I'll take what I've paid
dearly for. I'm tied to you for life, and don't you forget
it!'

Then he had slammed his fist right on her cheekbone,
under her eye.

That was the beginning of the brutality. At first Bella,
proud and beautiful, and still with some of the spirit of
her forefathers in her, tried to fight back. One day her
mother came to see her, and while she was there, sitting
quietly talking to Bella, he came in.

'Oh, it's you, is it? Well, we don't want you here, so
get off home – back to your church. Go on, and don't let
me catch you here again. Bella doesn't need you, and
she's got more to do than sit and gossip to anybody. Go
on, get out.'

Bella tried to argue with him – tried to stop her
mother leaving, but Flora left, fearful for her lassie. When
she had gone, he took his leather belt, and beat Bella to

her knees. Then he picked her up and flung her on the bed, and took her, savagely, lustful, careless of her pain or bruises. After that, she could only gather strength during the day to withstand his demands and brutality in the nights.

She could go out very little in the daytime – she was too ragged, and after he came home in the evenings, she dared not be out of his sight. If he went out for a drink, at a nearby pub, she had to be home when he came back. He was not a heavy drinker, but he liked two or three glasses of whisky, and some beer.

Occasionally, he would fling a half-sovereign on the table and tell her to go out and buy some food. Once, he had locked her in because, in sheer desperation, and in an agony of fury from the pain of bruised limbs, she told him she would run away from him, and he would never find her. He laughed at her, and told her she would have to come back to him. He had the law on his side, she was his legal wife and he would take what he wanted, whenever he wanted.

'And to make sure you don't get away, my girl, I'll lock you in. You won't let the neighbours see you climbing out of the window, and it's a twenty foot drop anyway!' And he laughed again. She was locked in for the whole day, until he came home about six o'clock.

After that, she was quiet, and tried to avoid any excuse for blows. She lived in fear and terror of him.

For a few days in early April he was at home, and did not go out to work.

He told her nothing, except when he would want a meal. He started bringing home new clothes for himself, never anything for her. The few dresses she had had when she came on her wedding night were in rags, and she could not even wash her clothes properly. She could not buy the soap and cleaning materials that she had taken for granted all her life.

He had been buying thick jerseys, socks, and heavy woollen underwear; big boots and reefer jacket, and even woolly caps. He had said many times that he wanted to go deep sea again, she was no use to him, 'might as well be in bed with a statue . . . sick of her and her puny ways . . . plenty of women in the world . . . '

On theWednesday night she had made the drab kitchen as tidy as she could. He had a passion for intense cleanliness around him, and she had had to do the best she could to keep it clean without soap or scrubbing brushes, which she dared not buy out of the small amount of money he gave her. The fire glowed red, because he insisted on a good fire and a hot meal when he came home.

She wore only an old coat over her thin cotton nightdress.

She heard the thud of his footsteps along the landing. He had obviously had a few drinks. She heard his heavy breathing, and the fumbling of his key in the lock.

She waited.

He lurched in and leered at her.

'Aye, waiting for me, my beauty, eh? So I've trained you who's master at last? I said I would. Pity I won't get the benefit of it now. I'm away to sea in the morning; so get my supper and then get into that bed, quick.'

She shrank a little, although she had tried to school herself to show no emotion.

'Oh – ho! Did you think that just because you're three months gone that you'd be having nothing more to do with me? Well, you'll soon see different. You thought I didn't know, did you? Think I don't know anything about women? Let me tell you, I've had plenty better than you under me. Now, my supper, and then – Come on, I've got to be up early. Move, curse you!'

He slapped her full on the face, and she stumbled and fell. The little whimper of pain that she could not keep back seemed to incense him even more. He kicked her, and moved over to the dresser and opened his parcel. He pulled his seaman's bag from under the bed and filled it with the clothes from the parcel.

Bella pulled herself up, scarcely breathing with relief, and release. It seemed he really did mean to go this time.

He ate his supper in silence. She gathered up the dishes and cleared the table.

'Leave them, and get into bed,' he snarled at her. She looked at him fearfully. He *never* let her leave any dishes.

'B – but . . . ' she stammered. 'You want . . . '

'I'll show you what I want. Leave them and get into bed.'

He tore the coat from her, picked her up and flung her on to the bed. He took off his leather belt and raised it high, to bring it down with a terrible crack on her body. She buried her face in the pillow and screamed in agony as the first vicious stroke stung right across her backside, tearing the nightdress already torn and bloody from other beatings.

'Aye, you'll soon see different; turn round, you stupid bitch, if you don't want another leathering. I'll be away in the morning, for three months – so you'd better be ready for me when I get back. Move, blast you!'

The last night of his savage lust and brutality passed, leaving her worn, exhausted and sick. She was already humiliated, degraded and bruised; she could go no lower.

'Oh God – let him mean it this time!' A tight little prayer inside her.

Something must have decided him at last. Perhaps the life on the river boats was too tame. He needed the broader seas. Or perhaps the latent cruelty in his nature found only irritation in the calm beauty of the Firth.

At four o'clock in the morning he flung her from the bed. She could feel nothing but relief that she would have three months without his demands. Shivering, she lit the fire, and made tea – and he only laughed obscenely when she shrank from him as she poured it into his cup. But all she could think of was that he would be away for three months. In three months *she* could be away somewhere – anywhere – anywhere in the world – away, from the brutality and lust and savagery. She would feel clean again.

He picked up his seaman's bag and checked over its contents. He put on his jersey and reefer jacket and a seaman's cap. She stood up and backed away from the table. He looked at her, and said:

'I'm away – you'll be ready for me when I get back.'

A parting slap on the side of her head as he went out, sent her sprawling against the table, and she fell to the floor. She slid down beside the dresser and lay there, stunned and breathless. She stayed there, helpless, and somewhat surprised. She tried to remember all he had said this morning. He had flung down on the table three gold sovereigns, and said, 'There, that will do you while I'm away. The rent's paid. You'll keep out of mischief anyway. I'm going to Canada. I'll be back in July.'

She must have slept. She woke and found the fire had died down. The gas, in its broken mantle, had gone out. The kitchen was cold and dismal, but quiet. She wondered for a moment why she was there, but then the pain of her bruised body came back, and she moaned a little. Slowly, weakly, she tried to move, and at last she reached a chair. Outside, footsteps sounded over the pavements. Quick, hurrying feet clattered past her door. It was nearly six o'clock now. Men were going to the shipyards; women would soon be going out to work in the big houses; and in a few hours, children would be going to school. She could not face anybody yet. She knew that all her neighbours knew how she lived – but many a woman got an occasional beating, and none of them would have dared to interfere. She would have to keep out of the way until it was dark again. But yet, she must somehow get help . . . she must get to her mother. The surging need of her mother at that moment overwhelmed her, and she buried her head in her arms.

A faint sound reached her.

She started up. Could it be . . . ?

No. He would not come quietly or timidly.

A gentle knock at the door . . .

She walked with difficulty to the door and whispered, 'Who's there?'

'It's me, Maggie Leith. I thought – Are you all right?'

'Oh, oh yes, Maggie – just a minute.'

She opened the door, and even managed a laugh.

'I tripped over a hole in the linoleum, and hit my head on the table. I think I was stunned for a minute.'

'Tut-tut.' Maggie made tutting noises.

'Treacherous things, holes. Have you had a cup of tea? Would you like a wee dram, or something? I heard your man go down. Is he away to sea, then?'

'Yes, he sails this morning, He'll be away three months.'

'Oh my! It will be near your time then?'

Bella stared at her. 'How, how did you know?'

'Och, lassie, I've had wee Charlie. Come away in with me and I'll give you some breakfast. Come away now.'

Bella tried to protest, but Maggie took her arm, gently, and led her across the landing into her own cosy, bright kitchen.'

Bella sank down with difficulty in the basket chair by the fire. She drank the hot, sweet tea that Maggie gave her – laced with a little brandy, she knew. Somehow, she must get word to her mother.

'Maggie, will you be going out?'

'I will, Bella. Do you want something?'

'Would you take a wee note to my mother, at the church?'

'Surely! I'll get a bit of paper and a pencil.'

She wrote the words with a struggle – her hands were swollen, and her arms felt numb.

> Will you come and bring me home when it gets dark? He's gone to sea for three months. I'm ill.
>
> Bella.

'Now you stay there till I come back. Rest is what you need, you poor lass. I'll bring your mother back.'

She dressed the baby, and wrapped him in the big shawl which she put round herself – after the manner of mothers who carried babies safely long before the perambulator was invented.

Flora took the letter when she had asked Maggie into

her kitchen. She couldn't read it, so she passed it to Jenny, while she poured a cup of tea for Maggie.

'What is it, Jenny? Is it Bella?'

'You might know it's Bella. She says she's ill, and you're to come and get her when it's dark. When it's dark, indeed!'

'Be quiet, Jenny. All right, Mrs Leith, and thank you for coming. I'll be over to see her as soon as I possibly can.'

'She needs rest – she's had a bad time,' said Maggie, as she turned to go, and settled wee Charlie more firmly inside her shawl.

Flora took her down to the big outside door, and said again that she would come very soon.

'She's a disgrace,' said Jenny, when Flora came back. 'Why doesn't she want to come till it's dark?'

'*Be quiet,* Jenny! She's ill, and I'm going to see her. I'll be back soon, and your father and I will go and bring her when he comes home from the yard.'

Jenny, grumbling still, went to the cupboard and got the brooms and went up to the church. Flora put on her bonnet and a warm coat, and hurried away along the streets, now busy with shops opening, school children running.

'My poor lassie, what has he done to you?' Her thoughts ran ahead of her, and she was breathless as she climbed the two flights of stairs in the shabby tenement. A woman washing the stairs looked at her with some hostility as she trod on her clean steps.

Flora said, 'I'm sorry, but I must come up. I'll be as careful as I can.'

Mollified, the woman said, 'Oh, that's all right. You'll be Mrs Morrison's mother?'

'Yes.'

'She's in Maggie Leith's house. She's not so well. It's just across the landing. I'm Mrs Foster.'

Flora thanked her, and knocked on the door with the brightly polished name-plate. Maggie opened the door wide.

'Oh, come in, Mrs McGarvie. Bella's a lot better now. Your mother's here, Bella.'

Bella now lay on the ancient horse-hair sofa, beside the bright fire. She seemed too weak even to raise her head, and as Flora knelt down and put her arms round her, tears flooded Bella's eyes. She had not wept real tears since that night when she was twelve, and she had flung herself at Flora's knee – as Flora now knelt with her.

The hurt she had endured over the last three months had been more of shock than of sorrow, and tears then were no relief.

Flora held her close, and let her cry herself out. Maggie hovered, with the inevitable cups of tea.

When Bella's tears stopped, she slept again: her head drooped, and her arms hung limply at her side, with no strength left to lift them.

Flora whispered to Maggie,

'We'll come and take her home when John gets home from work. Will you take care of her till then?'

'Aye, that I will. I'll take her back to her own place, because my man will be in for his dinner, and it might disturb her. But I'll watch over her, never fear. But . . .'

Her voice trailed away. Flora waited.

'What about . . . about when he comes back? It will be near her time, then?'

She stopped. Flora had gone white to the lips.

'Her time? She . . . she's like that, then?'

'Aye. About three months. When he comes back, it will be a bad time for her.'

Flora nodded grimly.

'I think the minister will help us then. We won't let her come back to him. I'll speak to the minister, and the doctor. Well, thanks very much, Mrs Leith, for looking after her. Will you take this. Buy a bit of something nice for her dinner. I'll see we don't forget you.'

'Och away with you! She can share our bit of dinner.'

But Flora forced the half-crown on the kindly woman, and whispered a soft goodbye to Bella, who stirred a little, but slept on.

It was a long while after she had gone when Bella woke, restored – at least mentally.

'My mother?'

'She's just gone, Bella love. I've been into your house and lit the fire again, and tidied a wee bit. Go you in now and start getting ready, because your mother and father are coming for you about six o'clock. I'll bring you some soup when my man has gone back to work. Come now, I'll help you.'

Tender hands lifted her from the sofa. Bella laughed, a little shakily. 'Oh – you'd think I was drunk!'

She let Maggie help her into her own kitchen. Maggie had opened the window, and the fire was burning brightly – with some of Maggie's coal, Bella was sure. On the corner of the table, Maggie had set a little white lace cloth, with a tea-pot and cup and saucer, and on a little plate, some thin bread and butter cut in dainty triangles – for Maggie had once been a parlour-maid, and knew how things should be.

Bella spent the rest of that day in a semi-stupor. It seemed that she had no sooner eaten the bread and butter and drunk the hot sweet tea, than Maggie was in again.

'Bella, lass, are you coming in for a bit of dinner?'

'Good gracious, what time is it, Maggie?'

'Nearly one o'clock. Eddie's had his dinner and gone back to work; and he says you're to come in, and I've to give you a wee dram. It's rest you need, you poor soul.'

'No, no, Maggie. I don't need it. I must have slept – just sitting at the table. It's gone so quick . . . ' She stood up. 'Oh Maggie, I'm stiff and sore.' Tears ran down her face; weakly, she just stood there and wept, quietly and helplessly.

'Hush noo, hush noo. Come away in with me, and you'll be all right.'

She lay all that afternoon on Maggie's sofa. She dozed – and woke – and always the impression she had was of wavering red firelight . . . soft little sounds, that meant nothing at all, and the rain, pelting steadily down the windows.

Fear woke her sometimes . . . she seemed to hear the heavy footsteps . . . and the loud voice shouting obscene words shuddered her into wakefulness – and there was another hour gone, and he would come back . . .

She did not know that she had endured his bestial attacks for the last time, and that other, even more helpless victims were to feel the lash of his belt, and his ferocious savagery.

XIV

Millie enjoyed her trip across the Atlantic in the big red-funnelled liner. Rob met her at New York, and took her in the train to the little town. So that, when Millie walked in to the splendid house, and saw it all so clean and sweet, with flowers in every room, the kitchen loaded with home-made pies and cookies, she was completely enchanted.

'Who did all this?' she asked.

Jimmy cut in before Rob could speak.

'Oh, Martha Hallam looked in, to make things tidy. She left these pies and things, and said she'd be over tomorrow to welcome Ma, and see if she can help some more.'

Rob could only think of the cold words that Martha had said. 'You're a fool.'

Millie's visit extended over the New Year of 1868. Letters passed between the families at frequent intervals. Millie was taken on all the usual sight-seeing trips, and it seemed the only subject Robbie wanted to discuss was the new idea that he put to his mother.

'I'd like you to stay here, Ma. And I'll ask Willie to come over. We can have a good life here – I wish you would, Ma?'

To a letter asking Will if he would come, Will replied that he wanted to marry Jennie McGarvie, and he was going to ask her soon: that he was getting on fine, managing by himself, and Auntie Flora and Uncle John sent their love.

Tell Ma just to enjoy her holiday and not worry.

Love, Will.

XV

AMERICA 1868—1872

Apple blossom hung fragrant on the trees in the garden that led on to the lake shore. Millie sat on a low chair and thought how lucky she was. Rob brought out a jug of home-made beer and two glasses on a tray, which he put on the grass beside her. He squatted, relaxed and comfortable, beside his mother. The hurt of the New Year had dimmed; and he had decided on his future. He had felt rather a set-back when Willie had refused his offer of bringing him out, to join him and mother, but he thought he would go somewhere, over this wide country, and then, in a little while, a year perhaps, he would come back and ask Martha to marry him.

The madness of his dreams about Bella had been made

clear. He had stayed here – like the fool Martha had said he was – all this time he had taken it for granted that he only had to go back, and Bella would be his. He had assumed that she would be there for the asking. Well, she had shown him that he was wrong.

'Robbie, do you not think it's time I was going home?'

Robbie sat up straight.

'Would you like to stay, Ma?'

'I'm not sure, Rob . . . '

She stopped as footsteps sounded on the flagged path round the house, and Jimmy came across the garden.

'Hello, Rob – how are you, Ma? Just met the postman.'

'Have a drink, Jimmy. Some of Martha's beer.'

'Sure. Letter here for you, Ma.'

'For me? Goodness! I've never had so many letters in my life! Who is it from, Robbie?'

'It's from Auntie Flora – I expect Jenny wrote it for her.' He opened it.

'Read it to me, Rob.'

Rob laughed as he opened it.

'I think we'll need to teach you to read, Ma, if you keep on getting letters from across the sea!'

He began

Dear Millie,
This is just a line hoping it finds you as it leaves me. We have had a bit of trouble. John was never keen on that sailor, Jim Morrison, but we didn't tell anybody because Bella seemed to be fond of him, and we thought she'd be all right.

Rob's voice choked, and he looked up at Jim.

'What is it, Rob? What else does she say?'

'It – it's bad news. But she, she's all right now – but –

Scarcely could he frame the words, as they danced on the paper in fiery letters before his eyes.

. . . so we went and brought her home . . . she . . . a mass of bruises . . . and she's three months . . .

He dropped the letter and stamped into the house.

'Jimmy! What is it? Read it to me. I can't read.'

Millie was nearly in tears. Shaken and horrified, Jimmy took the letter and read a few words more,

> . . . he's away to Canada for three months – but the minister will help us when he comes back.

Jimmy felt deeply for his friend, but he was beginning to think that this Bella, whoever she was, seemed to have made havoc with everybody's life, including her own.

'Is that all?' Millie broke into his thoughts.

'Just they hope you're enjoying your holiday and send their love.'

Millie put her hand out. 'Help me up, Jimmy.'

He gave her a gentle pull, and he put his arm across her shoulders as they went slowly into the house. He thought he knew what was the best thing to do with Rob. He had plans and ideas.

Rob could not trust himself to speak, out there, but he knew what he was going to do. Even if he could not marry her now, he could make sure that this lout, Morrison, would never lay a hand on her again. He would take his mother home, and go and get Bella to keep her here, with him; where she would be safe, safe, with a fool . . .

He looked round and found that he had stamped out to the garden in red fury. Turning, he went back into the living-room, and found Millie and Jimmy there. 'Mother, I'm going home. If you want to come, I'll book two passages, but if you want to stay, that's all right. But I'm going home to bring Bella back here. She'll be safe here.'

Jimmy gave a huge, disappointed sigh.

'There. I was just thinking I only had to say one word to him, and now he's going chasing off to Scotland.'

Rob turned on him, white-faced, with his fists clenched. 'What is it? What the hell are you talking about?'

'Well, it's like this. You remember the first night we came here, when we decided to jump ship? That first bar where we had a drink, I heard the men talking at the bar, and somebody mentioned gold, and we took no notice of it. Well, it seems there's been another gold strike, 'way up north. And I figured we might have one last adventure, before we settle down, make enough to see us through the rest of our lives. Come on, Robbie! A last trip before we get stuck in a rut? Louise says she wouldn't mind, and Mar . . .'

He stopped suddenly. He had been going on to say that Martha had no real claim on him.

Millie looked from Jimmy to her son, and then back to Jimmy. The moment was tense, with an under-current that was different for each one of them.

Jimmy, eager and irrepressible, bursting with vitality, the lure of change, the challenge of the unknown, and only incidentally the thought of reward at the end.

'Gold? We need *gold*?' said Robbie.

'No, we don't *need* it,' said Jimmy. 'We've got land, and property, and a transport company, and miles of forests, but we're not *old*, Robbie lad. And there's enough of the Scots in *me* to take a chance on something new.'

He hesitated. Then he said, 'Come on outside a minute.'

He stamped out to the porch.

Robbie followed him slowly.

Jimmy faced him, four inches taller, two years younger.

'Rob, we've been mates for twelve years. I never asked again, about the lass in Scotland, when you told me she was too young. But she's *married* now, Rob. Get that into your skull. You can't interfere. Do you think she'd want you to see her as she is now? She'll be all right. She's with her mother and father, and Ma will go home and help where she can. Let's go and find gold or something. A couple of years – you'll get her out of your system by that time – come back and marry Martha, and start a family. A man needs a family.'

Robbie leaned on the porch rail. He saw a ship battling in heavy seas, he saw a man on the bridge, and he

saw a slender, brown-eyed girl, and he could look no
more.

What Jimmy said made sense. What a fool he'd been!
A selfish fool.

'A couple of years?' He turned.

'About that,' Jimmy nodded.

'I don't think Martha will have me, but I can see
you're right. I'll send my mother home, and then we'll
go. *Now!* As soon as we can.'

Millie knew as soon as she saw her son's face that the
danger was over.

'You'll not be coming home then, Robbie?' she asked
quietly.

'It seems no. Not yet, Ma. Jimmy's a hard master!' (He
felt he could actually make a joke.) 'We're going to find
gold – maybe!'

'Your laddie will be a millionaire before long, Mrs
Munro!' said Jimmy.

'I can do without that,' said Millie, 'so long as I have
my son safe and sound again.'

Since that first day when Jimmy had carried an old
woman's parcel on horseback, he had gone travelling... in
California, Virginia, and all over the rich, opening
country. Some journeys were by train, some on
horseback, some in the covered waggons. Wherever he
went, he bought land, or simply staked his claim and
registered his ownership. Land in Texas, California,
substantial shares in the great railways, forest land, virgin
country.

Now, he and Robbie took time to make sure that all
their wealth was safely, securely, and legally registered.
Banks and lawyers held their documents. Louise and the
three children were as comfortable as money could make
them.

Robbie's properties, land-holdings and shares, if not so
extensive as Jimmy's, were willed equally between his
mother and his brother Will. With a home for Martha, if

she should ever need it. Then, hesitantly, he said,

'Put in a note for Will to – to see that Bella is looked after.' He managed a grim laugh. 'You'd think we were never coming back!'

'You never know,' replied Jimmy. 'It's a chancy business – only don't tell Louise I said so! And I'm not going to let all my hard work go for nothing. Young Bobby will soon be able to take an interest, at least in the carriage business. He'll be seven next year, so in a few years, he'll be able to figure where it all comes from! But, Robbie . . .'

He hesitated. Robbie looked up.

'In case we *don't* get back, or one of us doesn't, what's to be done?'

'If *you* don't, I'll see that your family are all right. If I don't, then just see that what I've put in my will gets done. If neither of us comes back . . . well, what are we paying expensive solicitors for?'

'And the girl in Scotland?'

Rob turned and looked at him. Then he shook his head slowly. 'I'll never forget her. But she doesn't need me,' he said.

But some day, *some day*, he would go back and claim his own.

*

Rob and Jimmy had set off in early September. Martha wished them a fond goodbye, but Robbie knew that whatever the future held for him, the homely life with Martha was finished.

With Jimmy's incredible luck – Robbie always said if he fell in the river he wouldn't get wet! – they struck gold after four years of travelling: after they had left the long line of gold-maddened men struggling up the snow-covered lands to Klondyke.

There, with a new dog-team and sledges, and Jimmy always on the look-out for new land and forests, they turned north-westwards, where the area was deserted. It would soon be time for the snows to melt, so after travelling for a week or so, they turned again and headed south. In the near distance, stark against the whiteness, they saw a dark shape of a small hut, with smoke coming lazily from a squat chimney, where an old trapper lived, in contented isolation. Tracking over the hard snow, pulling the sledges and carrying packs, they covered very little distance before the sun began to set.

The snow levelled everything – Rob took a step forward – into nothing. A block of frozen snow hit the back of his head, Jimmy yelled, and tried to lift him, but the snow slipped off his gloves. With thudding heart, he scrambled up the bank which had trapped Rob into the fall. Stumbling and staggering, he tried to hurry across the few hundred yards to the hut. It seemed such a short distance, but Jimmy was exhausted and breathless when he reached it.

He fell – then felt strong arms pulling him up. He looked up into bright eyes, in a dark face covered with dark beard and moustache. A hood of fur over the head and a jacket over leather trousers and tall boots completed the picture of the man who lived in this snow-bound corner of Canada.

'Come along, steady now. What's up?'

'My – my mate – fell – he doesn't move – For God's sake, help me.'

'I'll go on; follow as you can.'

Jimmy watched the short, squat figure stride through the snow, and slowly, his heart sunk with fear, he followed him to where Robbie lay in the deep, snowy hollow. The old man turned Robbie over, and felt all over his legs, then over his heart. Then he put some strain on his arms, and heaved on the right leg. He looked up and shook his head.

Rob's face was a sickly purple; there was no life in the pulse, and no tremor from the heart.

'What are you doing?' Jimmy demanded truculently.

'Setting his leg.'

'What's the use of that? – he's not walking anywhere!'

'Might as well – be tidier in his grave.'

'You callous old wretch. Leave him alone!'

'Listen to me, young 'un. I – no, never mind.'

'Go on.'

Something had happened to the old trapper – 'Old Benny', as he was known among the gold-seekers, the fishermen, and hunters, and diggers – just 'Old Benny'. But suddenly Jimmy saw that he wasn't old. His beard was matted and his hair straggled all over his head and shoulders. But what could be seen of his face was rough, but unlined; his eyes were clear and his hand steady. The voice, cool – county – from generations of wealth and security.

'You're . . . not American – or Canadian?'

'Nope.'

'You're not Scottish? – Irish?'

'No. I'm . . . I *was* English.'

'English?' Jimmy was astonished.

'Help me get this leg set. He'll be easier to handle, and much better when I *can* get him buried!'

'God! Don't keep on about that!'

'Want me to leave him to the wolves and bears?'

Jimmy shuddered. 'No.'

'Then shut up, and help me.'

The task was easy – easier on a man not yet cold, than it would have been on a man who might regain consciousness at any moment.

They carried their burden on a blanket, as an improvised stretcher, and laid him gently down on planks at the back of the one room in the hut. Jimmy draped a blanket over him.

'Have some coffee – got no brandy.'

'Coffee? I've got whisky in my flask – there's brandy in Robbie's flask.'

Jimmy was numb. Shock was delayed, and it was a long time before he felt the full effects.

'How long have you been here?'

'Me? Oh, eight – maybe ten years – lost count.'

'You said you were English?'

'Yes. You've heard of us – there are so many of us – the black sheep of the family. Got a girl into trouble, spent my inheritance, disgraced an honourable name, ordinary things. Started when I was sent down from Oxford – too much money, no brains, sent out here on remittance. It's . . . well, however long it is since '66 – that was the last time I drew my remittance. God knows if it's still being sent. Haven't thought about it since then. I don't think I want to know how it is; and yet I get a mild curiosity sometimes. What year is it?'

'It's 1872.'

'Is it so? 1872? Ah well. We'd better bed down – you'll need an early start. The thaw and floods will be on us any day now, and it would be November before you could get away with your dog team. Fine outfit, that.'

'Yes. We got the best that money could buy; a last adventure before we settled down.' Jimmy's tone was bitter.

'Married?'

'I am. Rob was going back to Scotland to get his girl and bring her out.'

'Family?'

'I've got two boys and a girl.'

'Time *you* settled down all right!'

'Oh, Louise doesn't mind – but she'll be glad to have me back.' He hesitated. 'Do you want to go back to your own country?'

'Back? To *that*? To the *county* – and the City – and the Court? Is Victoria still Queen?'

'Yes.'

'I've had enough of Court life. My father's a Duke – there are two older brothers – they can do without me. I like it here. Now get some sleep. I'll wake you before sun-up.'

'What time is that?'

'No idea. Haven't had a clock for years. I live by the sun.'

They settled down to sleep, and early, early, Jimmy

got up. He had slept little.

'Old Benny' made him a pot of steaming coffee and a mush of stuff that was like the pease brose he used to eat as a child.

He cooked over a fire of logs gathered in the summer time from the forest about half a mile away. Once a year Old Benny went into the city and stacked up with oil and candles and flour and potatoes, and some foods he kept packed under the snow. 'They keep for months when they're frozen,' he said.

Jimmy went back to take a last look at the still body of Rob.

Was there a faint flicker of the eyelashes? But no, it must be a trick of the light, or the tears in Jimmy's eyes. The face of his old friend was cold and grey, like dark marble. Jimmy touched the cold forehead, and said, almost to himself, 'Goodbye, Rob, old friend. God bless you.'

Benny hitched his dog team, and gave him some provisions, and Jimmy left. (Five months later, when he had reached home at the end of May, and when he felt he could face the task, he wrote to Willie.)

Old Benny stood and watched the sled disappear to the south-east, across the snow. He turned back into the hut, and went to look at the cold, still body. He must get it buried, right away.

Suddenly, he dropped to his knees, and laid his head to the chest, hurriedly tearing coat and shirt open. He muttered thickly, 'God in Heaven!' and then he took a deep breath and laid his mouth to the cold lips in the dark face. Gently, gently, he blew his own breath on the cracked blue lips that were so slightly open. His hand found the point where it had seemed there was a faint heart tremor. He rubbed the place lightly, slowly, and blew another breath on Rob's lips.

'Christ! I could have sworn I felt a beat, old son. Maybe I'd better let you rest in peace. But, if I warm you a bit . . . I'll lie close to you, and put some rugs over us. God! I'm an idiot! It must have been imagination. I'm only trying to breathe for you, old boy! Don't lie there and say nothing! I'll try again. You're so cold, cold . . . '

His breath was gathered again, and he pressed his mouth firmly on the lips, while his hand still massaged the heart now with greater pressure.

And again. And again. He sweated with exertion, and the heat from the rugs that covered his body and Rob's.

And suddenly he felt the lips under his lose their cold clamminess. The first realisation was sudden, but then they got warm slowly, and he burst out laughing, with relief and hysteria, when he felt the real thrill of a faint, irregular beat under his hand; yes, there it was. Thud-thud-thud, thud, thud – thud.

The breath was coming, the mouth opened, and Rob gasped in pain.

He tried to open his eyes, but they were too heavy.

'Don't do anything. Thank God I tried, anyway. No, don't move, you're safe. Don't try to speak. You've been in a coma. All right . . . that's right. Go back to sleep, just try this . . . '

He knew he was babbling, but he couldn't think coherently.

He stretched over to the table and opened the flask of brandy; it was Rob's own flask that Jimmy had said Benny might as well have as not. He had plenty. Benny had not tasted brandy for twenty years. He put a little on a spoon, and raised Rob's head very gently. The brandy, whether it was the right treatment or not, seemed to help. It stimulated the heart for a few moments, but Benny was wise enough not to give him any more.

'There, now I'll tuck you up nice and warm, and you should get some sleep. I'll bring my bunk over here, and move the oil stove. Don't move. Just lie there.'

Benny went over to the door of the hut. It was about half an hour since Jimmy had gone. He was about two miles away, across the white expanse of snow, a small black dot travelling into the rising sun. He could not have heard if Benny had called him.

Benny went back to Rob, with the oil stove and more furs. Rob lay as he had left him, but now his eyes were open.

'Awake, eh? But you'd better sleep. Feeling warmer? God!,' he thought, 'if you could only know how *cold* you were!' Rob slept again, and soon his breathing came more easily, and regularly. He even snored a little. Old Benny smiled and settled down to work on a fur, and watched over the sleeping man.

'Well, for a chap who's just been dead for twenty-four hours, you're doing a lot of sleeping! A hell of a lot!'

It was nearly sunset when he woke. Benny was cooking a stew of some game; the smell was good. The hut was warm and cosy, from the glow of a log fire and an oil lamp.

Rob's leg gave him some pain, but there was no flicker of knowledge or intelligence in the grey, unshaven face. He was alive, but only barely so.

Benny went to him, and fed him like a baby. Rob just looked at him without speaking, occasionally winced with pain, and slept again.

Benny just watched, and mused, and fed him, over the long nights, until the spring days came again.

PART TWO

World Enough For Me

XVI

Whatever elements had combined in forming Jenny, the first-born, so long delayed, one element had been left out: Jenny loved only Jenny.

She left school at thirteen, and went to work in the little grocery shop near her home. The sudden impact of menstruation sent her screaming to Flora, in hysterics. Helpless, Flora tried to talk to her, reassuringly, but since these subjects were never discussed, she could find no words to calm the tears and hysteria. Jenny was sure she was dying, and it was even worse when Flora managed to tell her that this would happen every month. 'And if it doesn't, then that means you will be having a baby, but that won't happen until you get married.'

Whispers and giggles at school had been totally ignored by Jenny. And the little she did hear, she dismissed completely, as nonsense. Everybody knew that the doctor brought a baby in his wee bag: It was always so. So how could this – this – horror have anything to do with a baby?

She could not, nor would she, even contemplate the awful posibility of creation, neither in its conception or delivery. The whole idea was preposterous, and nothing would change her mind. And when, two years later, the phenomenon stopped as abruptly as it had started, she suffered agonies; she didn't believe, of course, that she could be having a baby. But Flora had said . . . She waited in agony, for weeks, but nothing happened.

She began to feel irked and discontented with the boredom of slicing ham, digging into huge slabs of butter with the wooden butter-pats, and weighing out sugar. It was on the day that Bella had been brought home, bruised and beaten. Jenny hated the talk and whispers all round; she sulked all that evening, and went to bed still scowling and angry. Flora spoke to John as they were preparing for bed.

'John, you'll have to do something about Jenny. She wants to leave the shop and go to service.'

'Oh? Well, what do you think, Flora?'

'I expect it would do her good. I don't think I would have liked working in a shop either. We'll talk to her when she comes home tomorrow night.'

Jenny was still in a stormy mood. She ate her meal angrily, but she was determined to get her own way.

'Well now, lass, what's all this? Do you not like the shop?'

'I'm sick of it! I want to go to service. I want to be a –' She stopped.

'Well now lass, if that's what you want, we'll see what can be done. What do you want to do?'

'I want to be a lady's maid, and then . . .' she broke off.

'A lady's maid?' Flora echoed. 'What would you have to do at that job?'

'Oh, look after a lady, keep her dresses nice, do her hair and all that kind of thing.'

'How do you know all this?' John asked.

'Mrs Barber's always talking about how she went to Paris with her "lady", and all the wonderful clothes she had, and she gave them to her when she had finished with them. She only had to leave her when Lady Ann was thrown by a horse, and was paralysed. So then she needed a nurse, who could also do some hairdressing and make her look nice. Then she got married. Mrs Barber, I mean.'

'Well, if that's what you want, lassie, I'll speak to the minister. Maybe Mrs Christopher will know how to set about it.'

Jenny jumped up in excitement. 'Oh! Will you father?

I'm sure the minister's wife will know somebody.'

The best she could get, for a start, was as a general maid up in the small country town of Kilmacolm, seven miles over the hills, on the old Roman road. Here, she cleaned out fireplaces, including the big kitchen range, as well as the drawing-room and dining-room fires. She polished floors, and dusted furniture. She learned to make beds, to do washing, and ironing, and she lapped it all up, because it would lead to . . . she knew where it could lead.

After a year, she applied for, and got, a job as third housemaid, in a grandly beautiful Highland castle, near Oban, with Lord and Lady Granfield. The castle stood at the shore of a lovely loch, set near a forest, and with gardens glowing with green bushes, the red of beech tree, the purple of fox-gloves against the blue of the loch, almost royal blue in the golden sunshine. She had been met at the pier, and driven over the hills in a pony and trap, to arrive at this once-fortress against Scotland's foes, the first Edward of England. And it was one of the wealthiest estates in Scotland, although Lord Granfield, of course, would never have admitted that.

For the next two years, Jenny took it all in her stride. The hard training as general maid, had given her an advantage, in that she knew the right way to do things. The staff went to dances in the village hall, and Jenny danced in sheer natural enjoyment. But she remained untouched by either the excitement of the strenuous Highland dances, or the amorous efforts of every boy on the estate. If any of them over-stepped the touch of arms or hands in the dance, or afterwards, he was left in no doubt that Jenny would have none of it. She would not be 'pawed'.

Young Helen, the second housemaid, a pretty girl who was not so wise – or cold? – was in disgrace, and was bundled off home. Jenny seized her chance. Timidly, but respectfully and firmly, she asked the housekeeper if she could take over Helen's job. Not only for the sake of promotion, or extra wages: no, there was something

much more important to Jenny. For traditionally, the
second housemaid travelled with the family – to London,
to Paris – to Austria – even to New York! And she would
be among those exquisite dresses, those warm, luxurious
furs. And if she could drop the occasional curtsey, or
even a small bob . . . She had her tongue firmly in her
cheek all the time.

Jenny worked, and dreamed, and hugged her dreams
to herself. She was not going to be condemned to a life of
dusting and making beds, and laying out wonderful
clothes that she wanted to wear herself. She knew that
she would never find her dream below-stairs, and it is
only in the cheapest novelettes that the young master of
the house seduces the pretty parlourmaid. In any case,
Jenny had no intention of being seduced. From all she
had heard of this procedure, it was altogether disgusting
and unthinkable. Jenny was cold, hard, and beautiful.
Jenny was not to be shared. Somehow, she had to get
from below stairs, to the other side of the green baize
door: to exchange frilled cap and apron for a purple
velvet gown and a hat with sweeping feathers. To ride in
a carriage instead of horse trams: To be, in short, some
day – 'Oh yes, I will – some day I will be . . . '

She was darning white linen dinner napkins one day,
after lunch time, when the bell rang from Lady
Granfield's boudoir. She went quickly along the stone
passages, through the green door, and into the carpeted
hall, up the small stairway to the exquisite little room
facing on to the loch.

'You rang, m'lady?'

'Ah, yes, Jenny. Come here.'

Jenny stood demurely beside the chair facing the
lady.

'Mrs Carter tells me you would like to be second
housemaid?'

'Oh yes, very much, m'lady!'

'Yes, well, of course, you are rather young, but your
work has been very good. You seem to have had
extremely good training.'

'Yes, thank you, m'lady.'

'I hope you would not do anything so foolish as Helen did?'

'Oh no! I would never do anything like that, m'lady! My mother would never have thought of me doing such a thing. She was so good, my mother.'

'Was, child? Is she . . .?'

Jenny gave a quiet, silvery laugh. 'Oh no, m'lady! She is still at home, in the church.'

'Ah yes. You were brought up in the church, I believe?'

'Yes, m'lady.'

'Now, you realise that as second housemaid, you would have to travel, when we go to London for the Season? And help to maid me, when Miss Bell is off duty?'

Eagerly – 'Oh yes! I would love to do that, and I will learn as much as I can from Miss Bell.'

'Very well, Jenny. We will advertise for a third housemaid, and I will tell Christine. I trust your parents will not object to your travelling with us?'

'Oh no, m'lady! No!'

She danced all the way through the corridors, into the servants' hall, and continued darning the napkins, with her dreams flashing before her in golden visions; it would all happen – she didn't know how, but it must all happen.

She didn't get to the London season of that year of 1871. But the winter passed quickly; she helped with the visiting ladies, and ladies' maids during the long shooting season, from August till February.

And it would all come to pass, she knew.

*

Without the disturbing presence of Jenny, Bella and Flora found comfort and a real companionship that had seemed to be lost, from childhood days. A message arrived, by magnetic telegraph, from America; at the Shipping

Offices on the Old Quay. An official account of the voyage and personnel of the sailing ship *Arran*. It was passed on to her owners in Glasgow, but despite the orders of complete confidentiality, the story inevitably leaked out, in various different versions.

Eddie Leith heard it at work, from a riveter whose wife cleaned the rooms in the Shipping Office.

'Maggie, I think you'd better go and see Bella, to tell her before she gets it from gossip outside.'

'What, Eddie?'

'That boat – her man was captain, or mate, I'm not sure which – Some boys got on it, stowed away, like; There's bad news, Maggie, and nobody's sure how bad it is, but that man, Bella's man, you know, he's at the bottom of it. It seems some of the boys have been drowned, and he battered them all. Anyway, it's all getting hushed up, and we won't know the whole of it until the boat gets back. But it's bad, Maggie, bad.'

'Oh, Eddie! And that was Bella's man that did it?'

Eddie nodded. 'Aye, so I think you'd better just go up to the church and tell Bella, and her mother.'

'I will. I'll go first thing in the morning.'

But by the time Maggie got to the church next morning, Flora already knew. She had gone to the shops, and as soon as she went in to the grocers', the talking stopped. The women stood in small groups, questioning, speculating, looking for someone to blame. Rumour grew wilder, spreading faster than fire. A dozen boys had been lost at sea . . . some had been flogged to death . . . some had been drowned . . . they had all been drowned.

And Flora McGarvie's daughter was married to the man who had caused all this. They turned on Flora, poor, angry, loving their children (inside them, 'thank God my wee laddie wasn't there'). Helplessly, Flora made her way out of the shop, and found Maggie sitting with her little son, Charlie in her lap, wrapped in the big shawl. Bella was standing, staring, as Flora came in the door. Stunned, and sickened, she just stared at Flora as if she saw a ghost.

All through the last two months, she had known, as everybody did, that there were some boys missing from the town. But this was not unusual; boys were always running away to the farms in the south or even further south, to London! Some had 'gone for a sodger'. But none of it had touched her, personally.

Her mind couldn't take it in, yet. She heard Maggie saying, 'So Eddie thought I'd better come and tell you, before you hear it. Four of the boys were rescued, it seems. But it was seven boys that went on that boat. Some fishing folk in Newfoundland got these four.' She stopped, and looked at Bella.

Whether it was three, or twelve boys, her husband – dear God, that she should call such a man husband – had treated these children as brutally as he had treated her. And caused death, to some of them. Because they 'wanted to be sailors,' because they 'wanted to go to Australia.'

Resolve and contempt – not hate for hate is too much effort – strengthened in her from that moment. She turned, without a glance at either Flora or Maggie, and went into her own room.

Flora walked down to the door with Maggie, and it was the first time in her life she had not given a visitor a cup of tea!

XVII

If Margaret Preston's daughter had not married a missionary, it is doubtful if Bella's life would have taken the turn it did. Margaret passed a cup of coffee to her husband, while he unfolded his *Times,* and spread his napkin.

'Oliver, there's a letter from Elizabeth.'

'Oh?' He looked up at her over his glasses and saw her expression of sorrowful resignation.

'Oh no! You don't mean she's . . . again?'

'Yes, dear.'

'Oh good Lord! Beg your pardon, my dear, but really! This will be the third time. Can't a man go out to convert the heathen without giving his wife a baby every year?'

'Hush, Oliver. She's our daughter.'

'I know. I'm sorry, my dear, but we've done our share. Bessie must come home and look after her own children. I'm sure there's plenty of heathen in Scotland to be converted, without going all the way to China.'

'Have some more coffee, dear. I can manage the children, but I could do with some help with the washing. No, hush, dear, we don't want the servants to hear. I'll get another maid. She can do the washing and help Ellen in the kitchen, and give a hand with Ivy in the drawing-room, and that kind of thing. But we must tell Bessie that she mustn't do it again.'

She blushed as she realised what she had said, and then smiled.

Oliver leaned over and patted her hand. 'There, there, we won't go into that, eh? The washing . . . yes, you do wash beautifully, but it's not the thing, my love.'

'I was only a laundrymaid when you married me, Oliver.'

'Yes, I know, and I'm sure the Duke and Duchess never forgave me for falling in love with you! But you were such a *very good* laundrymaid!' he twinkled.

'Oh stop it, Oliver. I've always liked to do the nice washing myself, but with a new baby coming, it *is* too much.'

'Well, get another maid. There's still a spare room at the top, isn't there?'

'Yes, it will need decorating. We could get that little Irish fellow who did your office, could we? What's his name? He's got his own business in the town, hasn't he?'

'Joe Mulligan, you mean? Yes, I could go and see him today.'

'I could teach her to wash properly, and she could take the children out, and look after Bessie, and help Ellen and Ivy.'

'Well, you see to it, I'm playing golf with the Reverend Christopher this afternoon, if the rain keeps off.'

'Oh! That's what I'll do!'

'What, play golf?'

'I'll go and see Alice Christopher. She's sure to know of a nice young woman. There's a meeting at the Manse this afternoon.'

'All right, my dear. I'll go and see the children and then I must get to the office. I'll be home for luncheon.'

On his way to the office of the sugar-house of which he was managing director, he pondered that he should soon exchange his pony and trap for a carriage and pair. A managing director ought to have a carriage and pair. And he thought rather angrily about his daughter, the tomboy of the family. She had grown up from schooldays into a forcefully active, tweedy woman, like a Punch cartoon of British womanhood. That was bad enough, but soon after they came to Greenock she had met this earnest young evangelist, throbbing with desire, not for a woman, but with the need to help the persecuted millions in China, waiting, he insisted, with patient hope, for him to come and show them the True Way.

Something in him appealed to the strong, rebellious Bessie, and in six months she had married him and sailed away to China. That was six years ago. She came back after about eighteen months, proudly announcing that she was pregnant, and in the troubled state of China at that time (when is it not?) George Clark, her husband, thought it best for her to come home and have her child there – and really, it would be best if she left it with her mother. In view of the troubled state of China at that time ...

She came home, and for the next five months she up-
ended the whole house. For exercise, she marched round
and round the green lawn below the kitchen window; she
insisted on a special diet. Some doctor on board had
managed to convince her that her diet was most important
to her child, and herself.

When the baby, a girl, was three months old, she
sailed back again. And George must have been waiting,
hungrily, to take her to bed again, for in a year she was
back with another baby coming. The performance was
repeated. The marching and the diets, and then the birth
of a boy. He too was left in the care of Margaret, and
now, two years later, here she was again!

Oliver sighed, as the trap and the trotting pony
brought him along Eldon Street and along Union Street to
the dark ugly sugar works at Kilblain Street. He could
think of no one in his family, or his wife's, to account for
the peculiarities of Bessie. When he had come to be
educated at Edinburgh University, he had had no
thought of spending the rest of his life in Scotland. Then,
in his last year, when he was twenty-one, on a visit to a
ducal household, through a University friend, he had
seen Margaret, a little laundrymaid in service. The
picture of her stayed with him when he went back after
the holiday, and when he had taken his degree, he wrote
to her. After a long time, he persuaded her to marry him.

He was entirely happy. Meg, as he usually called her,
was sweet and gentle and kindly. She brought to his home
a sense of belonging. Every room was soft and warm-
looking, inviting and restful. For his sake, she learned to
do things the right way, and when he was offered a seat
on the Board of Directors of Watson's Sugar Refinery,
with its works in Greenock, she uprooted her lovely
home and set about putting her imprint on another one.

They chose one of the first houses at the western end
of the Esplanade, looking out over the Firth. A solid, grey-
stone house, with a wide garden and spacious rooms, and
at the back of the green lawn that faced on to Eldon
Street, there was a well fitted wash-house. This, of

course, was hidden from the view of the back windows by a clump of trees that grew with the years, and their leafy branches in the spring and summer hid the lines of washing from the dignified house,

The Ladies' Combined Churches Guild did not often meet on a Saturday afternoon, but this was a special meeting to discuss the Charities events for the next year, for the Town's Poor. At a quiet moment, Margaret found a chance to talk to Alice Christopher. The minister's wife smiled at Margaret, a wholesome, sweet smile of sincere liking.

'Margaret, I'm so glad you could come. How is all the family?'

'Oh, fine, Alice. I wanted to ask you, do you know of a suitable young woman who could come and wash for me?'

'Wash? For *you*, Margaret?'

Margaret smiled. 'Yes, I know. I'm an expert, but I need someone now. Bessie's coming home again.'

'Oh, Margaret! Not another baby?'

'Yes, I'm afraid so. So it will be too much for me.'

'Indeed it is. Now, let me see. I should know of someone . . . good evening, Mrs Heathley. No, we're not being confidential; Mrs Preston has just asked me if I know a washerwoman. There's my own girl, of course, but I couldn't spare her all the time.'

Mrs Heathley snorted. 'You'll have to be mighty choosy. Servants *these* days! But at least they're cheap and plentiful.' She spoke as if they were something she was going to buy at her grocers'.

Margaret said quietly, 'I wonder if there will ever come a time when they *won't* be cheap and plentiful?'

'It's very unlikely. There's so many of them, that class.' Mrs Heathley stamped off.

'Never mind, Margaret, I know how you feel. I've just thought of someone. Do you remember that dreadful case of the young woman who was stoned? Her husband was put in jail for ill-treating the boys at sea?'

'Oh yes. I remember. Poor girl, I often wondered what

happened to her after all.'

'Her parents live in James's church, you know. They clean the church and look after it. I know they've been very hard-pushed since Bella came home with her baby. Bella has been doing most of the heavy work too, to help her father. Her illnesses don't seem to have affected her strength. She's still a good strong girl.'

'She seems to be just what I want. Do you think she would come to me and live in? She could bring her own little boy too. There's plenty of room.'

'I will certainly ask her, tomorrow. It would put a lot of the work back on Mr McGarvie, but it would ease the position. Of course, Bella's husband has completely disappeared after he served his sentence. Four months, for what he did!'

'Will you ask her then, Alice?'

'I will, my dear. You're very generous, Margaret.'

The two women moved away, and the meeting gradually dispersed. Margaret went home, very thoughtful.

*

Bella listened to the minister's wife, and it all seemed very reasonable:

'And you will learn a lot from Mrs Preston.'

'I can do a good day's washing with anybody,' Bella said sulkily.

'I'm sure you can, Bella. But there's a difference between a laundrymaid and a washerwoman.'

'A washerwoman and a laundrymaid?'

'Yes, and of course your own boy can be with you, you know.'

Bella thought for a long minute. Thought of one who, with a word, could lift her from the despair she felt so deeply. If only, if only she wasn't tied to that brute Morrison. If only Willie Munro would ask her, she would go to the ends of the earth with him. Before this time, in fact, up till this moment, she had been simply someone who lived here, or in the hovel in the east end, with a man who was her husband. Or who had been near death in a hospital. She had been a thing that Fate had buffeted about, something caught in a whirlwind, and dropped, bruised and injured on a stony, steep hill.

Now, suddenly, she was a person in her own right. Now she had to make a decision for herself. A thousand leagues of impossibility separated her from the man she would love till she died; three thousand miles of water separated her from a man who loved her, and would have given his right arm to save her pain, and had been waiting till she was old enough so that he could ask for her hand in marriage.

'What would I have to do?' she asked Alice Christopher.

(Down in the yards, bad times loomed again, unemployment and hunger faced them all, but although there was no kind of work for a man who was willing to work with his skill, there were always the West End ladies who could afford servants. A mad world.)

'Well, Mrs Preston would tell you most of it, but I think she would like you to do all the washing.'

'Everything?'

'Oh yes. She has a very fine wash-house at the back of the garden, and a good drying green. And the ironing room is fitted out in quite the latest style, all the newest tables and stoves. A big circular stove, I'm sure it has about twenty irons. It looks most efficient. And of course, when the washing's done, you could give a hand with the two children, and maybe help Mrs Clark till the new one comes, and help the cook. There will be plenty to do.'

Alice Christopher was a good woman, as a minister's wife should be, but she was brought up in a house where she did not even have to take a handkerchief out of a drawer. And it quite literally never occurred to her that the servants she had always had around her could possibly get tired. It was a state quite out of her imaginings, like a man going to the moon, or flying in the

air. They were *there*; they did their work. They went to
bed when *you* said they could. Especially after a ball, or
any gala occasion when they had to help you out of your
dress, but that they actually had *feelings* . . . she never for
a moment suspected it.

Bella looked at her, and saw all this. But what did it
matter? She was tired anyway. And if she went to this
Mrs Preston, she would at least not be parted from young
Sandy, and she would be earning; not much, but even a
few pounds a year would be good, if she had no rent to
pay, and no food to buy. And she could help her mother.
What was it? A laundrymaid, or a washerwoman?

'All right, I'll go. When does she want me?'

'I'm so glad, Bella. I'm sure you'll be very happy. I
think she wants to get a man in to decorate the room
you'll have. I'll tell her tomorrow that you'll go, and she
will very likely write to you, or come and see you.'

Bella lay sleepless that night, Sandy's small body
warm beside her. She went over her happy childhood,
and she suddenly realised that she had grown up without
having the least idea how she got there. The incident of
the Sunday Breaker had caught her just on the borderline
between child and woman. She could never recapture
the glowing happiness of her life before that Sunday.

She must, then, make the best she could of her life for
the future, for her son. The picture stretched away to
eternity – she was tied to a man who was a natural brute,
a sadistic murderer, and a stab of foreboding went
through her. She knew in an instinctive flash that he
would reach out, somehow, even if she never saw him
again, he would reach out and destroy any happiness she
might find. She was in love with a man who, she knew,
did not like her at all – and there was no hope for her
except in work, and perhaps the comfort of her son, if
they could be spared to live, to comfort each other. And
perhaps she could be spared to give, at least, some
comfort to the mothers her husband had bereaved.

Dawn was streaking the sky before Bella slept, but a
chapter in her life had closed. She found courage from a

remote ancestry to take up her new life, a life that held no meaning, she thought, and no hope.

She learned quickly: the different irons for doing Mr Preston's shirts, and the thickness of blanket she had to put under embroidered cloths, or blouses. She learned – she worked – and she ate well. Ellen was a good cook, and Bella had never tasted the kind of things that were provided even for the staff meals, and when she got the chance to taste any left-overs from the dining room, she ate them with enjoyment. Ellen knew nothing about calories or vitamins, she only knew what was good for you, what went with what, and how much of it, and there was nothing synthetic, there were no substitutes, in any of her dishes.

Bella slowly regained her enjoyment of life; the work she did was hard, but constructive and rewarding. There was constant joy in the piles of spotless clothes every week, and practice in the intricacies of faultless ironing made her perfect. She knew, now, the difference between a laundrymaid and a washerwoman.

The months passed. Bessie Clark came home, stamped around the garden, and eventually produced another daughter. But this time, Oliver put his foot down, firmly.

'George has got to come home, and either find a church, or take a job somewhere and get a house for you. Your mother just can't do this any more.'

'I do see that, father. I was thoughtless. Of course mother must have some rest. That's a very good woman you've got. Bella, is it? She seems to be doing very well.'

'Yes, a fine girl. She seems to be making a good job of bringing up her boy. Incidentally, she's been looking after your two as well.'

'I know. I'm very grateful. I'll write to George and tell him he must come home. I don't think he will really mind. China is very unsettled, just now.'

XVIII

For Bella, the days and the seasons were divided into the washing and ironing; and the week-end walks when she took the three children along to the Battery Park from where she could see the Lyle Hill, and she could see the gradual building of new red-roofed houses. She could dream about one day living in a house on the hill, but deep down she did not really believe it would ever happen.

Hard work – good food, sound sleep, her boy beside her, and occasional visits to her mother in the church; what more could she want? Her beauty blossomed again, her eyes sparkled and she felt it was good to be alive. But there was something . . . something she needed as much as she needed the air to breathe.

She only let herself think of this when she went to bed at night – young Sandy had his own cot now – so she had the whole bed to herself. She knew, and blushed at the thought, and the shame of it. She wanted to love, and be loved. She wanted a man's arms around her – and her face grew hot as she slid into sleep, for she knew only one man she could bear to think of now in the peculiar position of lovers in the act of mating.

Remembering how she had been taken by the drunken lust of her lawful husband, she felt it was absolutely wrong and sinful that she should think like this. But the call of her blood, the passionate Spanish blood in her, was clamorous and insistent. She shuddered and hid her face in the blanket. Tiredness took over, and she slept – but her dreams were jumbled and she woke early.

Her longings and dreams had to give way to stark reality, and the months and seasons passed, until it was time for Sandy to go to school. Five years, five years out of her life, and she felt she had become a vegetable. Work, eat and sleep, the same as Ivy and Ellen, although they went off for holidays back to their distant Highland islands, in the summer time.

It was funny how Joe Mulligan had seemed to grow into one of themselves over the last three years. He was so nice; he had the gift of the gab, it was true, like most Irishmen, but it was at least coherent gab, it had meaning and argument. They got used to him and he was always nice to young Sandy.

After the departure of Bessie, Margaret and Oliver Preston went off to Paris for a holiday, and Margaret decided that it would be a very good idea if Mr Mulligan stayed to do the other rooms, while they were away. The drawing-room was rather shabby – the kitchen really needed attention – best to be done while they were away, and perhaps during the girls' holidays?

So Joe came every day, and worked, and the house brightened.

And one day Joe asked Bella if she would come with him to a social in a hall in the town. It was a town council affair, he said, and there would be tea and games and dancing.

'Oh, I'd like it fine, but I have to see to the wee ones.'

'Surely Ivy and Ellen would look after them for one night? I'll bring you home by 11 o'clock – earlier if you like. I'd like it fine if ye'd come, Bella; I think you could do with a wee dance.'

She laughed. 'Oh aye; I'd enjoy a dance – it's such a long time since I . . . since . . .'

'Since you had any fun'?

'Yes, I suppose so. I'll ask Ivy if she'll watch the bairns.'

Ivy was not only pleased to watch the bairns, but she helped Bella with a dress for the social.

Mrs Preston had left her instructions to give away

several of her dresses, and had shown her exactly which
ones she had no further use for.

Mrs Preston was bigger than Bella – but that was
better than being too small.

'Oh!' and 'Ooooh! Isn't that lovely?'

'Try this dark red one, Bella.'

'Oh, it's too grand.'

'Not a bit of it. I used to wear this colour when I was
your age.'

Bella looked at her. Ivy seemed ageless.

'But you're not that old!'

'I'll be fifty-four next September.'

'Oh goodness. I was twenty-five last month.'

'Aye, well, you must get a bit of enjoyment while
you're young. It's a pity you're . . .' She stopped.

'You mean it's a pity I'm still tied to that man?'

Ivy flushed. 'It's none of my business, but I think you
should have some enjoyment while you are young.'

'I had some good times when I lived in the church. We
used to have Sunday School socials – and all the children
got an orange and a poke of sweeties going out the door.
I can't believe it's all these years ago.'

'It's no' that long – you've got a long time in front of
you. You'll see a few summers yet – and you'll see a few
changes.'

'Do you think so? I'd like to live a long time if I
wouldn't be a burden to anybody.'

'Try this dress; it's a kind of thin serge stuff; it won't
be too warm. And you could put a nice white lace collar
over it – a big yoke collar, and a wee bow. It's a wee bit
big in the waist, but I'll take that in for you, and there's a
velvet belt to match the bands down at the hem. It's a
nice dress; I think it will bring you luck.'

'Yes, I need some.'

*

'You'll come to the social then, Bella?'

Joe Mulligan's face puckered into a sort of hopeful

grin. 'I'll bring you home whenever you like – it should be a nice night, if you don't think the walk will be too much for you.'

'No. I think I'd like to come. I've got a red dress. At least, Ivy says I can have it. Will it be too grand, do you think?'

'I haven't seen it, but I'm sure it will look grand on *you*, not *too* grand at all!'

He had a nice turn of phrase, had Joe – the gift of the gab.

Mid-April, with a wet, drizzly day that drew the mist down to hide the far mountains and, as it so often does, cleared to give a soft spring evening of purple velvet shadows and shafts of moonlight across the grey river.

Joe met her at the corner nearest to the house, and they crossed the wide Esplanade to walk along by the rippling water. She walked a little fearfully because, although she had known this insignificant little man for three years now, he was still a stranger; she had never been alone with him.

They arrived at West Burn Street, and went along a narrow opening and into a hall, where gas lights glowed and flickered in white globes round the walls. At one end was a small raised platform, where stood a piano, and a table with two or three chairs round it. There was a man with an accordion standing near the piano, and when Joe entered the hall holding Bella's arm, he was met by a cheer.

'Joe! Here he is . . . Hello, Joe!'

A chorus of goodwill met them from all sides.

Joe showed Bella into a small ante-room to hang up her cloak, which was of soft, black cotton stuff, with a hood, and she put it hurriedly on a hook and went back to the hall. The excitement of the people, the shouting and laughing and the gay music from the piano and the accordion – and somebody tuning a fiddle – made her feet dance.

Her face was bright and flushed, her eyes shining, and the first person she saw as she went into the hall was –

Willie Munro.

Her heart jumped – it seemed right into her throat; her head was swimming, and her legs felt like wet dishcloths. She saw him in a haze of exaltation – she could see no one else.

But he was not alone. He nodded briefly to her, and said: 'Hello, Bella – didn't expect to see you here,' and turned to greet the girl who came forward in a blue muslin dress.

Jenny.

'Oh, Jenny! Hello! I didn't know you would be here. How is mother?'

'Fine. I'm surprised to see *you*. I'll tell her you were asking for her.'

Willie nodded again, and took Jenny's arm in his own and led her away.

'Are you all right, Bella?'

The voice at her shoulder was subdued, and she realised she was standing still, fiercely looking at the retreating forms of Willie and Jenny.

'Joe! I didn't know my sister would be here.'

'Is she your sister? The girl with Mr Munro?'

'Yes. Is he – ?' But the words were drowned in the babble of voices.

'Now then, ladies and gentlement. Please take your partners for the Circassian Circle, to open the evening. Away you go, boys . . .'

The man at the piano played a big opening chord, and the band struck up a tune in waltz time.

Joe danced well. He was light and agile, and Bella very soon lost herself in the lilt of the music, the movement of her feet, and the sounds of laughter and talking all round her. It had been so long . . . so long . . . since she felt this surge of happiness. Although she was not with him, Willie was *there;* she could see him, and sooner or later she would be dancing with him.

The Circassian Cirle was followed by a waltz, then a polka. Then they all thankfully sat down, while trestle tables were hurriedly put up. White cloths were draped on them, and tea was handed along the tables. There were plates of sandwiches, some hot pies and sausage rolls, and cakes, and everybody ate a great deal and drank many cups of tea, before the evening's festivities started again.

The MC stood up, and hammered on his table.

'Ladies and gentlemen – pray silence for the Provost.'

Provost Grey stood up, and proceeded to give a long speech. He was not a good speaker, but Bella found Joe listening intently to every word. Part of it was about new buildings, extensions to the railway, another station, some land now occupied by tenements in the centre of the town to the south-west at the top of Inverkip Street. The Council proposed tearing them down to make 'fine dwellings for professional men and their families,' the repairs to the Town Hall plumbing. He went on and on, and finally stopped to a burst of applause. Joe was quiet, until the dancing started again.

'Bella, will you sit over there where I can see you . . . and listen?'

'But what – ?'

'Wait a minute. Just listen.'

The MC stood up on the platform, and spoke again.

'And now, ladies and gentlemen, we are to have the pleasure of hearing Mr Robert Bailey sing, accompanied by Mr Thomson at the piano, and our old friend Mr Joe Mulligan on the fiddle. Mr Bailey, please. Mr Mulligan.'

Joe got up quietly and looked a little shamefaced at Bella. She was astounded. He climbed on to the stage, and Robert Bailey, a fine, tall man, with red hair, and a pock-marked face, came on, to thunderous applause.

Music was placed on the piano, and Joe took a violin out of a case hidden behind the table. He quickly tuned the instrument, and the MC announced, in ringing tones,

'Mr Bailey will render "Bonnie Mary of Argyle." Yours, Mr Bailey.'

Robert Bailey's voice was strong and tuneful, and soared in an ecstasy of music, and the tribute paid to him was silence until the last pure top note had died away, and then there were many furtive handkerchiefs at moist eyes, in the hall. The applause was loud, sincere and prolonged, and Mr Bailey was more relieved than grateful, for he suffered badly from stage fright, and after his song, the audience demanded more, with loud cries of 'Encore! Encore!'

Another sheet of music was produced, and the MC announced that Mr Bailey would now sing 'Dark Lochnagar'.

His father had told him, when he was young, that he could not call himself a singer until he could sing 'Lochnagar'. As it turned out, Robert was a better singer than his father – a fact which the father was glad to know.

The last verse was particularly popular.

> England, thy beauties are tame and domestic,
> To one who has roamed o'er the mountains afar.
> I sigh for the land that is wild and majestic,
> The steep, frowning glories, of dark Lochnagar.

Wild, enthusiastic clapping greeted this one too, so Mr Bailey obliged with a comic one about 'a ram that had a tail sir, most wonderful to tell, it reached from here to Ireland and rung St Patrick's bell, singing a fal-de-diddle-i-dum, fal-de-diddle day, it was the fattest ram sir, that ever was fed on hay.

'The butcher that killed the ram sir, was up to the knees in blood, and the boy that held the bucket was carried away in the flood, singing a fal-de-diddle-i-dum, fal-de-diddle day, it was the fattest ram sir, that ever was fed on hay.'

The laughter and applause thundered round the hall. The MC stood up and raised his hand for silence, which eventually fell on the crowd.

'And after that excellent rendering, Mr Bailey has to leave us. I think he might just be in time.'

The gold chain across his waistcoat gleamed in the light, as he pulled a watch from his pocket. The audience laughed, and Robert Bailey slunk out of the hall knowing the laughter – and hating it – and hating the compulsion that drove him to the nearest public-house, before they closed. He did not leave there until he was thrown out helpless, with all his money spent.

But people loved him – and gave him drinks – and he lived to sing another day.

The MC went on: 'So now I must call on our good friend Mr Mulligan to give us his rendering of the Londonderry Air on his violin – accompanied by Mr Thompson. Yours, Mr Mulligan.'

Loud applause greeted this speech, whether it was because of Joe's playing, or the qualities of Joe himself, no one really knew. But Joe played the Londonderry Air, then followed it by 'Comin' through the Rye' – then 'A Hundred Pipers' – and to repeated calls of 'encore', he played – 'My Love is but a Lassie yet'.

Bella sat entranced – she had never heard such sounds in all her life. The only music she knew – and loved – was the organ in the church, and the singing of hymns.

When the musical interlude was finished, the dancing and games started again. The tables were cleared away, the women volunteers went to the task of washing cups and saucers and plates – and putting away some left-overs for the bairns at home.

The second half of the dancing was opened with the Quadrilles, and Bella found that Willie and Jenny were in the same set as herself and Joe. In the figures of the dance, she was for a brief moment in Willie's arms. And in those moments, his touch set her on fire. But now she grew wary. She mustn't let anybody see this – least of all Willie.

She didn't mind about Jenny, because she guessed – rightly – that Jenny didn't care enough about anyone, except herself, to see whether or not Bella showed any sign of her feelings, anyway.

During one of those mad moments, during the 'visiting' figure, Willie said in a whisper: 'I didn't know you knew Joe Mulligan?'

'He came to do some painting, where I work.'

'He's a fine man.'

'I believe so.'

And then they were separated, and she was back with Joe, who swung her round, and laughed, and looked happy. It was true, his plain, rather melancholy face looked really happy.

But Bella could endure no more. She could not go on watching Willie, as he danced with several girls, and although she herself was never without a partner, Willie did not come and ask her to dance.

'I want to go home, Joe.'

'Do you, Bella? It's not ten yet – but we'll go whenever you say.'

'It will be nearer eleven when I get home – and I've got the drawing-room to finish off. They'll be back tomorrow.'

'Right; get your cloak. Aye – we're off, Jimmy, we'll see you soon. Goodnight, Andrew – goodnight, Mrs Wilson – aye, it's been a lovely night. No, I'll call for my fiddle tomorrow.'

'See your lass safely home, Joe. She's no' a widow yet, you know!'

Joe turned to where the voice had come from, and his face went as white as chalk. The small crowd round him turned too – but the man who had said it had squeezed through and was out the door.

'Never mind him, Joe; the lass deserves a bit of fun. She's had the rough end of the stick long enough.'

'Aye, she has that. We're not all against her. She didn't know that her man would do such a thing – she's well rid of him. Look after her, Joe!'

Joe's colour came back slowly, and Bella came out of the little cloak-room. He took her arm, and shouted, 'Goodnight, goodnight, aye, goodnight.'

Bella felt the tension in him as they came out into the soft darkness – the darkness of a misty rain, with the pavements shining under the few gas-lamps.

'What's the matter, Joe?'

'Oh, nothing.'

'Somebody said something about me, didn't they?'

'Well – '

'Tell me. I'm used to it, ever since that letter got back here from Canada – about the boys. I've had to live with it, all these years.'

'Bella, none of it was your fault – a man just shouted at me to take you safely home, and then said that you weren't a widow yet.'

'Oh, is *that* all! Maybe I never will be a widow!'

They had reached the main street, West Blackhall Street and turned west, and instinctively they crossed over to the other side of the road, nearest the river. Joe talked easily, and well; he changed the subject of the remark at the hall, and went right on to how she had enjoyed the evening.

'Oh, it was grand, Joe, just grand! I've never enjoyed myself so much. But you didn't tell me that you could play the music.'

'Ah! I wish I could, lass; I've only taught myself, by ear. I would have liked to learn music. I tried to teach myself, but it was too hard going. I couldn't make any sense out of the wee dots and lines. I wanted to play the fiddle in a big band, an orchestra, you know. And then. when I knew enough, I wanted to be a conductor.'

'A conductor? What's that?'

'The fellow who stands in front of the orchestra or a band and waves his wee stick.'

'And that was what you wanted?'

'Aye, but we couldn't afford it in Ireland, where I came from.'

'How long have you been here, Joe?'

'Oh – about twenty-six years. I came with my sister, Bridie. My mother and father died in Ireland. Bridie, she . . . went away; I never saw her again. My wife died seven years ago. We thought we'd be all right here, there was plenty of work; Annie was a milk-maid. She could milk a cow better and quicker than anybody. She got diphtheria, and died.'

'Did you have any family, Joe?'

'Aye, a wee lassie. She died when she was three. We were on a farm in Ayrshire, near Largs. I've always been good at papering and painting, so I started up on my own. We managed fine, but when Annie died, and the baby after her, I came here. I thought I would look for my sister, Bridie, but nobody seemed to know where she had gone. Even Father Manahan, in the church, had left, and I couldn't find any trace of her at all. I've got a nice workshop now, look, just below West Burn Street, with a wee house up above and it's just behind the Bakery. So it keeps nice and warm. There's plenty of room for my paints and ladders and things.'

They walked on, but as the rain was growing heavier, they quickened their pace, and for some while, they did not talk. Her head, covered by the hood of her cloak, was bent against the rain. Joe nudged her elbow to turn the corner, and it was only when they were a few yards down Campbell Street that she realised where they were.

She stopped dead. 'No! Not down here!'

'What's the matter, Bella?' Joe asked gently.

'I can't go down here. I've never walked on this street since – It was five years ago.'

'Yes, it *was* five years ago, Bella, do you realise that? And can you get it into your head that it can't happen again?'

'No. Yes, I know that, but . . . '

'I heard the noises, that day. I didn't know what was happening. It was you, wasn't it, Bella?'

She nodded. Then, as if she felt she wanted to tell it to somebody sympathetic, she stood at the railings on the edge of the river, the rain still pouring down.

'The ship he was on – he put two little boys who had stowed away on to the ice at Newfoundland. They fell into the icy water and were drowned. Crowds gathered on the dock to watch them. They would have lynched them if they could have got at them. I – wanted to see him. I wanted to see what it was I had seen in him the summer before. It was just four months before Sandy was born – the end of July.'

She turned away from the river, and they walked on again slowly.

'The crowd was angry when the police managed to get the men, the captain and my husband off – and they looked round and somebody saw me. I can remember a shout: "There's his wife! She's as bad as he is".' She stopped again and looked out over the angry grey clouds covering Ben Lomond.

'Go on, Bella. Get it all said. It will do you good. What happened then?'

'Somebody threw a stone at me. It struck my shoulder: I remember the pain and then there was a lot of stones thrown at me, but I didn't feel them.'

They walked on again, in silence for a few minutes.

'I heard the shouts, then I saw a cab coming down, fast, to the dock. And the crowd seemed to fade away. The police were running, and whistles blowing. Oh Bella lass! I wish I could have helped you then. But it's over now. He will never hurt you again. Come on, love, we're nearly there.' He coughed again, a little rough cough. 'Come on, lassie, or I'll get my death in this rain.'

'Oh Joe! I didn't think. You've got to go all the way back. I'll manage fine now. You get home.'

'Nonsense, we'll walk quick now, and be sure you get something hot when you go in.'

'What about you? Will you have something hot?'

'Aye. I'll have a wee toddy. It's nice and warm in the place. I'm just at the back of the bakery. Remind me to tell you the story of the Duchess when I see you again. Will I see you again, Bella?'

'I don't know. You'll be at the house doing some more painting, I expect?'

'Very likely. But I'd like to take you out somewhere, up to Glasgow for the day or Edinburgh, or take the boat to Dunoon?'

She shivered. 'No. I don't want to go anywhere. I want to stay here, where I can see this.' She pointed northwards from the Esplanade to where the mountains merged like shadows into the deep gloom of the sky, and the river flowed black and sullen, with white horses near the shore.

They reached the side door of the house at the far end of the Esplanade; she put her key in the lock and turned to say goodnight to him.

Very gently, very tenderly, he laid his arm across her shoulder. His left hand lifted her chin and he looked at her very steadily. He was only about an inch taller than Bella.

He kissed her quickly and lightly on the lips, said 'Goodnight, Bella, I'll see you soon,' and walked down the path to the gate. She heard the crunch of his feet on the stone path, and she heard his little cough. She went up the stairs to her room on the top floor, and lit her candle to undress. Sandy was fast asleep. Bella lay for a while, thinking . . . of the social, Joe's playing, of Jenny and Willie, and inevitably, of Joe's kiss when he left her. And she could have cried in despair.

Was this to be all that life had to offer her now? Second best? Joe was a good man, but then . . . she couldn't read too much into a social evening, a walk home and a goodnight kiss.

She blew out the candle, and fell asleep seeing only Willie in the darkness.

XIX

Margaret Preston made her way up the garden to the laundry. The days were darkening early; soon it would be Christmas and New Year. She shivered. There was snow in the air. She heard the sound of not unmusical singing as she came near the open door of the laundry.

Bella was ironing, her face flushed with the heat, and shining, not only with sweat and the cleanliness of soap and water, but with a kind of inner happiness that she had not felt for many years.

'Good morning, Bella.'

The voice broke in on her humming as she held a hot iron up to her cheek.

'Have you nearly finished, Bella?'

'Oh yes'm. Only the aprons to do.'

'That's good. We won't be working on New Year's day, so we must get as much done as we can now. When you come down to the house, will you come and see me in the drawing-room?'

'In the drawing-room, m'am?'

'Don't worry, Bella. I just want to have a talk with you.'

She went back to the house quickly. It really was draughty in there, especially when there was an east wind. She supposed she should do something about it, but there, they wouldn't be here another winter, and she was inside now . . . It wasn't really so cold, after all.

Bella felt sick with apprehension. Something had happened. Morrison had come back. He had found out where she was. He would take little Sandy and batter him, as he had beaten her.

What could Mrs Preston have to say to her that had to be said in the drawing-room? It couldn't be a rise in her wages, because each time that had happened, it had been Mr Preston who had called her into the dining-room and made a little joke about it. She was now getting £12 a year, and had nearly £20 in the savings bank.

She finished up quickly, and put on her cloak and ran down to the house. Sandy would be home from school. That was it! Sandy had had an accident. He was always near the boats. Maybe he had even tried to stow away! She went through the kitchen, where the girls were sewing, and drinking tea.

'There you are, Bella. I'll pour your tea.'

'No, Ellen – I've got to see the missus, in the drawing-
room. I'm frightened.'

'Och lassie, there's nothing to be frightened of. It's all
right.'

Timidly, she knocked at the white door of the
drawing-room, when she had pulled down her sleeves
and straightened her cap.

'Come in, Bella. Sit down, here, near the fire. How
long have you been with us, Bella?'

'Six years m'am.'

Margaret saw the terror in Bella's face.

'You mustn't be frightened, Bella. I only want to ask
you if you would like to come to America with us. Mr
Preston has had a very good offer, and we would like
you all to come. Ellen and Ivy are coming. Of course,
Sandy would come too. It would be a wonderful
opportunity for him. Such a great country.'

'To America? Goodness, I never thought . . . I don't
want to leave here.'

'Leave this house, you mean, or leave the town?'

'Just *here*. I want to stay here. I won't leave.' She shook
her head.

'Will you think about it, Bella?'

'Yes, but I think I want to stay here. I *never* want to
leave this.' Her arms went round the room, vaguely. 'I
sort of promised . . . '

'Promised? Promised who?'

But Bella only shook her head and would say no
more.

Mrs Preston was disappointed, and somewhat
annoyed, as she said afterwards to her husband, 'I can't
think why she wants to stay *here*. After all the trouble
she's had, with that dreadful stoning, and then the fever
when she was in hospital – did you know they thought
she was going to get smallpox? You'd think she would
have been glad to make a new life for herself and the
little boy. But you can never tell with these people.
Anyway, I'll give her a good reference. She's a very good
laundress now. She should get a good job.'

*

On a windy day in January, she took Sandy up to the brow of the Lyle Hill. They stood facing the Argyllshire mountains, trimmed with peaks of snow, and heavy with brooding clouds. The river was dark and sullen, with an angry undercurrent, and white horses right across to the opposite shore.

'Look, Sandy.'

'What at?'

'Just look. All round. All this. Do you see?'

'I don't know, it's awful cold.'

'Sandy, do you want to go to America?'

'Do you?'

'No. But I want to do what's best for you. Mrs Preston says you would get college and all that, there. But I think you'll get a better education here than in any place in the world. And I don't want to leave all this.'

Suddenly she knew that she must teach him the real beauty and meaning of this spot. She would one day tell him about the hard brilliance of that summer day, and her finding the wild, savage possessiveness of the broad-bosomed firth.

She spoke very softly. 'I want to stay here, all my life, Sandy. It's too big to explain, but this is *mine*. I found it, long ago, and I'll never leave it. Never. Look, Sandy: *Look!*'

Young eyes could not see as she had seen on that day of horror, because he had nothing to compare it with. But he wanted to please his mother. Yes, he could understand, a little.

'It's better on a summer day,' he said.

'Yes, it's brighter. But it's beautiful, any time. Will we go to America?'

'No. I'll stay here with you. Can I go to the Academy when I'm older? I'll go to sea when I'm a man, and I'll take you with me wherever I go.'

Bella laughed.

'I won't go anywhere, even with you, Sandy. Education, yes, you should have that. I only need this; they can't take this away from me. It'll *always* be here. Come on Sandy. Race you to the bottom of the hill!'

They ran, laughing, and the child was away in front of her. Then he waited, and they walked, hand in hand, down through the quiet streets to the Esplanade.

*

The upheaval of packing was nearly finished. Joe, versatile and willing, had not only decorated: he had been a valuable help in nailing up crates and boxes, and packing precious furniture and china. It was an evening late in May. The two girls had gone out, since Margaret and Oliver were dining out. Oliver brought Joe into the kitchen.

'Ah, Bella. Could you make a cup of tea for Mulligan? And give him some supper? Don't wait up for us, Bella. We'll be home about 11 o'clock. Goodnight, Mulligan. If you'll come early on 1st June, I'm sure we'll be glad of your help. Have a good supper. Goodnight, Bella.'

Joe sat down on a kitchen chair.

'Well, it'll soon be here, the first of June. Are you going with them after all, Bella?'

'No. I won't leave here.'

'Got another job?'

'No. not yet. I'll go home for a wee while. Would you like some cold beef?'

'Aye, fine. Thanks. Have you any views about what you want to do?'

'What else is there but service? I've got to work to keep myself and Sandy.'

'And Morrison?'

Her face darkened. 'I'll never see him again if I can help it.'

'All men are not like him, you know.'

'Fine I know that. But it doesn't make it any better. Oh! I'm sick, and tired.' She sat down suddenly and put her head on her arms.

He leaned over and gently stroked her shoulder.

'Don't cry love. I don't want you to cry any more. I'd like to take care of you, Bella. I would indeed. If we could get married, I'd ask you to marry me tomorrow. Bella, will you come with me? I've got a nice cosy wee place. I've done it all up nice. Put my paints and stuff in the room below, and made a nice wee room and kitchen up on the top. I've done it for you, Bella. What I'm trying to say . . . I love you. If you can get a divorce, we can get married. I can help you with money. We'll be comfortable, lass. You'll never want for anything while I'm alive. I'll take care of you, and Sandy too. Will you come, Bella?'

She was staring at him.

'He wants to go to the Academy,' she said, stupidly.

'And he will that. The more education the children get, the better for all of us. Bella . . . ' He was quiet, firm, and gentle. 'I'll be good to you, lass. I won't ask for anything until you can . . . like me enough. Bella?'

'I don't know. It's a terrible thing to do. My father . . . Oh! he'd be *terrible* angry.'

'I'll go and see him tomorrow.'

'No, wait. I never even thought of such a thing.'

'I couldn't ask you before. I wanted to wait to see if you would go to America with them, if it was best for you.'

'I'll never leave here.'

'Never? That's a long time.'

'Maybe.'

'We . . . '

'Oh, your tea, I forgot. And some supper.'

'Never mind the supper, I'm not hungry. I'll make the tea.'

It was cosy, sitting in front of the glowing fire on hard kitchen chairs. He was so quietly placid. She felt suddenly at ease with him.

'Sandy likes you, I know.'

'I think he does. Does that mean that you . . . ?'

'I'll have to think about it, Joe. I'll need to come to it myself. It's not the kind of thing I can ask advice about! I know it's wrong.'

'You mean it's been drummed into you that it's wrong. There's only black and white, isn't there? It couldn't be a bit of both, could it? You were married to Morrison. Was that *good?*'

'Oh don't, Joe!'

'So if you come to me, and I take care of you, will that be bad?'

'I can't think! I can't think! Let me be, Joe.'

'All right, lass. I'll come and see you tomorrow night.'

'No. I'll meet you at the corner at half-past eight. I'll tell you then.'

'I'll be there. Goodnight, Bella love.'

'Goodnight, Joe.'

She went up to bed and looked in on Sandy. He had a tiny room to himself now.

While she undressed, and when she had put out her candle, she pictured the loneliness ahead of her. She could go on, in service, until she was an old woman. Or till Sandy was working and able to support her. And was there any guarantee that he would, or could? For he would very likely get married, and she would be alone again, and at the mercy of the women who employed her, and she had seen so many old people, working their hearts out, and thrown aside, with little of mercy, after years of devoted service. *Of course,* there were other kinds of people, who did have feelings and care for their old servants. But it was a chancy business, never a sure one.

She was tied to Jim Morrison, until death took him, or her. Wicked it might be, to go and live in sin with a man, but it would be a safe haven. And Sandy? Joe would be good for Sandy. What this would do to her mother and father she could not dare to think. She saw the long rows of heavy seats he shifted every Sunday for Sunday-school. She heard the minister say, 'to present us spotless before

His Presence with exceeding joy,' and she remembered the simple pleasures of the socials in the church hall.

How uncomplicated life had seemed in the shelter of the church! Before she slept, her mind was clear, and firmly made up.

XX

'Your breakfast's ready, Willie.'

'All right, mother – just finished shaving.'

'There should be a letter from Robbie; there's usually one about the end of the month.'

'Gold hunting in Canada – I thought he had enough gold by this time. Your big laddie's a rich man now, you know, mother!'

'I don't need a rich man; I just want my boy back. I've a feeling I'll never see him again.'

'Och, get away with you, mother! You saw him six years ago. I haven't seen him since he went away – when he was twenty-one.' He broke off, because he didn't want to say that he knew, now, why Robbie had gone off.

'Mother, I'm going to ask Jenny McGarvie if she'll take me.'

'Aye, son, I know; you've always had an eye for Jenny, but – '

'But! It doesn't matter what anybody says – ' he was angry – 'if she'll have me, I'm going to marry her. When she went to service two years ago, she said she wanted to think about it. Well, I've waited; so I'll ask her again tonight. I'll need to go, mother – cheer up. There'll be a letter from Robbie in a day or two. It's going to be a lovely day. I'll take you doon the watter on Saturday . . .

I'll away.'

He picked up his coat from a hook in the lobby and ran down the stairs. At the bottom he met the postman.

'Hello, Mr Munro. Letter from America for you!'

'Oh, thanks; I'll take it with me. It will be from Robbie.'

He pushed it into his pocket, and walked quickly down the street.

He reached the outbuildings and offices that proclaimed, in white letters: 'Colin Campbell & Son, Ltd. Coal Merchants.'

Soon – very soon – Campbell senior would be gathered to his fathers, and Campbell, Son, and Willie Munro would be in partnership. Then it would be: 'Campbell and Munro, Ltd. Coal Merchants.'

Willie had gone through the whole coal business, from a hungry schoolboy filling the sacks of coal, and selling them. The youthful adoration he had written about to his brother in the laconic phraseology of the inarticulate Scot, 'I like her better than anybody I've seen,' had grown into the passion of a man for the one woman in the world who would ever hold his heart.

Jenny, beautiful, cold, neat and adored, was his. He *would* have her.

He enquired about Campbell senior. He was not so well. He had lunch with young Campbell at the Unionist Club; he liked the atmosphere of wealth and leather chairs.

When his day's work was done, he turned his steps eastwards, towards the church, where he was welcomed with real affection by Flora and John. Flora was a little stooped, but her hair was thick and brown still. A little inclined to forget her immediate happenings, but clear about all the years that had gone.

John was as upright as always, but his eyes had lost their light; almost, he had lost his faith. Inside him, disguised as yet in slight indigestion, a cancer was eating his life away.

'Going out, Andrew?' Willie asked the boy who was

cleaning his boots by the fireplace.

'Yes. Up the burn.'

'Got a girl yet?'

'Got a few, when I feel like it.'

'None so smart as Jenny here.'

'Och! You're a blether, Will,' said Jenny.

'Coming out for a walk, Jenny?'

'Yes, all right. I'll put on my hat.'

She went into the big room which she had all to herself now. She had come home when Bella went to Mrs Preston. In a way, she was quite pleased to queen it at home without Bella. And she had got out of her frilled cap-and-apron when she gave a month's notice to Lady Granfield. She didn't think she would be wearing them ever again.

She combed her hair, and arranged the folds of her dark green dress. Her straw hat had seen four summers, and now she put a green ribbon on it, and tied it in a bow at the back. It was really her Sunday hat, but defiantly she decided to wear it tonight.

When she had gone, Willie turned to John.

'Uncle John, I want to ask you . . . I'm going to ask Jenny if she'll take me, and I hope you'll give your consent. I've got good prospects. I'm thirty-six now, and there's never been anybody but Jenny for me. I'll be good to her.'

'Willie lad, I couldn't wish her any better. She's a lot younger than you, but if she's agreeable, then you'll get my blessing. I just wish – ' his face saddened again – 'that our Bella had been as lucky.'

Willie just said, 'Aye, it's a pity.' He had no interest whatever in Bella or her troubles. 'Then all right. I'll ask her tonight. I'll not be late bringing her back.'

Jenny came in.

'Oh! Your Sunday hat, Jenny!'

'I don't care. My other one's terrible. I like this one.'

'Never mind, Jenny. I'll buy you a new hat tomorrow. We'll go up to Glasgow and get some new clothes.'

He took her arm, and they walked up through the

railway arch, and on to the green hillside, over heather clumps, and yellow broom. They sat down on a patch of grass, and watched the busy town below.

'Jenny?'

'What?'

'I've asked your father . . . I've asked him if he'll let me marry you, if you'll have me. Will you, Jenny?'

She laughed, a delighted, girlish laugh.

'Marry you? A coalman?'

'I'm not a coalman now, Jenny; I'm a coal merchant, and very soon I'll be in partnership.'

'You mean you'll be rich?'

'If you want me to be.'

'Well, you might be, but that's not all I want.'

'What *do* you want, Jenny?'

'I couldn't tell you. I don't see how I'm to get it.' She spoke in a worried, impatient tone, as if whatever it was, was going past her, and she would never be able to catch it.

'What is it you want, love, and if it's humanly possible, I'll get it for you.'

'I want a big house.'

He nodded.

'And servants.'

He grinned, but nodded again, and said, 'Usually every girl wants these things.'

'And a carriage and pair.'

'There's nothing impossible in all that.'

'Ah, but . . . I want the servants to call me . . . ' she hesitated – then said it, 'My Lady!'

He sat up. 'Jenny! You're daft! How could I . . . oh, I don't know, though.'

She went on, ignoring him. 'I want to be Lady Jenny something or other.'

He burst out laughing.

'Well, lass, that's finished it. *That* you can never be.'

'And whit way can I no'?'

'Because, my dear, lovely Jenny, to be a Lady Jenny, or Lady Mary – or Lady *any* first name, you have to be the daughter of a Duke or an Earl, or some such thing. Your only hope is to marry a Lord – or a Sir somebody... or else . . . ' He drew her into his arms, 'or else somebody who will one day be a Sir . . . and, by God, Jenny, I believe you've made me see what *I* want. *I'll* make you a lady, my Jenny. I can't make you Lady Jenny, but I can make you Lady Munro. Will that do?'

'How can you do that?'

'There are ways and means. I'll do it. Will you marry me, Jenny? Oh, Jenny, I've loved you for such a long time. Let me hold you close.'

She wriggled away from his arms and stood up.

'None of that, Will Munro!'

'Oh, Jenny! I didn't mean any harm. I love you.'

'Well anyway, there's to be none of that. I don't like being pawed.'

'God in Heaven, Jenny! I wasn't pawing you! I love you! Do you realise what that means? I want you, for my wife, for always.'

'Yes, but . . . '

'All right, Jenny love. I'll wait, only don't keep me waiting too long. There's nothing to stop us.'

'You're a lot older than me, Will.'

'I'm fifteen years older. But I've been saving for a long time. I've got enough to get a nice house. I'll take care of you.'

His passion, in the face of her coldness and disdain, had calmed a little. But the nearness of her, the heady beauty of her, the tilt of her lovely head under the pale straw hat, kept him tied, and only the thought that of course he mustn't expect a nice girl like Jenny to be used to the force of a man's love, made the journey home in the June twilight bearable.

'Well, lad, had a nice walk, eh?' John asked.

'Aye. We went up the Whin Hill. I've asked Jenny, and I think she will.'

The big outside door at the bottom of the passage banged, and young Andrew's footsteps were heard clumping with youthful vigour across the wood floor of the hall.

'Oh hello. You still here?'

'Just got back. I suppose you'd better know. Jenny . . . me and Jenny, well, we're getting married.'

Andrew looked up from the chair he had slumped into, to take off his boots.

'Gimme a cup of tea, ma. You and Jenny, eh? You're getting married?' His tone was slightly incredulous.

'That's right.' Tightly.

'Oh. Thanks, ma, no, nothing to eat, just the tea.'

Andrew stood up, and took his boots by the laces in one hand and his cup of tea in the other. He turned and faced Willie, and looked at him strangely. He seemed grown up.

He said, 'Well, I'll tell you this. You'll no' have your sorrows to seek. Goodnight, ma, goodnight, father.'

He nodded briefly to Willie. Jenny had gone into her room to take off her hat. Willie was furious. (What the hell had he meant? And yet, deep down, some strange sensation told him that what he had said was true.) But he pushed the thought away from him when she came in. The sight of her drove all reason and wisdom from his brain. She was so perfect; even Flora looked at her with a new vision. Perhaps she had really cared for Willie, and hadn't known it?

But it wasn't love that delighted Jenny's heart. It was the promise in Willie's voice when he had said he would make her 'm'lady.' She was shrewd enough, in her selfishness, to know that no other man would take her on her terms. She had accepted, at last, the facts of creation, by the occurrence at Lady Granfield's, when her daughter-in-law had come for three months prior to the birth of an heir. But *she* would have none of it. She would not be pawed. Willie would be malleable.

The future, as a rich lady, beckoned: the thrusts of love were not for her. Such things were not 'nice.'

John said, 'Well, I know you'll look after her. When will you be wed?'

'Nothing to wait for. Have you any idea, Jenny?'

'Oh no . . . Whenever you like. I'll need a new dress.'

'I'll buy you a new dress, lass. We'll go to Glasgow on Saturday and get one. Well, lad, we maun get to bed. I'll see you to the door.'

John and Willie walked down the hall to the big door. John offered his hand and Willie shook it warmly. They spoke very little; John was gruff, and Willie was not quite sure of his ground.

He was going to be married to Jenny . . . that was all that mattered. And then he remembered she hadn't even kissed him.

He walked home, his mind full of the incredible idea that Jenny had given him.

'A title! I never thought of that, but what a do that would be! I'd have to do something for the town. Politics. Should I try for the MP? No, I'd be up against that Joe Mulligan. He's a good lad, but he's got these new socialist ideas. I'm afraid the town's going to listen to him. But it won't catch on. Pity there isn't a war. Not that I want to see anybody killed, but it doesn't matter so much when it's foreigners. Only thing is, it gives you a chance to do something *big*. I should buy some land. I could maybe get Robbie to help me there. Gosh! I forgot that letter! I'll read it when I get home. Jenny! Oh Lord, Jenny. I hope you'll be different when I get you into bed!'

He opened the letter when he had taken his boots off and sat down by the fire. His mother was asleep in the other room. He lived with his mother in a nice two-room and kitchen flat in a good tenement in Nelson Street, and his room was nicely furnished.

He now noticed that the letter was in a strange handwriting. It opened:

Dear Mr Willie Munro,

I'm writing this letter as I have to because him that should be writing it can't, he's dead. I'm sorry I've to tell you this and I'm not very good at the writing my wife is helping me. Rob and I have been friends since we jumped ship in New York fifteen years ago, and a better friend a man never had. Louise will tell you how it happened I can't write any more.

The writing on the letter changed and Willie read on with mounting horror. It told of the accident, and went on:

Jimmy says will he send all Rob's papers, and instruct his Bank to send you all his affairs, or will you be likely to come here. If you do, we will be pleased to see you. We hope your mother is well, and we only wish we could help her get over this shock. That's why we've written to you. We thought you could break it to her.

Willie could read no more. His eyes were filled with the tears that flowed down his cheeks quite unheeded.

'Oh God! Oh my God! Robbie! How can I tell my mother? You should never have left us. Oh God!'

He fell weeping on his pillow, choking back sobs he had to stifle for fear of waking his mother.

All his thoughts of Jenny, marriage or future had gone in an instant. His brother, his untidy, honest, fearless brother, had gone. He would never see him again. But to die in such surroundings, with not even a Christian burial!

He would have to go. He must sail to America, and bring his body home.

Jenny.

Oh God! He couldn't take Jenny on a bridal trip . . . to bring a dead body home! He couldn't take Jenny to the frozen wilds of Canada.

Robbie was dead. Jimmy, he was sure, would have done everything that was necessary and decent for his friend. He must write to Jimmy, and ask him to get word to the old trapper, whoever he was, to put a stone, or even a wooden cross, on Robbie's grave.

The hardest thing was going to be telling his mother. He could not wake her now. It would have to be told in the morning.

Willie slept only in snatches that night, and he was up at five o'clock making tea. He took a cup in for Millie. It had to be done. Somehow he had to tell her. He thought she had died, when he told her as gently as he could.

She broke down and sobbed. 'My Robbie! What a terrible way to go. In the cold.' (Was there a faint echo of the other mothers' laments over the laddies who had slipped through the frozen Arctic Seas?) 'He should never have gone there. It's all Bella's fault! Oh God . . . what have I done!'

Then she stopped suddenly, and looked . . . at him and beyond him. 'I don't believe it! I don't believe it! He's *not* dead!'

He hushed and comforted her, and when it was time, he went down to the office and said he would be taking the day off. He walked over to the church and told Flora and John.

'Will you go over there, Will?'

'I thought about it, but I can't leave mother. And I'm promised to Jenny.'

'Jenny can wait. If you want to go, Millie can come to me. I'll go and see her now, anyway. Jenny!' Flora called.

'Yes, mother.'

'Come and see Willie. I've got to go to your Auntie Millie.'

Somehow, he got through the day. At the end of it, he had decided. Nothing he could do could bring Robbie back, and he and Jenny would be married, in two weeks. The days would go on. He was head of the family now. Soon he would be head of his own family. He would have sons . . .

*

There had been a time when Willie believed that his tenderness and devotion would bring Jenny to the understanding of his love and his need of her. Jenny

tantalised him, not consciously, because she had none of
the feeling of the coquette. She had said she would
marry him, hadn't she? Well, she would, but he had
promised, hadn't he, that some day she would be
'm'lady'?

When he saw her, in the church hall, dressed in a soft
white silk dress for their wedding, he told himself that she
had been quite right to deny herself to him until they
were married. It was the right thing for a nice girl to do.
He was almost afraid of his long-suppressed desire; afraid
that his passion might frighten her. She was so delicately
fragile.

He was not so entirely innocent himself. There were
always the lads who 'knew a place'. This was the kind of
thing a man had to take in his stride. And he would have
no need of the experienced professionals once he was
married.

Perhaps, too, it was as well he *had* gone to that house
in Glasgow. He had discovered how ignorant he was!

He had taken a flat in a very exclusive tenement in
Finnart Street, just one room, and the kitchen. He had
furnished the room as a real bedroom. The kitchen would
be used for eating and sitting and having friends in. It still
had the usual alcove for the traditional set-in bed, but he
had put a good sofa there, and it was cosy and soft, and
almost luxurious.

They arrived in a cab, and Jenny was thrilled at really
having her own home. But of course, she was going to
have a really *big* house some day, with a drawing-room,
and bedrooms and bathrooms, and a kitchen and
servants' rooms, all quite apart from her rooms.
Especially, she would have bathrooms.

Willie put the kettle on and made a cup of tea. He had
expected her to be shy, and a little diffident about being
alone with him at last. But she was excited and happy,
like a child at a fair.

She went into the room, and when he had poured her
tea, he found her undressed and sitting up against her
pillows in bed. She was dressed in a white cotton

nightdress, and a lacy bed-jacket. This was a treasured possession given her by one of the ladies when she was in the Highland Castle.

'Oh Willie, isn't this lovely?'

'You like the room, love?'

'Oh yes. And my lovely bed. Oh, a nice cup of tea. I'll just drink it, then you can say goodnight to me properly, and I'll see you in the morning.'

She put her cup and saucer on the chair beside the bed, and looked up at him.

He sat down on the edge of the bed and put his arms round her, caught her fiercely to him, and kissed her, hungrily, hotly, on her lips. She made little protesting sounds, and struggled to get her face away from him.

Her eyes were flashing. Her face was red and angry, and her voice was venomous.

'I thought I told you there was to be none of that!'

'None of what, pet? That was before we were married. You're my *wife* now, Jenny love, you do love me? It will be all right. I'll be very gentle. I'll be with you in a minute.'

'You what? You're not coming in here with me! It's disgusting. I told you, I won't be *pawed!*'

He went white, and stood up. 'What are you talking about, Jenny? I love you. I'm your husband. We were married tonight. Do you know what that means? Did nobody ever tell you?'

'I know what it means to *some* people, but I'm not that sort!'

'Not that sort? For God's sake, Jenny, what do you mean?'

'What do *you* mean? Is that all you married me for? Just to . . . to . . . ' Her voice trailed away.

'Just to what? Will I tell you, in plain language, Jenny? Do you want me to tell you in just one word?'

'I don't know. I don't know what you're talking about.

He breathed deeply and spoke again quietly.

'You know I can force you? I'm stronger than you. Oh, you needn't worry,' as she looked up at him with eyes cunning and filled with fear. 'I wouldn't force any woman. A fine thing if a man has to rape his wife on their wedding night! What the hell did you marry me for, then?'

She was quite sincerely astonished.

'But you know what for! You said you'd make me a lady. That's true, isn't it, Willie?'

He backed away and stared at her as if he had never seen her before.

'Christ Almighty!' he breathed. 'What have I done?'

XXI

The Municipal Chambers of Greenock Town Hall are in an imposing building testifying to the industry, integrity and importance of the worthy men who control the civic business of a growing seaport. They are filled with unexpected passages and stairways; the entrance hall is of inlaid mosaic marble, with tall pillars supporting the massive structure. Standing as a landmark outside is the Victoria Tower which, every decade or so, is declared unsafe. But it still stands, a nostalgic reminder of all that has taken place under its benign weight.

In the council chamber, whose windows, facing south, look on to Cathcart Square, was a gathering of men on this wet, windy May evening. Their business was the election of councillors and, in particular, the filling of the highest office of all – that of the Provost, whose term of office would expire next September.

Names were bandied about – and various offices were filled, and then a name was mentioned: 'Not a native of the town, but he has lived and worked among us for twenty years and more. A good, solid, respectable workman, sober and industrious . . . he's been a good treasurer.'

'Agreed.'

'Indeed he has.'

The name of a mild little Irishman, an honest painter who stood high in the esteem of his civic comrades, was mentioned for the highest honour his townsmen could offer; quiet, unassuming, self-effacing happy fiddler – Joe Mulligan.

'Well, maybe we'd better wait a wee while; we've got other men to consider, you know.'

'What do you say, Munro?'

'Me? Oh, I think he would make a fine Provost. A good, upstanding wee man. But is the town ready yet, for someone who is not a well-placed businessman? It's a pity he's not married. Widower, isn't he? Mind you, I like him. But I say we should take a vote. Anyway, should he not be here tonight?'

'He said he had some work to do; he works for himself, of course – so he takes as much as he can get. He'll be at the next meeting. The full council will be here. Now, other business. The Fire Station.'

When the meeting was over, Willie Munro walked slowly along the street, the pavements wet and shiny in the little pools of light thrown by dim street lamps. Down in the harbour, a ship hooted mournfully, and only an occasional passer-by disturbed the quiet street, although it was only ten o'clock. Greenock went to bed early – they were at work before the lark.

On an impulse, Willie turned down Charles Street and made his way through the innumerable intricate passages that lay in the maze of huddled buildings. He saw lights at the bakehouse, and heard the clatter of tins, and the upsurge of raised voices, and smelt the wholesome odour of bread being baked. Above this, on the corner, lived Joe. There was a light in his place, both in the new rooms above, and in the place below where he kept his paints and ladders. Willie knocked, and Joe called from the window:

'Who's there?'

'It's me, Munro. Is it too late to come in and have a chat?'

'Will! Not a bit; hang on a minute, and I'll come down. Mind that ladder there.'

When the door opened, he shook hands firmly with Willie, and showed him into the paint room. Then he led him up to the two rooms that he had nearly finished painting and papering. He had also partitioned off a wee scullery. He was still in his white overalls.

'There, sit ye doon, Will. You'll take a wee dram?'

'Aye, all right. It's thirsty work talking. I was at the council meeting, and as I was passing, I thought I'd look in.'

'Your missis will be worrying if you're late, surely?'

Did a shadow come over Willie's face, or did Joe imagine it? He must have done. A married man of only a year would not be unhappy going home to his wife.

'She'll be all right. She knows I'm at the meeting.'

'That's all right then. Now, how do you like your dram?'

'Just as it comes. Your health, Joe.'

'And the same to you, Will.'

There was a silence, then Joe said, without looking at Willie:

'I think I'd better tell you something, Will.'

'I came to tell you something, too: still, you go on.'

'I . . . I've asked Bella, your sister-in-law, to come and stay with me. I wish we could get married, but Morrison is still alive. I'd be willing to pay for a divorce, but she can get a legal separation. Anyway, I've asked . . . '

He broke off. Willie had stood up and was gripping the back of his chair while he glared at Joe with a look of madness and disbelief.

'Are you mad? What the bloody hell possessed you to do such a thing?'

'Will – don't think too badly of Bella. I would marry her tomorrow, I'm that fond of her. She's a good lass, and she's had a lot of trouble.'

'I don't give a bugger for Bella's troubles. It's *you!* You bloody fool!'

'Me? What do you mean?'

'Damn you! Do you know what you're doing? Do you know what this means to you, if you go on with it?'

'Oh!' Joe stopped, and coughed.

'I've just come from the Town Hall. I know I wasn't supposed to tell you, but I wanted to talk to somebody... some sense . . . my brain's getting smothered, I can't . . . oh hell! You've got to stop this. And for God's sake, that's a terrible cough you've got. You'd better have another dram.'

Joe filled the glasses again.

'Now, what's it got to do with anybody, except Bella and me?'

'Nothing, I suppose. If you were anyone else. Bella can go to hell, if she likes. But you know what will happen. ' He paused, and emptied his glass.

'Do you realise, Joe Mulligan, that you could be having the two lamps outside your door this very year? And you might easily be in the House of Commons at the next election?'

Joe sat down and stared at Willie. He whispered: 'The two lamps . . . ! The Provost's two lamps . . . is that what they said tonight? That's what you were to tell me?'

'I'm not supposed to tell you – but I wanted to talk to somebody about something sensible. I feel smothered. Oh Christ! What a mess!'

He drained his glass, and Joe passed the bottle to him. Then he looked up. 'I thought Bella was in service in the West End?'

'Yes, but the Prestons are going to America, leaving on 1st June; they asked Bella to go with them. The other girls are going, but Bella wouldn't. She says she'll never leave Greenock. It's funny, that. There seems to be something, when she was young.'

'Oh yes – She got lost one day – she ran away, up the Lyle Hill. We were all out looking for her.'

'Was she very young?'

'Oh, eleven or twelve. I'm not sure.'

His tone conveyed that he wasn't interested in Bella.

It was three o'clock in the morning when Willie staggered out of Joe's little paint shop – with Joe helping him out to the main street. Talk had flowed – each the perfect foil for the other; arguments, threats, pleadings, instances, consequences, confidences – interlaced with mellow whisky – and at the end of it, Joe was just as firm in his stand as he had been when they started.

He looked down the road of public acclaim. He looked at the hearth where he would come home to Bella . . . and he only smiled, a little sadly.

The thought of a career in Westminster had not seriously concerned him. His council work – and such plans he had for the good of the town! – yes, that would have to be given up. The Provost? – Deep inside, he had perhaps had a kind of feeling that it was something he could have wished for, and could have handled. But Bella, she would last. She would be with him to the end. He coughed a lot when he went to bed.

He was shocked at what Willie had told him about Jenny. But he agreed that, as a man of honour, there was nothing else Willie could do. He could not admit to the world that he had married a cold, empty, beautiful shell. Willie pondered this, too, in his befuddled state as he passed his mother's house in Nelson Street. He could go to Glasgow any time he liked; there was a nice, obliging woman living near the outskirts. He had his work; and if Jenny was frigid, she was at least a good housewife and a really good cook, and she kept his clothes in perfect order. She was lovely to look at, and given her own way, she was charming, and happy, often very funny and clever, intensely house-proud, and particular about herself. It just seemed as though the functions of womanhood had been left out of her make-up.

Willie had attempted, just once more, being gentle and persuasive, instead of hostile and sarcastic, but she was still disgusted and angry. His kisses could not induce any answering passion in her, and she thrust him away angrily, spitting at him, as she struck his hand away from her breast.

'All right.' He stood up and looked at her, and his eyes were hard and cold. 'Don't worry, I won't bother you again. I won't go without. That's something you'll learn, if you live long enough. A man will get what he wants, whether it's a good dinner, a warm home, or a woman to love him. And if he doesn't get it at home, where he should get it, whatever it is, he'll get it somewhere else. I know where I can go. There's always somebody ready to oblige.'

'You wouldn't do . . . ' Her tone was horrified.

'For God's sake, Jenny! How do you think *you* arrived in this world? How do you think the world keeps going at all?'

She shuddered. 'I don't want to talk about it. It's disgusting. If *you* do – that sort of thing – I don't care. *I* won't do it, that's all.'

Her mind was closed on the subject. She would neither discuss it nor be wooed into it. She was perfectly happy, left in her virginity. And so Willie had settled down to this unreal marriage that, on the surface, seemed so happy.

He stumbled and shuffled along the deserted streets in the early May morning. He could only vaguely remember the conversation with Joe . . . something . . . House of Commons . . . MP . . . Even in his fuddled state he could grasp that part of it.

And why not? Why shouldn't he, William Munro – a respectable, rich coal merchant, with one or two fingers tentatively in other pies, why shouldn't *he* become the MP for Greenock? The Unionist MP, of course, because, dearly as he liked and admired Joe, he could not agree with his politics – all this equal shares and socialism. Well, it was only a minority group – would probably never get any more.

Yes. He put his key in the door: he would have to think seriously about it.

He stumbled into the kitchen and lit the gas. Soon he was going to move into a bigger house, which he would fit and furnish with two, or even three bedrooms. He would never again try to enter his wife's bed.

He put out the gas, and fell into the blankets on the sofa. Just before he drifted off into a drunken stupor, he remembered what Jenny wanted – to be 'm'lady'. Well, why not? Now he could do that for his own sake. It would sound very nice, he thought, drifting . . . Sir William Munro, MP. Yes, why not . . . why . . . n . . .

*

Now that Bella had gone, openly, to live with the well-known and well-loved Joe Mulligan, the harpies opened their attacks on her. Everywhere she went, spiteful eyes followed her – sniggers reached her back as she walked on. Once she heard the distinct sound of a spit as she passed a group of women. She came in, white-faced and shaken, to Joe, who held her in his arms and let her cry her fill.

'Hush, lassie, they don't know what they're doing. It will all die down soon, you'll see.'

'Oh Joe! I can't bear it! You'd think we were the only ones in the town, and I know we're not. Joe, you'll have to go to the doctor with that cough.'

'Aye, I'll go and see him tomorrow – maybe. Now lass, if it happens again, you just walk on. Don't think about it any more. Be happy, sweetheart.'

It was the first time he had called her that.

She wished she could love him as he deserved. She was content and happy, and his love-making bore no resemblance whatever to the agonies of the lust of Jim Morrison.

The next four years were full, and rewarding, and the most instructive she had ever known. Tranquillity settled on her gradually, and Joe's love, constant and true, was a tower of strength. The irritation of the cough had quite gone. He had been afraid – but the fear was gone; he had seen much of the dread disease, and the summers had been kind. Only an occasional small dry cough bothered him.

In time, the outside whispers died away, and she got a nod from one or two women. She nodded and smiled and made a remark about the weather.

She went to see Flora one day some weeks after she had come to live with Joe. Flora had changed, and was surprisingly sympathetic to Bella's position.

'Your father won't like it, but as long as this man's good to you . . . '

'Oh he is, mother. He's nice – and kind. I'm very fond of him.'

'Bella, we don't talk about these things, but . . . are you – do you love him?'

There was an awkward pause before Bella spoke. Could she tell a loving mother that there was only one man she truly loved?

'I thought what I felt for Jim Morrison . . . I thought that was love. But it was only – I suppose just the attraction of him, at first. No, I'm not in love with Joe, but I like him and admire him, and if Morrison was dead I would marry him. He wants us to be married; he says he would pay for a divorce. He's been reading books to me, there's such a lot of things in the world I didn't know anything about. All the different people: the great writers and musicians; the war in America about slaves. And he wants to see *everybody* having enough. He says that some day there will be no poor people, no starvation or unemployment, no old people put out of their homes and separated. Oh! That day – I'll never forget it. Yes, Joe's a good man, mother. I'm very lucky.'

'He used to be on the town council, didn't he?'

'Oh? Yes, I think so. He says he's too busy now, but he always reads about them, when he goes to the library, to read big books and old papers. He's looking for something special – he was telling me about it the other day. About a visit King Charles the second made to this old town. He didn't stay long, because it was raining! But Joe says he gave a piece of land to somebody, for . . . '

She broke off as the door open and John stood there.

Suddenly the air was stiff with anger – and hate. Bella stood up nervously. 'Hello, father.'

He strode forward, his small stature detracting not a bit from his bitter anger.

'Don't call me father! Don't ever come near this house again. This is a house of God – you're no daughter of mine! And *that's* true anyway! *You're no daughter of mine!* To think we took you from the gutter and gave you all we had – and you've thrown it back in our face. You strumpet!' (he was shouting now) 'You harlot! Just like your mother.'

He raised his hand and struck her across her face. Then he turned and went out of the kitchen, shut the door, and went stamping down the hall. (A man had to be master in his own house, or a man was a henpeck, and a hen-pecked man was only half a man. John was going to be master in his own house).

They heard the bottom door close with a crash. Bella was shaking, not so much from the blow, as from the shock of hearing such words from a man who had, all her life, given her nothing but love and goodness; who had slaved to feed and clothe her – and suffered *her* agonies when he had seen her bruised and battered body.

She could not speak to Flora. She put on her coat and bonnet and walked quickly away, out of the church and down through the streets back to Joe. He could only comfort her, and hold her. He could not take away the knowledge that John's anger was just, if narrow.

John came home that night, and said not a word to Flora about the incident. He had his bed-time cup of tea, and then they went to bed. Flora lay awake for a long time, but neither made any mention of it.

The other incident that nearly destroyed Bella's simple happiness was the sight of Sandy when he came home from school one day. He went to the same school as he'd gone to since they were at Mrs Preston's. He was bloody and torn; it was obvious that he had been savagely beaten, and had given as good as he got.

Joe saw him first.

'God save us, laddie! What's happened?'

'Aw nothin'. Fella set on me.'

'*One* fella? You've had a good thumping, haven't you, lad?'

'Naw. I thumped them back.'

'Looks like it. What was it about?'

'Where's my mother?'

'At the shops. What happened?'

'Boy said something.'

'About your mother?'

A nod.

'And me?'

Another nod.

'I thought they might, sooner or later. How old are you now, son?'

'Eleven.'

'When's the school holidays?'

'Week after next.'

'Aye, Fair Fortnight for the yards.' He seemed to talk more to himself than the boy. 'Holidays? More like lock-out without pay.'

He spoke to Sandy again. 'Would you like to go away for a holiday to the sea-side? Paddle in the sea?'

'Fishing?'

'Aye – fishing too, if you like.'

'Will my mother come too?'

Joe laughed. 'I don't go anywhere without your mother now, son.'

The boy's face darkened again. Joe sat down and drew the boy to him, standing beside his chair.

'Listen, Sandy. You're a bit young to undertstand all about life just yet, but I want you to think a bit. Your father – he was married to your mother, and before you were born, he beat her, just like you were beaten today. Then he went away, and nobody has seen him since. She was very ill. Then you came along, and she was happy.

She worked very hard, and you've grown up a good boy. God grant that you may stay like that, and not grow like your father! But you see, according to the law, your mother is still married to him – that's a kind of legal arrangement, and she can't marry anybody else. Well, she could, if we went to a lot of trouble with lawyers, and tried to find your father, and all kinds of things. A legal separation, or a divorce for desertion – but at the first move we made, he might come back; then he might take her away from me – and I couldn't let that happen. So you see, son, whatever the boys said to you, it was likely true. I'm not married to your mother, although God knows I wish I could be! But I'm trying to be good to her, and look after her.'

'We had a bathroom at Mrs Preston's.'

Joe looked at him, and burst out laughing.

'Bathroom, is it you want? Aye lad, it will be a long time before working folks have bathrooms in their houses, but I'll see what I can do. Now we better get you cleaned up, before your mother comes.'

'They won't bother me again, Uncle Joe!'

'Won't they?'

'No – I smashed them.'

Bella came home from the shops with her basket of groceries, and saw the state of the boy's clothes.

'Oh Sandy! What happened?'

'He had a fight – and he won. It will be all right. You'd better go out tomorrow and get him some new clothes. We're going for a holiday – doon the watter, Bella. Where would you like to go?'

'I'm not going anywhere away from here.'

'All right. Helensburgh, Dunoon, Largs, Rothesay, it's all the same corner of the world, love.'

'Are you sure, Joe?'

'Positive, lassie.'

'All right – wherever you say.'

'Do you need money, love? Don't go short. I've got enough to keep us in comfort.'

'I'm all right, Joe. I learned a lot about cooking from

Ellen. I don't waste anything. But, Joe – ?' She moved over to the window that looked out on to the narrow passage, and the backhouse door. Sandy had gone into the small scullery that Joe had blocked off with a light wall of sawn planks. 'What was Sandy fighting about?'

'About us, and I think the others got the worst of it.'

'About us? You mean even school-children know and talk about it?'

'They hear their mothers and fathers – it will die down, they'll find a new scandal soon.'

'I'll take Sandy away from that school!'

'You won't! He's got to learn to stand his ground.'

'But he's only a baby!'

'He's eleven, Bella. At eleven I was out at four in the morning, milking cows, in Ayrshire.'

'But I don't want that for *my* son!'

'Nor do millions of other mothers – and your children will want better for their children – and so, the world *must* get better – if only men had as much sense as children! Sandy will go back to school, the lads might tackle him again, but he'll beat them. If he doesn't beat them this time, he'll beat them next time. Come on, lass – give us some tea. I'd like a bit of cold ham.'

Sandy had a black eye next morning, and a cut under his ear. His arms ached, and his knees were bruised and cut where he had fallen in the scuffle. He was gruff when he said good-bye to his mother, and almost afraid to look at her. ('Leave him alone' – Joe had said, 'he'll find his own level.')

Inside the gates of the school, a small crowd waited to watch the meeting between the two contestants of the day before. Standing apart, was the boy who had been the chief participant in the fight. As Sandy came in at the school gates, he hesitated only a split second; then, his heart thumping inside him, he walked firmly over to the enemy.

What is the electricity that passes between two small boys – or that can measure up grown men? Face to face, they looked at each other. Then Sandy put his arm out and gave Bob Murray a shove, on his shoulder. Quick as a flash, Bob shoved him, in the same way. They looked blankly at each other – and then turned away, and went into school. Honour, it seemed, was satisfied. It was the nearest either of them would ever get to an apology.

The little family set out for Rothesay on the first day of the holiday, the first Saturday in July. The boats lay at Princes Pier, and the raucous voices of the seamen, the loungers on the shore, and the clanking of the anchor chain proclaimed the busyness and the start of this brief time of leisure to which the working folks looked forward every year. It meant scrimping and saving a few shillings each fortnight from a small wage – it meant patching and darning old clothes to save buying new ones – and it meant a complete removal of all but furniture to the 'rooms' in the coast town of their choice.

Whoever, in his delirium, graced this period in people's lives with the name of 'holiday' – may he roast for ever in a hell of hordes of children all screaming for 'jeely pieces', and be smothered under an avalanche of blankets, knives and forks, sheets, cups and saucers, jam and tea and butter – and an empty purse.

'Packing the hamper for the coast' was a national pastime. Carrying the hamper to the train or boat was a job for hefty fathers, and grown-up sons. Getting to the room and kitchen in Dunoon, or Saltcoats, Millport or Helensburgh was another part of the day's drag. For the mother, it was the same round of work as it was at home – except that it was actually worse, for appetites were sharpened by the salt air and freedom from school and work – air that was not laden with smoke and fumes and gas.

But holiday it was not.

Standing listening to the German bands was good, but what could music do for a tired woman who still had to shop and cook and wash and iron in a strange house?

There were, of course, the holidays 'with attendance', that meant that you simply paid your landlady for your rooms, did your shopping, and she would cook your food, and clean the house, and make your bed. But naturally that cost more, and it was not always easy to get a holiday at all.

Joe and Bella and Sandy went the way of all the others – except that Joe did a little more to help Bella than many of the men who took their families for a holiday.

They walked along the seashore; they walked right across the island to Ettrick Bay – in later years there was a little electric tram that ran through the leafy woods to the stretch of golden sand which lies facing the long vista of the Mull of Kintyre in the distance.

The people made their own enjoyment – there were the bands on the promenade, there were Pierrots on the shore, and Punch and Judy stands. There were fairs and roundabouts, and there were excursions in the big horse-drawn 'brakes'.

Swimming was not such a popular sport. Some boys were brave enough to go in the water and get wet all over in their combinations, but no girl or lady ever did. A discreet paddle was permitted, that was all.

'You remember you were going to tell me about a duchess, Joe?' Bella asked one day as they sat in the sun.

'Oh yes, I was; Well, you see, there was this duchess, and she was coming home one night from a Grand Ball. It was freezing cold – the pavements were icy, and the horses clip-clopped on the frosty road. Well, she got to her house, and the footman put down the wee steps for her to get down, and she wrapped her fur coat tight around her. Then, when she got to the railing by the steps of her house, she saw a poor woman standing there. She was cold and hungry, and clad only with a thin shawl over her clothes. The duchess went into the house, and she said to the footman – "Oh James", she said, "bring me some hot tea, and take a cup of cocoa to that poor woman at the railings, and give her a penny." So he said, "Very good, your Grace," and she went in to the drawing-room, and there was a great roaring fire, and the flunkey brought her a silver tray with cups and saucers on it, and a silver teapot, and she took off her fur coat and sat down by the fire. Then she said, "Oh James, I don't think you need trouble about that cup of cocoa after all. It isn't *nearly* so cold now."'

Joe stopped, and for all his playful language and tone, his voice was bitter. Bella didn't know whether to laugh or cry.

'Oh Joe! Such things can't happen, surely?' (But remembering Mrs Heathley, she knew they could.)

'They do, lass. If not exactly like that, near enough. That's why we've got to end it, some time. This carriages-at-eleven for some, and dustbins-at-dawn for too many others. Now, lass, when we get home, I want you to go to the library for me. I want you to find a paper for me – I told you about King Charles II . . . he came here once, about ten years after the Restoration. You should know, Sandy. When was the Restoration?'

'1661.'

'Aye, I thought so, Well, he came, to see the herring-curing factories. A great day that was, for Greenock, although we've had Royalty often, and we'll have some more. But I've read somewhere that he gave a piece of land to the town, for buildings for poor people, for ever.'

'He was good like that,' said Sandy eagerly. 'He said "Don't let poor Nelly starve".'

Joe looked at Bella and winked.

'That's right son; a wee bit different, but the same kind of thing. Anyway, I want to know where it was, because this town will get bigger, Bella, you'll see, and it may be that it could get overlooked. Come on now Sandy, bed-time!'

*

Winter days and summer sunsets – the thin autumn mists: now the measurement of time was the constant growth of Sandy, and Joe's winter cough. At the end of a day's work, Joe would gather books and papers round the table, and read to her. She gained in confidence; she learned how to express herself, and listened entranced to Joe as he talked of the world and the evils in it, and the good that could be. It seemed as if Joe felt he had to leave his life's work to someone else; as if he knew that he would never, now, take his place in the wise and worthy company of the town's municipal dignitaries.

Occasionally he would go out, especially once a year to the Burns Supper. This was a great event, at which there were speeches, and haggis and a piper, and mashed potatoes and poetry and whisky. Especially poetry, and perhaps a tune on Joe's fiddle, a song of love and bonnie lasses. And his heart was glad, as if he were a native of this gregarious land.

The sun shone, on rich and poor alike: the rain fell, on Christian and heretic alike. Somewhere, in the vast unknown spaces of the world, a people stirred and grumbled. The end of an era was coming: the beginning of the end of the splendid fabric of Victorian civilisation – in all its harshness, its grandeur, its superb complacence, its monstrous self-discipline, and its touching belief in human permanence.

Let them enjoy this – one of their few holidays, before their sons and lovers were called to the plains of South Africa: before the stern old lady passed, leaving behind the sorrows and mistakes, to a nation which is still paying for them.

XXII

In that spring and bright summer of the year when Joe
Mulligan died, he seemed to have taken on a new hold of
life. The irritating cough was gone – his steps were firm,
his eyes bright, and his vitality seemed endless. His work
prospered – life was fine, and golden; his love for Bella
was a deep, active, and satisfying delight.

With the end of September, he drooped a little: the
cough came back, seemingly deeper. Perhaps the sudden
cold spell had upset him? They thought it better he gave
up some of his decorating.

Quietly, Bella went out, and did some washing: not to
the West End ladies, because she knew her sin had been
widely publicized there. But to the lesser people; the
small shopkeepers' wives, and the wives of foremen at the
yards. She earned a few shillings, to help. Joe didn't want
to touch their savings.

It was one day, as she was carrying some clothes up
from the green at the back of the tenement in West
Stewart street, that Bella noticed a tired-looking little
woman washing the stairs at the bottom. The woman
looked at her, and Bella saw fear, naked and terrifying,
on the woman's face. And yet, it was a face she knew –
had known and loved, in the past that she had hoped to
forget.

'Maggie!' she breathed. 'Maggie Leith! Oh God! I
didn't know you lived here?'

'No, I just work for Mrs Foster. I do a bit for her now
and then. Are you all right now, Bella?'

'Oh, oh aye. I'm fine now.'

'I'll need to get on. I've to bring coal up.'

She turned and started scrubbing again with a desperation and energy that was nearer madness than cleanliness.

Bella took her washing up to the grocer's wife, who helped her to damp and roll it up for ironing.

'There you are, Bella. Here's your three shillings. Would you do some washing for Mrs Foster?'

'Is that the woman who lives at the bottom? There's somebody doing the stairs for her now.'

'Yes. She's really too stout to bend, poor soul, she has to have help. Mrs Leith does a lot for her. She's not been looking too well lately, either. She's had ten sons, you know.'

'Who? Maggie Leith?'

'Oh no! Mrs Foster. Will you do some washing for her then?'

'Yes, all right. I'll do it next time I come to you. Thanks.'

She went thoughtfully down the stairs. Maggie was just finished.

'Are you going home now, Maggie?'

'Oh aye. I'll just put my pail away. I'll catch you up.'

Slowly, Bella walked to the corner, and after some time Maggie came, with a hurried, shuffling step. She was breathless and sweating, and she wasn't over-clean. Bella was shocked at the change in her, for she remembered only too clearly the freshness of Maggie's kitchen, and the smell of hot porridge, that cruel morning.

'She's wanting me to go for some messages, but I said I had to get my man's tea. She said I was to get them in the morning and bring them. I've my washing to do. I'll have to get up early and get it done. Eddie goes to the yard early. I'll manage . . . '

Her breath gave out, and she shuffled along quickly... almost too quickly, for Bella; panting, and still with a look of fear, almost guilt, on her face.

'Oh Maggie! Wait a minute! You'd think it was the last day! Come in home with me and have a wee cup of tea.

I'm sure you could do with it.'

'Oh indeed I could, but I don't think I've got the time.'

It seemed as though just sitting down was a luxury for Maggie. She looked up at Bella, and tried to take the cup of tea that she handed to her. But her eyes filled with tears. Bella took the cup from her quickly and the poor woman broke down in a storm of sobbing and trembling. She was quite obviously at the end of her endurance. How long she could have gone on, if Bella had not met her that day, was not easy to judge. The end had to come some time, and Maggie had no strength left.

The story she told Bella was a pitiful one.

'You see, Eddie was working at Clydebank, on the night-shift. It was that year – the three boys on the ice – and I was working in a pub at the station. It was one night – one of the sailors off the boats, he seemed a fine man, he saw me when I finished, and said he would walk me home. Well' – she drank some of her tea – 'I didn't want to let him in, or anything, but I couldn't make a row. Wee Charlie was sleeping. I always left him sleeping. Mrs Tate across the passage always looked in at him now and then . . . he . . . he . . . made me let him in . . .'

'I know what you mean, Maggie.'

'He went away early in the morning. I didn't know.' She bit her lip. 'I didn't know that Nelly Foster saw him. She never said until I had Annie. She was born in April, the next year. She's just twelve. She'll be leaving school next year. She's a bonnie lass. Eddie didn't say anything. He was home sometimes from Clydebank. I . . . oh God! He's a good man, and I couldn't tell him. He was that pleased it was a wee lassie, what with having Charlie. He didn't bother whether she was full time or not. He's quite happy.'

'But Mrs Foster?'

'It was just about six months after Annie was born. She was having another one. She said, would I go and get her something for her dinner, so I did. Then the next week she didn't feel too well, would I take her turn of the stairs. Then her washing, then see to her when she had the baby, and do everything for her. When I told her I couldn't do any more, I had my own family to look after, she said, 'Your *own* family, Maggie Leith? Maybe yours, but not Eddie's, is she?' I didn't know what to say. She must have seen on my face that I knew what she meant. She said, 'Sailors, eh? You'll be getting the place a bad name. I saw him coming out of your house at four o'clock in the morning, when Eddie was on night-shift. *He* wouldn't like to know about Annie, would he?'

She was calmer now, and finished her tea.

'So – ever since then?' Bella asked.

'Ever since then, she's made me work for her – even after she moved over to West Shaw Street. She had two more boys after that. She's so fat she can't move, and the boys think the sun rises and sets on her. And she tells everybody how good I am to her. I hate her! She's fat, and dirty and evil. But she knows about Annie.'

'Maggie, what would Eddie do if he found out?'

'Oh God! He'd batter me silly!'

'Maggie.' Bella sat on the fender-stool beside Maggie's chair. 'Maggie, would it be worse than the way you're killing yourself with work for that woman?'

Maggie looked at her.

'Think, Maggie. Eddie thinks a lot of you?'

'Oh, we were sweethearts since we were in school.'

'And he's fond of Annie?'

'Dotes on her. No! I couldn't! He'd half kill me!'

'Are you sure?'

Maggie's tears came again – this time silently, and with a kind of finality.

'No – I'm not sure. I'm not frightened for myself now, but it would be terrible for him.'

'Tell him, Maggie. Tell him, and get this woman off your back.'

Maggie stared in front of her. She said, softly: 'She's taken thirteen years of my life, and nearly killed me – while she got fat and lazy. My Eddie . . . ' She broke off, and looked at Bella.

'Would *you*, Bella?'

'I don't know, Maggie. I think I would try . . . but I wouldn't submit to that woman any more.'

'You've helped me, Bella. I think maybe you were meant to help people. I'll tell him. If he takes the belt to me, it won't be any worse than all I've suffered the last ten years. I'll get Nellie Foster's messages in the morning, and take them to her. It's Saturday, I'll tell Eddie tomorrow night. Now I'll need to go, Bella. Say a prayer for me. Yes – I'll tell him.'

When Bella told Joe the story that night, he shook his head.

'Well, blackmail by demanding money, I've heard about . . . but blackmail by scrubbing-brush – that's something new! Poor soul; I hope she tells him.'

Haltingly, in fear, Maggie made her tawdry confession.

Eddie's anger was terrible. He stood up and struck her a blow on the face, and stormed out and got drunk. When he came home, staggering and sick, she took his clothes off, and helped him into bed. He did not speak to her for several days. He avoided Annie – until she climbed on his lap and asked for a story. His eyes met Maggie's – and he looked away again.

Time heals even these wounds, and many years of happiness were in store for Eddie and Maggie. Nellie Foster dropped dead three months later. Fatty degeneration of the heart, the doctor said.

Her sons mourned her as though she had been the Queen of Sheba, instead of the fat, lazy slut she had been; they mourned, and then in a few years some of them went to a far country, to kill some men they'd never heard of.

XXIII

Joe seemed to rally visibly, through the mild October, and even performed at another social in the same hall, where he had first taken her. Joe played his fiddle, Robert Bailey sang, his voice still clear and true, but his breath was short, and he could no longer sustain the beauty of his top notes. It was a great pity, everyone felt, but they all loved him so much, so they gave him another drink . . .

'The request is for you to give us a song, Joe,' the master of ceremonies said.

'Me? Now you know I'm no singer.'

But they wanted him: his voice was bad – off-key, with no ring to it.

Robert Bailey had sung a song of love – of first love – and his heart must have been in it, because it is known that he never sang it again.

> And yet the dream has passed away,
> tho' like it lived, it passed.
> Each moment was too bright to stay,
> but sparkled to the last.
> Here in my heart the dreams remain
> In gay unclouded joy,
> When I remember her again,
> My sweetheart when a boy –
> My sweetheart when a boy.

Joe sang from his memories, of his homeland, where the mountains of Mourne sweep down to the sea. That was

his last performance. He simply grew weaker: his cough
was dry and hard, and he complained of headache.

She watched him, one evening, sitting up against
heaped pillows: the autumn wind whistled outside. His
face was calm, sunken cheeks pink with the false glow of
advanced tuberculosis.

He was so quiet and peaceful; for a moment or two
she thought he had slipped away. Shallow breathing,
quick little gasps. And then he opened his eyes and
looked at her. The eyes were suddenly wide open, clear
and lucid.

He said, 'Bridie?'

Then, slowly, there came an expression of first,
surprise, then disbelief, and at last, such a look of horror
as she had never seen or known could be. A sound, like a
cry, or a sob seemed to come from the depths of his
throat.

He crossed himself, as in a gesture learned in
childhood, and but little used since then.

'Holy Mary Mother of God!'

'Joe! Joe – what's the matter? What do you want?'

He reached for her hands and held them, tight,
hurting her.

'Bella, tell me. I haven't got long to go. Quick, tell me.
John and Flora, your mother and father, you told me
they *found* you?'

'Yes, but Joe, you knew that. What's wrong?'

'Bridie, my sister. I was nine. I saw her go away with
that seaman . . . he looked foreign. I never saw her again.'
He stopped, fighting for breath. 'She was . . . *you* are
Bridie! Oh Jesus! What have I done?'

Bella stood up, trembling, and stepped away from the
bed. Her face was chalk white. When she spoke, her voice
was a whisper:

'Joe! Don't! It *can't* be: you don't *know!*'

His eyes were closed again. He spoke softly, as if to be
sure that he could say what he had to say, by preserving
what little strength he had left, and what little time, too.

'Bella lass, I *don't* know. And you will never know. But

you have done no wrong. I don't know if Bridie . . . I only
saw her laughing with the sailor. She was lovely, like you,
Bella . . . ' The words drifted away. He seemed to sleep,
but now he was fighting for breath.

Suddenly, his eyes opened again, clear and lucid.

He said, 'Bella?' and then he stopped breathing.

Quietly, she smoothed the eyelids down over the
staring eyes.

She looked at him, for a long time. Shock had gripped
her and she sat cold and rigid for several minutes. Then
she started shaking. She heard Sandy's footsteps outside,
and his whistle as he came up the stairs.

He stopped when he saw the still figure on the bed,
and he gently took her, and led her to another chair near
the fire.

'Go and get the doctor, Sandy,' she said, quietly.

*

It took a good part of the money they had saved to bury
poor little Joe, although they had had some money in the
new Insurance company.

She wept for the goodness of the decent man whose
love and care had warmed her, and consoled her when
the love in her heart for another man had almost overwhelmed her. He had always known of her love for
Willie – and cared for her in spite of it.

With a heavy heart she looked round the kitchen, and
wondered. She thought at last she had realised the depths
of despair. She would have to go back to service, to make
a living for herself and Sandy.

'I can get a job in the bakery, Ma, in the mornings, and
I can get into Scott's – and be a riveter like Uncle Andy.'

'No, Sandy. We'll manage somehow. I can still wash.
You go off to school. I'll think what to do.'

It was only when she glanced idly at the calendar that
a realisation struck her like a blow from a sledgehammer.

No! It couldn't be! It couldn't . . . Joe had promised –
he had always been so careful, always made sure nothing

like this should happen to her. He had said so often that he would have liked a child, but he wouldn't bring a child into the world that he couldn't give his name to.

She mustn't panic. She could wait a week or two. She could be suffering from the shock of Joe's death, and she must be a bit run down. But she knew that this was only false comfort. There was no escaping it.

It was just three weeks later, when she had come home after a long day's washing and ironing. She sat for a few quiet moments, wondering how long she could go on.

A loud, authoritative knock on the door stopped her day-dreaming.

When she opened it, a very young policeman took a note-book from his pocket and looked at her as he asked her,

'Name of Morrison? Mrs Morrison?'

'Yes, I'm Mrs Morrison.'

'Afraid I've brought you bad news, ma'am.'

'Bad news? It's Sandy – oh! what's happened to Sandy?'

'Couldn't say, missis. Could I come in?'

'Oh! Oh yes. Yes, come in.'

'Well, missis, I've been sent to tell you that' – he consulted his note-book – 'to tell you that a man, name of James Morrison, died in Liverpool day before yesterday. He was listed as your husband, in the shipping office. It's taken us a wee while to find you. You'll be sent a proper certificate and your claim to any property he left. But I was to tell you, ma'am, that it will likely take all he had to bury him.'

She looked at him stupidly.

'Are you all right? I thought I was breaking it gently. It's not an easy job, to tell a woman her man's dead – are you sure you're all right?'

She sat down, with her hands on her lap and she looked at him – 'looked right through me' he told his sergeant afterwards, 'and she just said "Dead" like that – and then she started to laugh – yes – *laugh!*'

She laughed, loudly and hysterically, until she cried,

while the policeman sat on a chair near her, and alternately patted her shoulders, and offered her a drink of water. It was only a moment or two, but to Bella it seemed that she had lived a lifetime.

When she was calmer, the now thoroughly shaken policeman asked, 'Is there anyone you'd like me to bring for you? A neighbour, or mother, or anybody?'

'No, I'll manage.'

'Are you sure?'

'Yes, my boy will be home soon. I'll be all right.'

'It was a shock. I was supposed to break it to you gently. I'm new to this district.'

'Yes. I thought you must be.'

'Our regular man, Sergeant Craig, is on holiday. He's been in the town for donkey's years, but I'm new. Well, I hope you'll be all right, missis. Just say if you'd like me to get anybody for you.'

'No, no.' (Just go away and leave me alone.) 'Thank you, constable, thank you. My boy will be home soon.'

He went away at last, and she sat staring at the wallpaper.

Where had she gone wrong? Why couldn't God have left Joe just a little longer? Was this the payment for their 'sin'?

It was long after six o'clock when Sandy came home, but she had not moved.

'Mother, where's my tea?' Sandy, hungry, impatient, and full of vitality, wanted to be off somewhere. 'Mother! What's the matter? I'm going down to the harbour. I want my tea. Are you all right?'

'Eh? Oh – Sandy, yes. I'll get your tea. Sandy – you know we never talked much about Morrison, your father.'

'No. Uncle Joe told me about him. What about him?'

'He's dead.'

'Dead? That means you could have . . . oh, mother!'

The boy broke down and flung himself into her arms, kneeling on the home-made rag rug in front of the fireplace. They sat like that for a long time, until the kitchen grew cold and shadows crept into the corners.

She said softly, 'You were fond of Uncle Joe?'

'M'mm'

'Are you not going out with your mates?'

'Naw.'

'I'll make your tea. Will you go and see your Uncle Andy when you've had your tea? And tell him I want to see him?'

'Aye.'

Alone, she could have battled. With Sandy beside her, she would have taken on the whole world. But it would be folly, criminal folly, to attempt to get through the next seven months without help.

Andy had always loved her, she knew: he would give her help and advice. What her father would say when he knew the whole sordid mess she could not bear to think about.

Andy and his wife, Mary, whose father was a baker, and kept a little shop near the railway station, came, with Sandy. He went out on a belated search for his mates, and came home near bed-time.

'Hello, Bella, how are you?'

'All right, Mary. I'll make you some tea in a minute. Andy, I had some news today.'

'News?'

'Yes. Morrison – he's dead.'

'God help us! Dead, *now*. As if he couldn't have died a year ago or more. Damn him! Oh Bella, I wish it had come sooner.'

What an epitaph for a cruel man: I wish his death had come sooner.

'Aye, it would have been fine. Joe wanted us to be married all along. But Andy, that's not all. I'm . . . oh Heavens! How am I going to tell *anybody*? What am I to do? What's to become of us?'

Now she was sobbing, and Mary held her in strong arms and 'shushed' her till she was quiet.

'Mary, it's a terrible thing. I'm going to have . . .'

'Oh my God!' said Andy. 'After all this time? Are you

sure?'

She nodded.

'When?'

'About July.'

'Well, there's nothing to be done. Joe's dead, God rest his soul. Morrison too, but the devil can have him. We'll do what we can, eh Mary?'

'Anything we can, Bella.'

'Don't tell father,' Bella pleaded.

'No, we won't tell him yet. He'll have to know some time. What's the best thing to do, Bella? Can you stay here?'

'That's what I wanted you to see to for me. I'd like to stay here; it's nice and quiet, and Joe was here. He was good to me, Andy.'

She looked up at him as though looking for assurance and comfort, and agreement that Joe was good.

'I'll go and see the landlord tomorrow. I'll pay the rent for a while.'

'I can wash for a while yet. My, when I think that Mrs Christopher said it was better to be a laundress than a washerwoman, and I went to Mrs Preston, and I met Joe. And now . . . I'm just a washerwoman after all.'

'No, Bella. You *are* better than a washerwoman,' Mary said positively.

'Well, we'll manage the rent, Bella, as long as there's work in the yards. I wouldn't ask Jenny, even if she was in the town.'

'Where is she?'

'Paris, I believe, or London. We'd better go, Bella. I've to be up at five. We'll help you till the time comes, and maybe by that time, things will be a bit better. Good-night, Bella.'

She felt comforted, and a little more secure, except for the thought of what would happen if the dreaded spectre of closing yards happened again. It seemed to come in cycles.

After the initial shock of the trick that Fate had played her, she gathered strength for herself and the child she was carrying.

She smiled, a little ruefully: it would have been nice, she thought, just once, to conceive, carry and give birth to a child in love and security; not fear, and guilt. But it was good, too, that Joe would be remembered.

XXIV

The Reverend James Christopher mounted his pulpit and John shut the door with the well-known little click and walked majestically back to shut the church doors.

The minister thought, as he waited for the organist to finish the Voluntary, that his old friend was ageing. There had been so many disturbances in his life, and he had been a faithful servant. He too, felt the years on him today – it was probably the sultry weather. How many years was it since that summer evening when he had clasped John's hand for the first time? Must be nearly thirty years. He felt older than he was, it *must* be the weather.

He rose to start the day's service, and he took as his text that day, 'Greater love hath no man than this, that a man lay down his life for his friend.'

The thunder and lightning came while he was preaching. A thunderstorm like nothing the old town had ever seen before, the worst in living memory, even to a town that was used to rain. It stopped for a short time that night, but it was still dark and sultry on Monday. For the next three days, there was a constant downpour, from dark leaden skies.

The minister was visiting in the district, his poor old horse standing draggled and patient, drawing the small carriage between visits. He called in to see John and Flora, talking with John over their pipes and tea. He tried, as always, to persuade John to forgive Bella, and take her back home. But John was sulky and adamant.

The rumbling and slushing was distant, and yet coming nearer – and the farms at the top of the hill took the full onslaught of the overflowing of the waterfalls that trickled all summer over cool, clear rocks – that spring water that has no equal anywhere in the world. Now they were black, and muddy and angry – and they moved with a terrible, slow ooziness. A sea of black mud took the back of the church, slithered through cracks and broken stones, and slushed down the steps leading to the kitchen. The force of the rain broke windows, and Flora saw – almost the last thing she did see – her brass bedstead, with its spotless white cover, floating, nearly submerged in the evil, encroaching mud.

In blind panic she ran – anywhere – anywhere away from there, and fell, face down, into the mud which was now nearly three inches deep.

John tried to get to her, and would have fallen too, but the Reverend James caught him by the coat-tails – the doors had burst open, and water, as well as mud, covered the floor, upsetting tables and chairs; dishes fell out of the lop-sided cupboards – books and papers were reduced to pulp.

The minister held John against his body until he had struggled with him near the door out to the hall, where the water and mud were spreading, making a thick carpet.

John stood by the door, gasping for breath, and the minister went back for Flora. He hauled her up, not realising that his own strength was going, and she was quite unconscious. He left her beside John, and turned and slipped in the treacherous mud, and fell on his back beside her.

John tried to talk to her, but she was past all help. She opened her eyes once, but it was doubtful if she even saw him.

The minister lay half under the bed . . . and the

movement of the water and the mud kept it making little thudding noises on his skull. But he didn't feel them.

Andy ran, as soon as he was told about the damage to the church, and found his father sitting at the door with his wife's body across his knees. Both were covered in mud. Andy saw the white-covered bed, seemingly doing a macabre, dignified dance, advance and retire, and on each advance, it struck the head of the minister, in salute to a man who had practised what he preached.

Bella had never seen her father drunk, but he was very drunk that day when they got him home, to live out the rest of his life in remorse, and anger, and pain.

Bella saw the funerals, the two funerals together, of the bonnie, blue-eyed woman who had longed so desperately for a child, and lavished her love on a lost waif – who had lived in spotless cleanliness all her life, only to die in a slough of stinking mud; and of the minister, John's friend 'till death do us part'.

All the years of authority and responsibility had been swept away by an avalanche of mud – and it was a long time before John could take stock of where he was, or could appreciate his everyday surroundings. The yards were finished, for him. The church – well – would it ever be a church again? His minister, his wife: it was all too much for him.

Bella came to see him once, but he only looked at her, and turned to the fire. The spring days were wet and chilly, and now Andy could not help her as much as he had thought. He had a duty to the old man – and he was literally torn between his love for Mary, his devotion to his father, and the deep sense of admiration, as well as love, he had always had for Bella.

XXV

Jenny and Willie did not come home for the funerals of Flora and the minister. Jenny was having too good a time during the London season, and even at the August end of it, there was still some gaiety in town. Willie had made up his mind about his future: Politics: that was the answer. He could see huge gaps in the Unionist administration, and had been admiring the speeches and policies of HM Secretary for the Colonies, Mr Joseph Chamberlain. He had learned a great deal from him.

He was just too late for the by-election that winter. The result was no surprise; the return of another Unionist for the town. What was good enough for my father . . .

It came to February again, and Bella had given up most of the washing she had been going out to do. The small sum of money she had left after the death of Joe was nearly gone. Sandy needed boots, and clothes – a growing lad of twelve needed so much. He had been going out early with the farmer, delivering milk, and then papers. He looked at his mother sometimes with a new, sullen look.

He gave her what few shillings he earned, and she knew that she would have to tell him soon about the child that was coming. She thought he wouldn't need much telling: children at school these days seemed to know a great deal more than their parents!

One night he came home about seven o'clock, and ate his tea without saying anything. When he had finished, he stood up and walked over to the window, with his back to her.

'Ma, I'm going to sea.'

Of course: she knew it, it had to happen. He was his father's son, and those whom the sea has called, she holds fast.

'To sea? But you're too young! And you wanted to go to the Academy.'

'Well, I'll learn at sea. I want to go. The mate says I can go to the captain tomorrow. I can be deck boy. The ship's bound for Australia. I'd like to go there. Anyway,' he turned round, and looked at her, 'anyway, I'll be in the way when . . . when the bairn comes. You should have told me.'

She felt she was going to be sick. There were no more depths. What could she do? Who could she turn to for advice or help? Sandy would go: if she didn't let him go now, he might very well stow away, and God forbid that he should be subjected to the treatment that his father had dealt out to the poor unfortunates who had ventured on seeing the world on his ship.

No, twelve was too young. She had to talk to him, to make him understand, but he sat down beside her and said:

'I know what happened to those poor wee boys. I've got to show them that I'm not the same as my father. Uncle Joe told me a lot of things. If I can be like him, I'll be glad. But I'm going. If you like, I'll take you to see the Mate tomorrow, or I'll bring him here. I'm going out now. I won't be late.'

She supposed it would all end some time. There couldn't be much more she would have to bear. And yet, there must be: It was not only now, before the child came – there would be afterwards.

How to go out to work for money to feed and clothe a child, and still look after a child. The Parish Council had not bothered to consider that problem.

And Sandy was going – to the other end of the world.

XXVI

Andy stood in the doorway of the cosy kitchen, where Bella dragged her heavy body with despair.

'You're to come, Bella. He wants to see you. He can't last much longer. He's in terrible pain.'

'I can't go and see him like this. He'll be that hurt.'

'I doubt if he'll notice. He's only conscious a wee while at a time. Keep your shawl on, he won't notice.'

'All right, I'll come.'

Andy took her arm gently, and helped her on the long walk up Ann Street, along Roxburgh Street, to Trafalgar Street. They were on the ground floor, which was a relief to Bella.

John lay in the big brass bed, rescued from the flood, and cleaned up. The white bed-spread was still pure white. The gas was turned down to a low flame, and Bella was at the bed, and seated, with her wide shawl round her, before John opened his eyes.

His face was grey and emaciated, and drawn with the pain of cancer, long dormant, now active, and destructive.

'Father, Bella's here. You wanted to see her.'

'Bella? Oor wee Bella? Where are you lass? You got lost.'

'I'm here, father.'

'Aye, you came back that night. You were a bonnie wee lass, in a wee basket, and then Rob made you a wee cradle. Tell Rob I'd like to see him.'

'Rob? Rob's dead, father.'

He was silent, his eyes closed, as if the lids were too

heavy for him.

'No, Rob's not dead. Tell him I want to see him.' There was a deep silence, while he breathed, shallow and painful.

'Tell Rob to take good care of Bella. What was it the Minister used to say, Bella?'

'When, father? At the communion?'

'No, his Benediction. It was: "Now unto Him Who is able to keep us from falling, to present us spotless . . . present us spotless before His presence with exceed . . . ' His voice tapered away and he spoke again. 'Spotless before His Presence, Oh God! Flora, Oh my God!'

The sounds of his dying were terrible to hear. Andy came in with his tablets.

'One,' the doctor had said. 'Two, if he seems to be in any worse pain than before.' And he looked at Andy very straight, very hard. Andy held his father up and gave him two tablets.

The screams died down to a moaning, then a whisper, then he breathed very heavy, and slept, and then he stopped breathing.

Bella's twins were born late in June 1881, in the house where she and Joe had lived so happily.

One child would have been enough, but two! Where was she to turn to?

Mary, and faithful Maggie Leith between them, saw her through her labour, and it was a shock when the boy was followed, a few minutes later, by a lovely, fair-haired girl.

When she was able to get up and about, she found that there was only a few shillings in her purse. Mary and Andy had given her as much as they could. He could help while he was working, but if work slackened off? Maggie Leith brought a jug of soup occasionally, but to feed two babies well, she had to have good food herself. Andy paid her rent, and she had sold Joe's paints and ladders for a few pounds, to help tide over the next few weeks.

'Do you think you should go to the Parish, Bella? Or surely you could ask Jenny for help? She's got plenty.'

'No, Maggie! I won't ask Jenny. But the Parish? Oh God! Joe! Joe!' She whispered his name again, but there was no answer. 'All right, I'll try the Parish.'

*

Mrs Heathley sat at a long table in the inner office of the Committee for Parish Relief. When, years ago, she had made the remark to Alice Christopher that servants would always be cheap and plentiful she had been a young wife, twenty-one, newly married, and had just come to the town from the rich country lands near the Borders. A forward, pushing, self-opinionated woman, over-bearing and loud, she had very soon talked herself into various guilds and committees, and eventually to the chairmanship of this Poor Relief Committee, and she had a heart of stone.

A pitiful collection of people sat on hard chairs in the dim waiting-room. One by one, sometimes a couple, went in to the inner office. What stories, or what tragedies the well-fed committee heard can be imagined, indeed, are known, *now.*

Women came out in tears, men shaken and white-faced with suppressed anger, and deep in their eyes the expression that said, 'Some day, some day, God help us...'

A woman came out with a baby in a shawl, and stood looking stupidly at the half-crown in her hand.

A voice boomed from the inner sanctum. 'Next!'

Bella went in and stood in front of the table where Mrs Heathley sat in splendour.

'Well, what do *you* want?' she asked Bella.

'I would like . . . '

'What's your name?'

'Bella Morrison.' She stopped, but Mrs Heathley gave her no help. 'I've . . . I've got twins, and I've got to go out to work, and I've nobody to look after them.'

'Where's your husband?'

'He's dead.'

'Oh, Oh well, that's different. When did he die?'

'Last October.'

'Oh. How unfortunate. What work do you do?'

'I'm a laundress.'

'A laundress? A washerwoman, surely?'

'No. A laundress.'

'Indeed. Who taught you this very fine distinction?'

'Mrs Preston – before she went to America.'

'Mrs . . . But surely you must be – I remember. You came to Mrs Preston. Mrs Christopher at the church mentioned you, but surely, surely, woman, your husband was away *then?*'

'Yes,' Bella said faintly.

'I thought so. You're the woman who went to live with that painter fellow, you wicked woman! So these brats are *not* your husband's, but this common Irishman, the agitator. I know all about *him*. And now because you've let your sins find you out, you expect the respectable people of this town to keep you in laziness. The very idea. No, Mr Septon – ' as one of the committee tried to speak, 'in this case I will take *no* consultation. The only thing *you* can do, young woman, is to go to the Workhouse, where your children will be fed and cared for. This committee is for *deserving* poor. You will go to the workhouse. We'll make an order out. Mr Septon, will you pass – '

Bella leaned forward and put her hands on the desk and her face close to Mrs Heathley. Her eyes flashed, her face was white with anger and hate.

'I'll see you in Hell first!' she said, and she walked out, feeling as if she was walking on air.

All the pride of her ancestry had boiled up in her, in one mad moment of defiance and power. Something swept through her, disgust that she had ever thought she could take this kind of charity, disgust at herself for not being true to Joe's principles.

She could work – she could do anything – if she had to take her children with her, and sit them on the wash-house floor, she would never again ask for organised charity.

Maggie came to ask her how she had got on at the Parish.

And Bella laughed.

'The Parish?' she said. 'I told that old bitch I'd see her in Hell. She wanted me to go to the workhouse.'

'Oh, Bella, I wish some more had the courage to stand up to her. She's only a young woman now; God knows what she'll be like in a few years. Aye, if only we could stand against her and her kind.'

'We will some day. Joe said we would.'

'Aye well, it'll be a wee while yet. I've come to ask you if you'd do some cleaning? Scrubbing and that, dusting and polishing.'

'Oh! I will! Where?'

'At the library, in the cellars. They're cleaning out some old stuff from the Town Hall offices, old books and stuff, and they want the shelves cleaned and the walls whitewashed – and there will be some of the library to do – to polish and dust.'

'But what about the twins? Who's going to look after them?'

'Well, that's it, you see. I can, because I go out in the mornings. I'll go home and give my bairns their dinners, and come over to you and watch your wee ones. You can work at the library whatever hours you like, and I thought you'd rather do it late in the afternoon.'

'Oh, Maggie. You're good. I'll pay you something for this.'

'Indeed you will not. If I can't help you after what you did for me, I'd be a poor soul. It will be heavy work, Bella. They'll want to shift a lot of books and papers – heavy and dirty.'

'I don't care – I'll do it gladly, and if you can get me any washing to do at home, Maggie, I'll do it and take it back – And maybe I can get a cheap pram; oh, I'll manage, thank God! Just to be able to work, and not go to that bitch of a woman, to send me to the poorhouse.'

The work was hard, the cellars were dark and low, and the gas jets had been put in roughly, to enable the joiners to put up shelves. The walls had been whitewashed, and the shelves ready to take the overflow of books, papers, and documents, hoarded in the council's offices for a century and more. Bella worked from four o'clock till seven – and was paid 2/6d.

In a few days, Maggie got her some washing to do, only a little at first, but she tackled it with the sure confidence of a craftsman.

The heap of papers and books, which the librarians were putting in order on the shelves grew less, and Bella was in a corner scrubbing the floor one night when two men came down to finish a section of papers. Bella went on quietly washing and scrubbing, and the men took no notice of her. She might have been one of the pillars for all they cared. Then she heard a name . . . and she listened.

'Must have been in that book all these years – Just an – acknowledgement of course. Doubt if we'll ever find the original.'

'That's the one Joe Mulligan was looking for, wasn't it?'

'Yes, it's a sort of confirmation: "Given under our hand and seal this day . . . " Can't make out the date – Oh, wait a minute. It says here, the twelfth day of October 1671, be it – oh, known – that's, "be it known that I, Albert Cameron of this burgh of Greeniog do hereby declare". Can't make out any more.'

'Oh well, best put it with the other books of that year. It's only a copy of the Covenant by Charles II after the Restoration – he bought a herring-curing factory or something. Anyway it will be quite safe here. Come on – I want to get home. I'm hungry.'

The footsteps of the two men died away, and Bella finished the corner she was cleaning. She went over to the shelves, but it was impossible to see where the men had been standing, or where they had put the books, or papers, she was not sure which they had been handling.

She must go now, it was closing time. But tomorrow she would work quickly, and look for that paper. If Joe had wanted it, it must be for something good; it became important to find it. She remembered what he had been telling young Sandy and her about King Charles II's visit.

In the days that followed, she searched every book or folder she could see, in this group of shelves. She really had no idea what to look for, or whether she would know if she had found it. And then, there it was: in a brown envelope, with the inscription on it, simply 'K.C.II.'

She pushed it hurriedly into her blouse, and felt that every eye could see it: she finished the work, and crept out of the library, holding on to the precious paper in the open envelope.

When she got home, she took it out of the envelope, slowly, gently. It was a piece of aged, yellowed paper, torn and mended at the back with gummed paper, mostly postage stamp edgings. Crushed and crinkled, it was still legible. She saw the words, ' . . . Hand and Seal . . . ' and 'Charles . . . ' and a date, 1671. Vaguely, she remembered Joe asking Sandy about the date of the Restoration, and it ran in her mind that he had agreed that it was 1661. So maybe this wasn't the right paper after all? What should she do? Without Joe to help her, it would be best, she thought, to put the paper back where she had found it.

Maggie was sitting by the fire, the children asleep, and as Maggie said, as good as gold.

'Thank you, Maggie. Do you think you could stay a bit later next week, one night – Wednesday. I want to go to the meeting, about the election.'

'Election? God save us, lassie. What have us women to do with elections?'

'Joe said that some day there will be women in Parliament – he said that women should have a vote in elections, and there's something Joe wanted done – I'd like to try it.'

'All right, Bella. I'll come as usual and stay till you come home. I'll bring Annie, and she can help me to bath the bairns. Although what you want at a meeting beats me.'

Bella was half afraid to go to the library – she was sure there would be a hue and cry over the papers she had taken. But things went on as usual – except that the big job was nearly over.

She would have no more work of this kind after the next week.

The election meeting started off with a speech of welcome by the Town Clerk. Another speech by the visiting member from Glasgow, and then 'our prospective Unionist candidate' rose to give his rousing address to the electors. There were a few women among the audience, but they were not favoured. They were looked on as an intrusion into a strongly male field.

Bella was up in the little gallery of the small hall in West Burn Street.

'And so, my friends, with every intention of leading this town – this *happy* town – to a better, stronger position in the world's trade, I urge you all to put your shoulder to the wheel. Let us pull together, shoulder to shoulder, with determination to make our country – and I mean our country of Scotland – our dear native land, a contented and happy land – with contented and happy people.'

His voice droned on. Bella thought – I feel sick.

'We are going to build better homes – we will see that the shipyards work to capacity, we will . . . '

His words were lost in angry murmurs. 'always *going to do* something.'

But the speaker was warmed up.

'Never in our history have we had as great an opportunity as we have now. And just look at what the council have done in the borough. They have built a new harbour. They have put down a number of fine streets – '

Bella could contain herself no longer. She stood up,

drew her shawl round her – and shouted: 'We canna eat streets!'

That was all they needed. The meeting rose to its feet as one man. They cheered, they booed, they clapped and laughed – and above the din, someone shouted:

'Good old Bella!'

With four words, in the plain vernacular of the people, she became one of them again.

All through the years, since the day when she had been stoned, and the beginning of her life with Joe, the townsfolk had felt guilty at their conduct, and outraged at hers. She had been a thorn in the flesh of the ordinary people, because she did things that ordinary people didn't do. And now, with four words, she had re-established herself in their hearts. It had only needed this faint impetus – because, deep down, they felt angry that they *had* to be angry with her.

She got away from the crowds, wondering at herself. It had been quite spontaneous – quite unintentional, and the reception was quite out of proportion. But they were glad, with relief, and the lifting of a burden of conscience. Bella was – all right.

Mr Simon romped home to victory with a slightly reduced majority. (After all, they had always had a Unionist MP, and what was good enough for my father...)

Bella went home, and in the quiet of the night, she read the paper she had taken from the library's archives.

Taken? Or stolen? She wondered.

XXVII

There came the day when Bella had literally no money at all. It was enough that Andy still paid her rent, but she could not ask him for more.

The fair was in town, in the park in Campbell Street – the gaudy trappings, and the roundabouts, the horses, and the stalls where you could try your luck, and over it all, the harsh tones of the organ grinding out its popular tunes. The July night was misty, a fine rain drizzling – the air was turning cold and the clouds turned dusk into darkness earlier than usual. In the space of a heart-beat, Bella had decided: she must have help, and there was only one person she could go to now.

She looked at the twins, rosy in sleep, their fretfulness and irritation forgotten in full bellies and warm bodies. She put out the fire, and left the gas jet burning low. She opened the window just a little at the top – there was no wind, so nothing could blow the gas out – she had never left them before, but this was desperate.

She knew that Willie often worked late at his office. She would have to chance that he would be there. She glanced at the clock: 8.30. Only five minutes walk and she would be there. Please God, let him be there. He must help me.

She looked round the kitchen, put her shawl over her head, and opened the door quietly, and shut it as carefully. She ran – ran until she had reached the coalyard – yes: mercifully – she saw a light in the office.

She knocked on the door, and Willie came and stood against the light.

'Who is it?' His voice was tired.

'It's me, Bella. Willie, I can't stay – I want to speak to you.'

'Bella? At this time of night? What's the matter, girl?'

He had not seen her since the funeral of John McGarvie, last year, and he had only nodded briefly to her – she meant nothing to him.

'You'd better come in.'

'No. I can't wait. I've left the bairns.'

'Oh yes, the bairns. Yes, I see. All right, wait a minute. I'll get my coat and walk home with you. Come in a minute.'

He locked up his desk, and put out the gas. He took her by the arm and when they were outside, he locked the door. She hopped with impatience, and wanted to be gone. But she just could not blurt out that she wanted money from him.

His long strides against her running steps soon brought them to the little alley, and she ran on ahead of him, and put her key in the door.

The twins lay as she had left them. The gas burned low, and the house was quiet and homely in the small flame that cast flickering shadows over the corners.

'God! It's cold in here.'

'I had to put the fire out when I came out. I've never left them before, and I was frightened. I'll soon light it again. I'll make a cup of tea. Would you like a cup, Willie?'

'Aye, I suppose so. Here, I'll light the fire.'

'The kettle's hot, if you just let me boil it up on the sticks, I'll make the tea and then you can put on the coal.'

The tea was good – hot and strong and sweet.

'Now – what did you want to see me about?'

'I . . . it's . . . oh! I never thought I'd come to this!'

'Come to what? What do you want? Some money?'

'Oh!' she gasped. 'How did you know?'

'I heard you'd been to the Parish. I didn't like it, and then you seemed to be doing all right. What happened?'

'The library job was finished. I was cleaning there,

and I was doing some washing. But the twins were ill, I
couldn't leave them. I didn't know where to turn.' She
sat down heavily. 'I don't know where to turn – ' she said
again.

'Well, I'll help you if I can. No, don't cry, for God's
sake, don't cry.'

'It's just – I didn't want to ask anybody. I'd rather
fight my own battles, but I've had Joe so long. He looked
after me and – '

'Yes, he did. You've made a fine mess of things,
haven't you, Bella?'

'Oh don't! I need help, or I wouldn't have come to
you. I can work, but the twins were ill.'

'You'll need something till you're stronger – till you
can work again.'

'If strength were enough, I've got that, Willie Munro.'

He looked at her quizzically for a moment.

'Yes, I believe you've got that, Bella, but in this case, it
isn't enough.'

She stood up and moved to the window.

'You're not going to help me.'

'I didn't say that.'

'Surely you know what it cost me to come to *you* for
help like this?'

He nodded, and there was a small still, silence. He sat
comfortably enough on the wooden chair with a cushion,
his feet on the fender-stool, and the light shining on his
handsome face, and fair hair with the reddish tints. Her
heart ached with longing and love for him.

He said, with a faint touch of amusement.

'You know I never liked you, Bella.'

Her face flushed; it was as if he could see right into
her heart, and know what she felt. It was something she
had always known, and had prayed that he might never
have reason to tell her of his dislike – that by never
speaking of it, it might not exist. But now, here it was, in
the open – in all its naked obscenity.

'You know *why* I never liked you, Bella?' he went on
softly.

She looked at him, and in his hard, dark look, she saw at last, the reason.

'Yes, you can see it now, Bella. Because you took my brother from me, right from the moment when he found you in the close. He never had a thought for anyone else after you came – and you a baby, thirteen years younger.'

'Don't, Willie! I never really knew Robbie. I was only eight when he went away. I didn't know . . . '

'Maybe you did, maybe you didn't. We don't show much affection, we Scots folk, but that doesn't mean that it isn't there. Robbie meant something to me when I was a youngster – and you came between us and spoilt that.'

'He was good, Willie.'

'Oh aye, he was a good lad. He looked after my mother, and me, *and* you. And then you killed him, Bella,' he said softly.

'No, Willie! Don't say that! I didn't know he would go away just because of me. I was young.'

'You used him, Bella. He was always there for you to pick up and use, just as it suited you. But you got married, and that broke his heart. But that wasn't enough, was it? You had to get *another* man – a good man.'

'After you married Jenny!'

And then she could have bitten her tongue out, but he didn't seem to notice the significance of what she had said.

'Another *good* man, and ruin his career.'

He stopped at the look of sheer amazement on her face.

'What in God's name, what do you mean?'

'Do you mean that you *don't* know what you did to Joe?'

'What *I* did to Joe?'

'Joe could have been – oh God! what he *could* have been! Before you came to him, he was in the council, remember?'

'Yes, but he said he was too busy.' Her voice died away.

'Too busy. Yes. Well – that year, or maybe the next year – he might have been, he *could* have been Provost. Maybe, come another election, maybe he could have been our MP. Although that wasn't so likely.'

'I never knew,' she whispered. 'He always said he liked staying at home with me. He was good to me, he read a lot of books and told me such a lot of things about – people, and the world. I never knew what . . . '

'What he gave up? All right. I didn't know you didn't know. But it ruined him, just the same. And then he got that terrible cough – '

'I think he got that the night he took me to that first social.'

'Well, I suppose I'd better be going. What time is it? Good Lord, it's nearly midnight! If anybody sees me coming out of here – they'd never believe we were only *talking!*'

'Nobody will see you – the bakery men don't often come to the door, they'll be leaving about four o'clock in the morning, but Jenny will be waiting for you, surely?'

'Jenny? No, she's in London. She won't be back for a couple of weeks.'

'Oh.'

'That reminds me – what did you mean when you said a wee while ago – "After I married Jenny?"'

'Nothing.'

He stood up and took her by the shoulders – and made her look at him.

'What did you mean, Bella?'

'Nothing.'

'You know, Bella, I never liked you, but you're a very bonnie lass – and a rotten liar. I've only just noticed how nice – how nice you are . . . '

She looked at him.

'There's stars in your eyes, Bella,' he whispered.

His arms went round her shoulders, she leaned her head on his chest, and then he lifted her face, and kissed her – and the blood pounded through her body. Her head was swimming . . . '

After a kiss that seemed to last a lifetime, he held her away, and looked at her again.

'God Almighty – Bella! What have you done to me?'

'Nothing, only loved you since I can remember.'

'Nobody ever kissed me, or held me like that in my life.'

'Don't be such a liar. What about your wife, Jenny?'

'Jenny is still a virgin, Bella.'

She jumped away as though he had struck her.

'Don't talk daft, Willie!'

'It's true. I can't tell you about it now. Bella, this is something I never imagined could happen in a million years. Bella, kiss me.'

She put her arms round him again. He lifted her easily in his arms and moved over to the bed. This time, she knew he would not leave her so quickly.

'What time did you say the bakery men left in the morning?' he whispered softly.

XXVIII

America

The snows had melted, and the green grass shone like jewels in the sun. The trees put on their green, and the birds chirped, and quarrelled, and arrived. Buffalo moved in slow procession, fewer than they were last year. Deer and their young ventured to the edge of the forests, and a mile away the broad streams flashed with the turbulence of fish, trout and salmon that had been carried away from the main river, and small fish that were good to eat.

Old Benny had nursed his unexpected patient back to life, but not to health yet. Rob spoke little, and when he did it was clear that the accident that had nearly killed him had left his mind a complete blank. He had no idea who he was, or where he was. He felt strangely content, and in the short summer season he simply existed from day to day, never questioning Benny's instructions, working when he could, and stopping when his strength gave out.

The usual foresters and fishermen and hunters who passed on their way to the sporting lands and rivers, came and went, nodded to him, and passed on, incurious.

Rob kept out of their way; he didn't know anything about them and they disturbed him. To anyone who asked about him, Benny would only say, 'Just a friend from way back . . . wants a rest from city life and some fresh air; been ill, you know.'

No one was interested; Benny called him 'Jock' and nobody cared.

Rob grew stronger; perhaps the medicine of the peacefulness and utter isolation did more good than expensive doctors or 'cures' would have done. His memory played tricks sometimes. He could remember fishing, but not in a stream like this. He could not understand the calm, green stillness. Sometimes he could hear in his mind the sound of steam whistles, the clang of hammer on iron hulls, the creak of swinging cargoes, the shouts of men. But it was all vague and momentary, and had no place in this sharp clear air.

Days, and weeks, and years, getting stronger, and the noises became clearer and were real in his memory.

The time had passed so quickly, and the snows were thick again, blinding against the dark line of the horizon, and the brilliant winter sun.

The two men were sitting near the door of the hut eating their mid-day meal.

'You've done a lot for me, Benny.'

'Humph.'

'How long have I been here?'

'Seventy-two, your friend left you.'

'What year is it now?'

'Far as I know, it's eight summers since then.'

'How long . . . I mean, I forgot who I was. How long did that last?'

'How long *have* you known who you were?'

'I think when the snow stopped last year, before the thaw. You were just getting ready to go away.'

'And you didn't say anything?'

'No. It's so peaceful here. I didn't want to remember. It frightened me. Is there any news from home?'

'Queen's ill. Been another gold strike near Alaska.'

'Jimmy left me and never came back. I thought he was my friend.'

'But – '

'I remembered him soon after I felt . . . I felt a kind of cloud, like a thunder cloud, and it was breaking, and the pain at the back of my head was torture. The cloud seemed to break all over me. I was sweating, and the sun came out, and the pain got less, and I saw a kind of picture. I saw the shipyards, and the river and the hills and, oh God! *Bella!* And I didn't know what I was doing here, or who you were, or what had happened. I only knew that I remembered Jimmy, and he isn't here. I thought he might be coming back that night or the next day. And then you went away. That seemed familiar. You'd been away before?'

He looked at Benny with his question.

Benny nodded.

'Yes, but – '

But Rob would not be stopped.

'So I just waited. The place was familiar to me. I thought you must have been looking after me.'

'The first year I took you with me. That was hell. But the next year you were able to do things for yourself. But Jimmy – '

'Aye, I remember him. What is it?'

'If you'll give me a chance, I'll tell you, Jock! You died, or as near as made no odds. A bit of an avalanche . . . you were going along that small valley and some overhanging snow fell on you. You got it in the back of your head, you pitched forward and broke your leg. Your heart stopped and I fixed your leg.' He paused. 'I told Jimmy it would make it easier to bury you.'

'To bury me? Christ!'

'Jimmy was heart-broken, I can tell you that. When I got into Dawson City the next year, when we both went in, I wrote and told him that you were alive. But there was a letter waiting for me, to say that he had registered your death, here in Dawson on his way down, and that he had taken care of all your property. He arranged for your property to go to your brother, and a nice sum for a Martha Hallam. But I don't think he could have got the letter I sent. And the doctor said it was severe concussion, and that maybe you *wanted* to be away from everything, and you seemed happier when we got back here. I never wrote again.'

'But how could I come alive if I was dead? What happened?'

'Jimmy had to go at sun-up. I left you out in the shed at the back. It was nearly time for the floods to come. Jimmy looked at you, he had tears in his eyes so that he couldn't see, and he went off with the dog-team. About half an hour after that I came into the shed. I came over just to look at you, and I thought I saw a slight movement of your finger. I didn't know what to do, but I tried what we did at Oxford sometimes. I breathed into your mouth, and rubbed your heart. You were cold, my God, you were cold! Then you began to breathe – and it hurt you. Then you were sick.'

He talked for a long time, and told Rob how the doctor had said that his memory could be gone for a month, a year, or for always.

The doctor thought that perhaps he ought to be left to find his own way back to health, which he did, and let nature work her own miracles.

'Apparently all your investments have been doing well. You're a very rich man.' His tone was laconic.

'Rich? What do I care? What about Bella?'

'Nobody mentioned Bella. I've no idea. But why did you not tell me that you remembered?'

'I wanted to wait to see if Jimmy would come. I didn't know why I was here without him. I remember leaving New York in the late summer of 1868. I didn't know. It could have been the same year except . . . ' He stopped and looked hard at Benny.

'You must have come here when you were young?'

'I was twenty.'

'That means you're – '

'Near as I can calculate, I'm around forty. Forty-one, I think.'

'You never had a woman here?'

'Not here. Sometimes, when I went into Dawson, not often though. Can't be bothered with all that now.'

'But you *can,*' persisted Rob. 'If you want to?'

'Yes, I suppose so. Can't be bothered. Why?'

'I *can't.*'

'Well, not yet, old chap; you've had your spine paralysed. Damned lucky you're still alive.'

'Thanks to you.'

'Anyone else would have tried. You nearly defeated me. But don't be worried about the state of your organs, my lad. You'll soon be back to normal.'

They sat and looked over the sparkling snow.

'Coming out to the traps with me, Jock? Bear there, if I'm not mistaken. Soon be over-run, this place. More railways cutting across the country. More roads . . . won't be any peace anywhere. I don't think I want the twentieth century.'

'It will soon be the twentieth century, won't it?'

'It will so. I've got a paper. I brought it back from Dawson last September, and I've watched the days since then, more or less. Could be New Year's Day today, or tomorrow, or last Tuesday! Anyway, Happy New Year,

Jock. It's 1881.'

'Same to you, Benny.'

'You know, I'll miss you.'

'I haven't said I'm going yet.'

'You must go. For your own sake, your brother's and your mother's, you must go.'

'I suppose you're right. What about you?'

'Me? I might visit you in Scotland. I'm a rich man too. I'm also a duke! My elder brother died. Father died seven years ago. Younger brother not a ladies' man, if you know what I mean? What a tale to tell! I suppose I ought to go back and look after the estate and do a bit of back-slapping. Hell and damnation! I suppose I'll have to marry and beget a son.'

That upset him more than anything, and he made a gesture of disgust – and spat.

'I'll never marry now,' said Rob, sadly.

'Don't know about that; you should. It's good for a man to leave a family behind him. I believe – do you know? – I think I'd like to try being back in the old country. I think I've just changed my mind.'

He left the door open and went over to the two bunks and spread some rugs. He came back to the door.

'Think I'll take a nap. Always feel I should sleep when I've got to make a decision. I'll see what comes into my head first thing, when I wake up.'

*

After that winter's snows, in the late spring of 1881, Rob and Benny left on the long trek to Dawson. They stayed there for some weeks, to get clothes, see their bankers and solicitors. Then they took the civilised journey to New York, and parted.

Perhaps they would meet again? Benny gave Rob a London address – his Club – patronised by the family for generations. Surely – they *would* meet again: the millionaire Robert Munro and the Duke of Peterbridge, had much of life in common.

Benny took ship as soon as he could. Rob waited – he had to adjust to the thought of getting to Jimmy. Would he be still there – still his friend, after nearly nine years?

XXIX

Golden September passed into misty October, and Willie came often, nearly every night, to stay, and talk, and love. This, then, must be her portion: to live in the twilight of stolen love, waiting, perhaps for another woman to give up her claim to this man. Or maybe . . . 'maybe she'll die. Maybe.' It wasn't even a whisper, or a conscious thought. It was a terrible thing to pass even as a momentary flash through her mind. Jenny was not likely to die anyway. She was young and lovely and blooming, enchanting and full of vitality.

Bella turned and looked at the twins again. They were at the interesting stage, with the cuteness of every baby. The small Joe had his father's eyes, and the serious look of little Florrie held the promise of beauty to come.

The sudden, sad death of the MP after his very brief office, gave Willie the chance he had been hoping for. The adoption of William Munro, coal merchant, as Liberal candidate, gave Jenny a brilliant chance to shine in local society.

There was no doubt she had been the toast of London society during that season. Her beauty, her unapproachable charm, her delightful 'Scottishness', were her entry to the exclusive world she loved. She had just accepted an invitation to shoot at the estate of Lord and

Lady Frenby, near Inverness. She would go home first, of course: when she had bought the correct clothes for a shooting party.

Now, at home, she lay, listening to the sounds of service: the metallic clang of long rakes against the sooty insides of the kitchen range. That was Cathie doing the flues. The clatter of a bucket, and the noise of a scrubbing brush on the front door steps: and then the gentle swish of a broom inside, the front hall and the dining room.

Jenny snuggled down again in soft linen sheets and thought how clever she had been to marry Will Munro after all. She decided she had been quite right to cut herself off from the rest of her family. She had never really liked Bella, and she knew that young Andrew had never cared for anyone but Bella, after his parents. So, when after the funeral of Flora and the minister she had said that she 'didn't want anything more to do with her mother's people' she had put them out of her life entirely.

She was in Paris when John died. She simply sent a telegram, asking Willie to get some flowers sent to the funeral.

Now she was free of all those memories of a hard childhood: she convinced herself that her childhood *had* been hard, forgetting the patience of Flora, and the loving discipline of John. Now she could live the life she wanted, swimming in the golden pond of court circles.

The one thing she had made up her mind about, however, (never for a moment having forgotten it) her one aim – her ladyship. Next to that, the decision that they must leave this forgotten town; this seedy, wet, dismal town with its constant reminders of Bella's connection with the two unfortunate children drowned from her husband's ship. And with its all-pervading atmosphere of poverty, only alleviated by the actual division of the West End streets.

She hated the women who looked coldly at her when she stepped from her carriage to go into one of the expensive dress shops. The sound of a ship leaving the

Clyde, giving her three blasts from her hooter in farewell, had no significance for her. It might never come back, but she cared not.

They really ought to go and live in London: or take a house in Sussex, or Surrey. This town was quite obviously dead. Nobody cared about it, nobody of any importance lived here. Yes really, they ought to leave.

The sounds reaching her now were the clattering dishes and cutlery; Sarah setting the table for breakfast. Cathie had finished the front door steps, and cleaning the brass knocker and letter-box, and was now in the kitchen frying bacon and eggs, and making porridge.

In the next room, she heard Willie move in his bed, yawn and stretch as the bed creaked. He had seemed different lately, too, Seemed happier, softer, kinder to her. It never occurred to her that he had really carried out his threat to her on their wedding night, to go to some other woman. Completely cold and sexless herself, in this instance only, she was a very stupid woman. A very beautiful, very clever, very stupid woman.

Willie knocked at the communicating door between the rooms, and came in.

'Good morning, Jenny. Nice morning.'

'Is it? Willie, can we not leave here, and go and live in London?'

'In London? Good God Jenny, not now!'

'Why not now? We've got enough money, haven't we? Besides, you could sell this house.'

'Money isn't the point, Jenny. I must spend a lot of time here, if I want to win the election.'

'If you win it, will you get a title then?'

He laughed. 'Not so fast, young lady. It might come very soon after, but it's not automatic, you know. Anyway, weren't you going to somewhere for the shooting?'

'I'm invited, but I've had to get some new clothes.'

'More clothes, Jenny! You're spending far too much on clothes.'

'Am I, Willie? I didn't think I was, but I can't wear the

same dresses I wore last year. But I will try to spend less. Will you come up to Inverness with me?'

'No, no, I must be here. You know, most of the money isn't mine at all; it's Rob's.'

'But Rob's dead! he can't use it!'

'Nevertheless, it's not really mine. You're living beyond *my* income. When do you go to Inverness?'

'On the tenth.'

'Oh. Seventh today. Do you want to do anything before you go?'

'Do?'

'You know, give a dinner or anything. And I'll need you here for meetings and canvassing and all that kind of thing.'

She made a little moué of distaste.

'Oh yes. All right, I'll come back as soon as the first shoot is over. There's only Lady Margaret. I want to see her again. She's in Edinburgh just now. Poor girl, she's practically on the shelf, if she doesn't get married soon. I heard a rumour the other day – somebody has heard from Canada – they've found the Duke of Peterbridge.'

'The Duke of who?'

'Peterbridge. He's been living in Alaska, or somewhere, like a hermit. Quite a romance. And I believe the families have decided that Margaret ought to marry him when he gets home.'

'Oh, how you can be bothered with all these empty people. Never mind.' He reflected that their very emptiness was mirrored in the girl who sat unconcernedly against the pillows of her virginal bed. Willie looked at her as he opened the door. It was no use being angry with her. She was like a child who is surprised to hear that she has been naughty.

The gong rang through the house.

It was lovely to sweep downstairs and into the dining-room, and choose breakfast from silver dishes. She could follow the thoughts in Sarah's mind, because she had often felt the same way herself.

'Hurry-up-and-have-your-breakfast-I've-got-the-flowers-to-do-and-the-washing-and-you-don't-give-me-time . . . '

Yes, she knew it all. But she had trained them well, because she knew how it should be. And they stayed: not for love of their mistress, but for their regard for their master. And anyway, good jobs were hard to come by; especially jobs like this, where the mistress was away such a lot, and there were no children. Children meant Nannies, and of all the trials of domestic service, the Nanny is undoubtedly the worst.

If the two girls wondered at the separate bedrooms, they never even guessed the real reason. After all, it was well known that the 'gentry' were – *different*.

A whirl of shopping, and then Willie took Jenny up to Glasgow, to get the connection for Inverness. And went as fast as steam and wheels could take him, back to Greenock, to wait for the night, for the friendly dark of the mean narrow streets, to see Bella. Now, over the past year, she had become a necessary part of his life. He was not in love with her. His love had been given to the doll-like Jenny when he was a boy, but he had taken her at least in gratitude, and with the whole of her heart.

Jenny came back in time to work with Willie for the election. Never did a candidate have such a charming, beautiful, tireless, and seemingly willing worker. And never did she question where he went in the evenings when she wasn't with him. She had a wide circle of friends . . .

With the prospect of the election in his grasp, Willie could talk easily with Bella, and it was now she knew the value of her education with Joe. They talked in her kitchen over tea and whisky.

'I want something that will make it *sure*. I think I've got a good chance, but I need a real *issue*.'

'What kind of thing, Willie?' Bella filled his glass.

'Something big . . . ' He stopped and looked up at her. 'Was Joe working on anything before he died?'

'He was always working on things. Trying to make life

better for working folk. But I've just thought. There was that thing he said before he died.'

'What?'

'He said – and mind you, it wasn't easy to hear what he was saying, because he coughed such a lot – but he said, "Tell Will . . . what he wants . . . to think of me . . . and this cough". I'm not sure what he meant.'

'Him and this cough.' He drank thoughtfully. Then he put his glass down with a bang.

'*I* know! I know what he meant! I'll build a hospital for TB patients – and fever. Out in the countryside, where they'll get fresh air. Oh Bella!'

He stood up and marched over to the window, and turned.

'That will do it! I'll put it before the committee tomorrow.'

'There was something else . . . '

'What was it, Bella?'

'He used to tell me that King Charles II came to Greenock. He gave a piece of land, for buildings for poor people, for ever.'

'God's truth, Bella! What *else* has been going on in this town that I didn't know about?'

'Plenty,' said Bella tartly.

'But why didn't you tell me about this before?'

'I didn't know it would have anything to do with the election. He said there should be a paper in the ark . . . arc . . . whatever you call them.'

'Archives?'

'Aye, that's right. A paper, he said, that would prove that the land was a Royal gift, and could not be abused.'

'Go on, tell me more about the paper.'

'I'll do better than that. I've got it.'

'You've . . . *got* it?'

'I took it from the library when I was cleaning there.'

'You just *took* it?'

Willie was almost speechless.

'Yes. I knew it must be for something good, when Joe wanted it.'

'Let me see it.'

Bella took a small wooden box from the sideboard. It had been a gift from John for her eighteenth birthday.

'These are what he had among his papers. I put that paper inside another envelope, after I brought it home. It is so fragile.'

Will took it gently.

'My God,' he breathed, 'I never knew such things were in history,' said this man who, as a boy of nine, had told his mother, with a mouthful of soup, that history was just battles and kings.

He sat and read the papers in silence.

They started:

> Be it known to whosoever taketh this Covenant to question that we, the undersigned, hath this day the twelfth day of October in the year of Our Lord sixteen hundred and seventy-one, witnessed the Deed Of Gift by His Gracious Majesty King Charles the Second of loyal memory as herewith presented: that He did, on the thirtieth day of August in the year sixteen hundred and seventy-one being the tenth year of his Reign, give, and in perpetuity, the piece of land on high ground above the harbours distant about 1/2 mile from the same, and extending over an area of 2 acres. And this given for dwellings for the poor people of this town, by His Majesty's Grace, for ever.
>
> > 'Given under Our Hand and Seal this thirtieth day of October sixteen hundred and seventy-one.'

The signature was written in, at the bottom, in a fair imitation of the monarch's hand.

Beside it, there was a crude little drawing, which gave a rough illustration of the land as it must have been two hundred years before. It seemed to be roughly at a point to the west of Inverkip street, which would mark the 'high ground' mentioned, and just over two miles from the docks, as they were now.

'My God!' breathed Willie. 'But I wonder why . . . Wait a minute! There's some more writing under here.'

It was very faint, but with care in laying out the fragile paper, it was just decipherable.

> . . . in that divers persons be not willing to respect and honour the Monarch's wish, and have destroyed or otherwise disposed of His original covenant, this is to state .that we, the undersigned, on oath before God, witness that we have seen and read the document written by His Majesty.
>
> We are:

Albert Cameron	: Clerk of the Council
Duncan Taylor	: Physician
John Smith	: Victualler
Alexander Tait	: Tailor
Robert Gray	: Master Baker

Willie sat, stunned. This just couldn't *be!* He handed the paper almost with reverence, to Bella.

'I never. . . in all my life . . . it didn't seem as if these people actually *lived*. But they did. And it seems there was as much skull-duggery then as there is now!'

'And,' said Bella tartly. 'It seems that they *expected* that there would *still* be poor people in this town, in two hundred years!'

'What now, Bella? Do you want me to go on with this?'

'That, and all the other things Joe wanted done. You must, Will – you're the only one who can.'

'Do you know what you've done, Bella?'

'No?'

'I think you've just helped me to win the election, and you might have committed a crime, for which you will probably go to jail!'

'If it gets homes for old people, who won't be

separated, I won't mind that.'

'There's been some talk about building new houses for better class people, just about there. But that can't be right, the railway runs just under there. Oh Lord! Bella, you do make life difficult! I'll have to look through old maps, and get a surveyor to check it all. But you know, I believe this will be the turning point, and if I win the election, Bella, *I'll* build homes for old people, just where the King wanted them!'

William Munro was returned as Liberal Member of Parliament for Greenock, with a large majority.

'Will you get a title now, Willie?'

Jenny sat up in bed leaning on her frilled white pillows.

'Perhaps, soon. It's not automatic, you know. I told you.'

'Can we move to London then?'

'Not yet. I've got a lot to do here. I've got to see about building those homes for old people.'

'Oh.' She wasn't very interested.

'Can we go and stay for a while, then?'

'Eh? Oh well, I suppose so . . . soon.'

A year later, the old buildings near the Inverkip street end where Willie had been born, were pulled down. Decent tenements were put up, and then, on the open country road to the west, the foundations were laid for a home for elderly people, where they would not be torn apart in the last days of their lives.*

*Author's note: This statement anticipates the happening by nearly a century, for the purposes of the course of the novel. Old people were still being separated in 1934. J.R.

XXX

During his journey back to his own town of Bessant, and across the Atlantic, Rob had wondered what was the best way to let people know he was alive. A letter would be cold and impersonal: 'Dear Willie, I'm alive after all . . . ' No, he couldn't do it that way.

But of Rob's arrival in Bessant, it is scarcely possible to tell in cold print. There were new hotels in the town – a new railway station: twelve – nearly thirteen years since he had left it. There were bound to be changes. He left his luggage at the station, and went to the adjacent hotel. He was tidy, but shabby: diffident, shy, inarticulate.

'Good morning, sir? Can I help you?'

The desk clerk looked at him superciliously. Rob just smiled quietly.

'Yes. Can you tell me if Mr Jimmy Miller still lives in town? And I would like a room.'

'A . . . room, sir?'

'That's right. A room. And Mr Miller, please.'

(But Jimmy tells it so much better, later.)

So, as the big liner nosed her way out of New York harbour, this tired man, this sad, lonely, shabby, very rich man, stood at the bows, leaving his place only to eat and sleep, and watched the ship's wake as she ploughed steadily eastwards.

No. It would be a shock to them all, he knew. He had sworn Jimmy to secrecy – anyway, he would be there before a letter could get to Scotland – but in that shock, he would see, in first discovery, how things were; whether the family were glad to see him: family? Did he have a family at all by this time?

His mother . . . then the McGarvies. How many of them were still alive?

The ship dropped anchor at the Tail o' the Bank, and the tender came out from Princes Pier. New since Rob had left.

He left his luggage, as he had done in Bessant, at the station, and walked slowly up Campbell Street, and turned eastwards.

He trod remembered streets, and he ached with longing. The street where he had lived as a child had changed, and changed for the worse: paint peeling off walls – doors fallen off their hinges. The cellar steps . . . down there in dim candle-light he had made the wee cot for Bella. Now the steps were worn and dangerous.

But children still played up and down them, shrieking, crying, laughing.

He enquired: 'Mr Munro? Oh no, he left here some years ago. He's got a coal business now, in Glebe street. Campbell and Munro. You can't miss it.'

So Willie had stuck to his coal-heaving, and made himself prosperous.

He found the place and went to the gate. A coalman came by and spoke to him.

'Were you wanting Mr Campbell?'

'No. Mr Munro.'

'He's just left, about ten minutes ago.'

'Thank you.' (He looked like an American, the man said afterwards.) 'Do you know where he lives?'

'Oh aye. It's the big house at the end of Eldon Street, it's called 'Braeside'.'

'Yes, I know the place. I'll go there. Thank you very much.'

Rob turned away, and the coalman looked after him.

'Poor old chap,' he thought. 'Looks a bit down on his luck.'

Rob walked slowly along Union Street, down Forsyth

Street, and into Eldon Street. These streets were quiet;
the very air breathed leisure and money. The scent of
flowers from hidden gardens, added to the always present
tang of the salt air from the river, and only faintly, if the
wind was blowing from the east, an overture of smoke,
and from the hills at the back, the heady nostalgia of
heather.

He found the house, with the name on the gate, with
steps up between rock gardens, beautifully kept, and
leading on to a path to the front door. The door was
wide, with a stained glass window, and through it, the
light in the hall gave a glow that spoke of money, and
good taste, plush curtains and rich carpets.

He rang the bell, and it jingled in the kitchen. A trim
maid, in black dress and white cap and apron, opened
the door, and visibly recoiled when she saw him.

'Good evening. I'd like to see Mr Munro please.'

'Oh! Goodness, yes sir. Who – Will you come in
please? Who will I say . . . '

'Tell him a friend from America.'

'Yes, sir. Will you wait here, please?'

She scuttled away and trotted up the green-carpeted
stairs and across the landing to the drawing-room.

Willie sat on a couch that stood opposite the
fireplace, where a log fire burned, although the early
September evening was not really cold. He had beside
him a bundle of papers, some newspapers, and a glass of
whisky and soda. He was studying the newspapers with
some satisfaction. His investments were doing well: his
own business was flourishing, he had completely come to
terms with his marriage to Jenny. They got along
together, like a favourite brother and sister. He loved her
still, but the early passion had died. She was happy,
decorative, a wonderful hostess when they entertained,
and she adored entertaining, and she was entirely
faithful to him. His plans for the evening were similar to
most evenings over the last months. He had his dinner,
and a good cigar, then he would stroll vaguely in the
direction of the town, and arrive at the dark little alley,

where a lighted window, with the blinds modestly drawn in the bright kitchen showed him that Bella would be waiting for him.

No one had seen him. He slept in her arms, till she told him the bakery men had gone, then before first light, he would walk quickly back to his home, and be there before the maids were up. When Jenny was at home, he usually went straight to his office, and saw his men start their rounds with the coal lorries, and made sure the horses were all in good health, and then went home. She never questioned where he had been . . .

He could see no reason why this very pleasant state of affairs shouldn't go on for a long time. Later, perhaps, he could put Bella somewhere down the coast . . . or possibly up in Paisley, where he could visit her more easily. But he would look after her anyway: it was a new experience, to be loved as Bella loved him.

He heard the front door bell and frowned. He didn't want any interruptions. He wasn't expecting any visitors. Surely it wasn't a telegram from Jenny? It was nearly time for dinner. The girl would be up soon to tell him dinner was served. (Jenny had certainly trained them well.)

Sarah opened the door.

'Dinner, Sarah?'

'Yes, sir. No, sir. At least, it's ready sir, but there's a gentl . . . there's a man downstairs who wants to see you. He says he's a friend from America.'

'Oh Lord! It must be that Jimmy Miller. Oh heavens, he should have told me he was coming. Ask Cathie if she can manage dinner for two. Will you set another place, Sarah?'

'Yes, sir. If you please sir, I don't think it's that gentleman, sir. He looks a poor old man.'

'What the devil! All right, I'll go down and see him. Hold dinner till I've decided.'

He moved to the door and Sarah stood aside.

He went quickly down the stairs and went forward to where the quiet man, who looked so old, was standing near the grandfather clock.

Willie stopped, as if a dead hand had rested on his shoulder.

'Hello, Willie.'

'Who . . . who *are* you?'

Sarah stood at the back of the hall and heard the moan. . . a sort of half-scream that came from Willie as he stumbled towards the other man.

'If I never move from this spot,' she told the cook, Cathie, 'I hope I never hear another sound like that.'

'God Almighty!' it was just a breath, 'but you're *dead*! For Christ's sake, am I going mad?'

'I'm sorry, Willie. I didn't know what was the best way.'

But Willie had Rob in his arms. He was thumping his back and shaking his hand. His initial shock was over. The reaction would come, but he was at least in the presence of the living, not a ghost conjured up by his conscience.

'Sarah! Sarah! Damn the girl! Sarah?'

Sarah came running out.

'Dinner at once. For two. This is Mr Robert, my brother. We thought he was dead. And make up a bed in one of the spare rooms. Come on, Rob. Come and have a drink. Oh God! You've got so much to tell me. Come on. Give me your coat.'

His words seemed to tumble over each other, as if he could not convey the sense of what he was trying to say, fast enough.

Rob left his coat, and walked up the stairs behind Willie.

'There – oh God! I can't believe it. Will you have a dram, Rob? Good. I need one too. Oh, Robbie, Robbie!'

And Willie sat down on the couch beside Rob, spilling the whisky, and laid his head on his brother's shoulder and sobbed: the sobs of a grown man are terrible things to hear, and Rob had heard them before. But the storm did not last long, and Willie was left weak and shaken. Rob got up and poured the drinks.

In a few moments, the worst of the shock had passed,

and Willie started questions, just as Sarah came in to
announce dinner.

'Come on, Rob. I expect you could do with a good
meal, and then bed.'

'I'd like some dinner, but I could go to the hotel?'

'The hotel? Surely to God you knew you'd be staying
with me, or mother?'

'Mother. I was frightened to ask. Is she . . . is she . . . '

'Yes, she's still alive. My God! she was right. She
wouldn't believe you were dead. And by God, neither
did Jenny's father. He said just before he died, "Rob's not
dead!"'

'*He's* dead then?'

'Yes, and Auntie Flora. A big flood at the church. Oh
I'll tell you all about that. Have some of this chicken,
Rob.'

Sarah handed the vegetables, and left the room.

'Mother. Is she all right?'

'She gets a touch of rheumatism now and again, but
she's just waiting for you to come home.'

'Where is she?'

'Ground floor, in Nelson Street. She gets out a bit, but
I haven't neglected her, Rob.'

'No, I knew you wouldn't. Jimmy told me you had
replied to his letter.'

'What happened, anyway?'

'That will keep till tomorrow. Just one more thing . . .
Bella.'

Bella.

The name fell into the cosy dining-room like a pebble
in a cascading waterfall.

There it was, between them, and Willie remembered.
He was going that night, to the arms of the woman his
brother loved, and there sat his brother – back from the
dead.

'Bella,' he said, and every ounce of strength he had
went into saying it with studied indifference. 'She's all
right now. Had a bad time but she's all right now.'

'Have you been looking after her?'

'Well, yes, I have been helping her a bit. She was a bit down.'

'But, Will – ! I left instructions with my lawyer that you and mother, and Bella, were to share in my property! I did that all clear and legal. Jimmy saw to it for me.'

'Rob, I've done all I could for Bella. She's not an easy girl to help – you know how independent she is. I *haven't* neglected her. She's all right, I assure you.'

Rob was somewhat comforted.

'Aye – well, I'll make sure she has everything she wants, not only what she needs.'

'Rob! This is terrible! You – just back from the dead, and fighting with me about *money!* And a girl! Stop it, Rob! I *have* looked after her. There's money there in her name in the bank, but she doesn't want a lot of money. So long as her rent's paid, and she has enough for the twins, she's quite happy. She gets a lot from me for the poor people she comes up against; she's always asking me for something for some charity, or some old people who can't pay their rent or something ... food and clothes ... '
His voice drifted away, and he dropped his head in his hands. Tears were very near. The shock was taking its toll.

Rob put his arm round Will's shoulder. They sat, silent, for a few moments. Had this girl come between them, after all the years? But no, it couldn't be. Will had eyes only for Jenny.

The tense moment passed. Will got up and poured another drink.

'It's not too late ... I think I'll go and see mother, and break it to her as gently as I can. God! I remember the day I had to tell her you were dead! And she *never* believed it!'

They went back upstairs to the drawing-room, and Sarah brought the coffee.

'Jenny likes it this way. You knew Jenny and I were married?'

'I guessed it. You said in a letter, that year when I had my accident. Any bairns?'

Willie kept his voice steady. 'No . . . not yet. We – we
– wanted to wait till I got really established. Jenny – she's
not awful fond of kids.'

'Oh.'

A small silence. Then Will said, standing up as he put
his coffee cup on the tray. 'I'll take a walk along and see
mother. Don't wait up, Rob. I've got a lot to think about.'

But he knew he was not going to see his mother.

He turned at the door.

'Why didn't you write?'

'I thought of it, but I wanted to see if . . . if anybody
remembered me. I thought this way was the best.'

'You're all right? I mean, your accident?'

'Oh yes. It was my head mostly. My leg got broken, I
believe, but it was mostly my head. The only effect I
have now is that I'm never sure what day it is! A week, or
six weeks, it's all the same to me! I look at the calendar,
and five minutes later I can't tell you the date! I think
that's partly because of the time I spent with old Benny.
He never worried about time.'

'Benny?'

'He's the one who saved my life. He set my leg as well
– Jimmy told me he said it would make it easier to bury
me! They thought I was dead. Funny, Benny is the Duke
of Peterbridge now.'

'The Duke of – ! Good God! That's the fellow Jenny
was talking about. But how – ?'

'All in good time. Tell me about Bella. What happened
after Morrison died?'

'Well, she got another man, you know.'

Willie used the word 'man' with the peculiarly
Scottish intonation which means husband, and Rob
accepted it in that sense.

'So I'm too late again!'

'No, no, Rob. He died – last year.'

'Good God! That poor lassie! Well, I'm maybe not
much use to her as a man, but I can look after her. Has she
– were there any children?'

'Aye, she had Sandy – he was Morrison's. Then she

had twins, a boy and a girl.'

There was nothing more to say. Nothing, until they could talk about the long years between, and the future. They looked at each other, for a moment, both a little wary, but with the deep feeling of contentment under the constraint.

'Right. I'll go and see mother. I might take a walk along to see Bella, but I'll make arrangements for us to go there tomorrow. Rob, it's a grand thing to have you back, lad. Sleep well. See you in the morning.'

He put his hand on Rob's shoulder, and shook his hand. The brothers looked at each other again, and then Willie turned away. But he knew he wasn't going to his mother. He walked quickly along the streets to Bella.

She had finished getting the twins to bed for the night, and sat with some knitting, and a cup of tea.

When his key turned in the door, she looked up, her face bright with welcome.

'Willie! You're early. I've got a cup of tea.'

'Wait, Bella. I've got something to tell you.'

'What is it? Is it Jenny? She knows?'

He waved that aside impatiently.

'No, it's not Jenny, and I wouldn't care if she did know. You remember what your father said just before he died? About Robbie?'

'Robbie?'

'Rob – my brother.'

'Oh. Oh yes, he said Rob wasn't dead, but we knew he was nearly gone himself then, so we didn't take any... oh! is he ... ?'

'Yes. My mother said the same thing all along. He walked into my house tonight. Oh Bella! It was such a shock, but a wonderful thing. Bella, he wants to come and see you tomorrow. I think he's going to ask you to marry him!'

'Marry! Me? Rob? Oh no! Willie, I couldn't give you up. I need you so much. I love you.'

'Wheesh, wheesh noo. I know, but I think it would be best for you.'

'Best for me!' she flared in anger. 'Best thing for me would be to spend the rest of my life with you. Why can't you divorce Jenny? She hasn't been a wife to you.'

'I would, Bella, but I'm going to get *something* out of this marriage, and I don't want a scandal. I told you what I'm aiming at, come another election, and she's making some very good connections. Very influential people.'

'People! What do we want with people? We'll go away, Willie. I'd leave here for you, nothing else in the world.'

'Bella, I'm telling you why we can't be married. I can't risk a scandal if I want to stay in Parliament. And something else – '

'What else?' she said sharply. 'What are you keeping from me?'

'I want a title, that's all, and I'm getting nearer to that too.'

'What's the use of a title if you have no son to leave it to?'

He stood back. 'My God, Bella! I didn't expect that from you! Anyway, it wouldn't be that kind of title, not a hereditary one. Only one that would last my lifetime.' He drank his tea.

'You'd better go soon then. I can't think. I want you with me all the time, not just now and then. *How* can I meet Rob?'

'How can I go on, knowing that he's wanted you all these years? But I didn't know he was alive. Oh hell! What's going to happen to us all?'

He left early. He kissed her tenderly, and she clung to him as though it was a good-bye. He walked out of the alley, and straight home.

Tomorrow. All would depend on how Bella felt about Rob tomorrow.

*

'You'd better let me go in and see mother first. I telephoned the office I'd be late going in. Wait just outside the close. I'll go in, and I'll give you a shout when she's ready.'

He turned his key in the door and called, 'Hello, mother!'

'Hello, son, you're early.'

She was up and dressed, a little slow, and lonely this last year since her friend Flora had gone, but spry and clean and cheerful.

'Mother, have you a cup of tea to spare?'

'Surely, son. What's the matter you're not at work?'

'I had a bit of news. I thought I'd come and tell you.'

'Oh? Is it Jenny at last?'

He flushed. 'No, mother, it's not Jenny. It's very good news, and I wanted to be sure you'd be all right.'

'It's Rob! You've heard from him!'

'No. I haven't *heard* from him. I've *seen* him! Steady, mother, sit down and I'll bring him.'

'Where is he?'

'At the close.'

'My boy, my Robbie. Oh Willie, where is he?'

Willie opened the door. Rob turned to him, and walked slowly into the house.

'I knew all along!' said Millie quietly, and the tears streamed down her face.

*

Afterwards, Bella wondered how she had actually got through that first meeting with Robbie.

She saw the two men come across the baker's yard in the bright sunshine, and Willie, the younger, stood a head above the slight, slow-moving figure of Rob. As always, when she saw Willie, her heart raced, and she wondered if Rob would see in her face what she felt must be there for all to see.

'Hello, Bella. I've brought him. Here she is, Rob, just like I said!'

'Bella. Is it really you? The last time I saw you, you had pigtails, and you had on a brown dress with a velvet collar, and a sailor hat and brown kid gloves!'

He held her hand and stared at her, as if he was afraid she would disappear.

'Well, I think I'll leave you two to get acquainted. You'll come to the office, Rob, and then we'll go back and see mother. I've sent a telegram to Jenny. Bye-bye, Rob, Bella. I'll see you both soon.'

'Aye, I've got a lot to say to Bella. I'll be up at your office when I'm ready.'

Willie left, with a backward look at Bella. She saw it, but she didn't look up. She poured some tea.

'I think I should never have gone away, Bella.'

'Would it have made any difference?'

'I should have waited, and watched over you – to see that nothing hurt you.'

'Maybe it was meant to be.'

'Maybe. These babies here – they look fine bairns.'

'Aye, their father was a fine man.'

(Why was she on the defensive? What was Rob planning, or thinking, in his mind?)

'I was angry when they told me that you had been – hurt – just after you married that man – Oh Bella! I couldn't *do* anything. I wanted to come. I wish to God I had. You wouldn't have been hurt any more.'

'Nobody hurt me after that. I worked hard, that's all.'

'There was a boy, wasn't there, before that?'

'Yes. Sandy. He's in Australia. He writes regularly every month.'

'Well, I've come to ask you Bella – and I *will* ask you. I can't keep trying to catch you between husbands! I've loved you ever since you were a baby. I've never loved anybody else. I want you to marry me, Bella. I'll take care of you, and the two wee ones, if you'll let me. You'll never want for anything. I can give you . . . '

'Oh stop! Stop! I don't want to think about anything, yet. And I'd better tell you before anybody else does. Joe and I weren't married. He died. The week before Jim Morrison died. And he never knew about the babies. Neither did I until he was gone.'

'Bella! Bella, my wee love. It doesn't matter. It doesn't matter at all. I've found you now, and I'm going to take care of you.'

And suddenly, she liked him. She saw him, all at once, as he really was. He was good and kind, like Joe, but there the likeness ended. Joe had been quick and fiery, and sometimes unpredictable. Rob was solid, slow, warm, and a safe anchor.

'It doesn't matter about that. Not being married, I mean. I'll adopt the wee ones. I've waited over thirty years, Bella!

'I'll need time to think. I had to go to Willie for help.'

'*Did* he help you?'

'Oh yes. He gave me two pounds a week. That was all I needed.'

'You shouldn't have *had* to go to him. He should have seen that you were all right.'

'Well, he's helped me anyway, and I can still wash a bit.'

'No more washing, unless you wash for me! Now I suppose I'd better go and see Willie. Will you think about what I've asked you?'

'Yes, Rob; I will.'

'I love you, Bella. I didn't know how it would be after all these years, but I still love you. Don't keep me waiting too long. I'll be back in a day or two. Have you enough money?'

'Yes, yes. Willie left me some yesverday.'

'All right, but don't go short. Is there anything you want?'

'Oh, well, if you're thinking of that. The one thing I want in this world is a house on the Lyle Hill!'

But she laughed. Funnily enough, he was easier to talk to than she had thought.

When he had gone, she dressed the twins, and got them ready for a walk. She had to think, and plan. This, she knew, was the turning point. It was madness to live in the hope that some day she might really belong to Will. If she married Rob, she wouldn't cheat. She would be true and faithful. That much she owed to her mother and father, and to the teaching of the church, so long ago. Church had never meant much to Joe: he said it was something made up by rich folk to keep poor people quiet: just let them think they would get everything in the next world, and they wouldn't ask for anything in this!

She shrank from the thought of letting any other man take her in love, after the ecstasy of being in Will's arms. But there had to be a last time, with Will. It had to come. She looked at the shops with a slight wonder; this was something new to her. It would be nice to be able just to *buy* things. She looked at the twins in the basket pram. They would have a name, anyway; a proud name; something dear Joe would have been glad about.

There could be only the one answer.

XXXI

Rob had written to Benny, at the address of his London house, and it was only a few weeks afterwards that he got the invitation to the wedding of the Duke of Peterbridge, to the Lady Margaret Rowland at St Margaret's Church, Westminster, on 20th December 1882. A personal note with the formal invitation said that the Duke would be very pleased if Rob would also bring his brother and wife: he felt he ought to meet them.

Rob was as pleased as a boy: Jenny too. This *was* moving in the best circles! She had met Lady Margaret – how Jenny wished *she* could be 'Lady Jenny'! Margaret, thirty-two years old, untouched, shy, and plain, had been offered as a suitable bride for the long-lost Duke. The marriage was so eminently 'suitable' in every way. Both from long lines of aristocracy, and the marriage would probably produce, in time, an heir to the title and considerable estates, and so the hierarchy of the landed gentry would be upheld, at all costs.

Willie sent a letter of thanks, but pleaded pressure of business for himself. But he was glad that Rob could escort Jenny. He needed some time to be with Bella.

It was ironic, he thought, that he could see his wife go away with his brother without a pang, and know that he was going to his brother's future wife for the love that his brother would never have. The short two years of his affair with Bella had to end. He knew it, and so did she.

The train pulled out of Glasgow Central, and Rob and Jenny settled for the long journey in their first-class compartment. Although he had always been a silent kind of man, Rob enjoyed Jenny's chatter. She made him tell her of his early days in America. She couldn't remember him, she said, she was only three when he went away. Now she was nearly thirty. Thirty! 'An old woman,' she said charmingly.

She listened, entranced, to the story of his first venture into property and land, and the gold mine that he and Jimmy had named, in a fit of happy madness, the 'Lou-Belle'.

The journey passed pleasantly enough, and they arrived at the terminus, where a hansom cab took them to Brown's Hotel. Jenny was thrilled to be among these distinguished people: although she had been accepted in society, as a whole, she had never been right in the exclusive upper bracket of the titles.

It had worried her a little that now Rob was back, the money he had left to Will would have to go back, and Jenny liked having money. Not for its own sake, but for what it could do. There was comfort for her, however. Rob was not concerned with what had passed: there was more than enough for the future. Willie had made his own way, and if Rob's money had helped him, then that was a good thing.

'Oh! That's good of you, Robbie! It would be awful to

have to worry about money now! We were so poor when we were young.'

Rob patted her hand as they waited for the carriage to take them to the reception.

'Well, you won't be poor any more, my dear . . . now, I'm sure you'll like old Benny.'

She was the loveliest woman at the reception. Her hair was piled in small curls on top of her head: where most of the women wore low-cut gowns, Jenny's was high to her neck, trimmed with silver lace, and the bosom tantalisingly outlined by the cut of her corset underneath. The heavy satin fell away in folds at the back, giving the effect of a small train. She wore white gloves, and carried a fan of ivory lace, just a shade lighter than the gown, laced with ostrich feathers. Not to outshine the bride, not pure white, but a delicate pale creamy colour. She looked exquisite.

She came into the room on Robbie's arm, and they were announced, 'Mr Robert Munro, and Mrs William Munro.' She nodded and smiled, as she passed through the guests; she did know some of these people. When they could get through the crush, a figure detached itself from a small group near the centre table, and dived straight for Rob.

'Hello, Jock! Hello, old son. Glad you could come. Is this your good lady?'

'Who? Oh no. This is my sister-in-law, Jenny. My brother is the MP for Greenock. Jenny, this is my very old friend, Benny – the Duke of Peterbridge.'

Jenny stood, speechless. She could not speak, or move. For the first time in her life, she felt the ache and hurt of desire. She could not know what it was; she had never even dreamed there was such a feeling. It was a wild, searing flame that went from her knees to her head; her heart pounded frighteningly. From far away she heard her own voice say 'How-do-you-do' and then someone said, 'Are you all right, Jenny? and then she was on a chair and somebody said, 'Give her air, it's too hot in here,' and the swimming in her head lessened a bit, and he was bending over her, kind, solicitous . . .

'Do you feel better, Mrs Munro?'

'Yes, yes thank you.'

'A glass of brandy. Where's my footman? Ah! good.'

Rob stood by and patted her hand, totally bewildered.
The Duke smiled at him and nodded.

'She's a lovely girl, your sister-in-law. There, I think
she'll be all right. I'll send the Duchess's maid to take her
to one of the bedrooms. I'm sorry it's so hot. She *is* a
beauty.'

'Who? Jenny? Yes, I suppose so.'

'Brother an MP, you said?'

'Yes. Liberal MP I'm afraid, not a Tory!'

The Duke shrugged. 'It's not important. We must have
her and you, of course, and her husband up to Yorkshire,
when we get back from Europe.'

Rob laughed. 'You'll spoil her! And she's already
spoilt. What she wants now is a title for Will, my
brother.'

'A title, eh?'

He looked at Rob. 'Not you, I suppose?'

'Me? Not likely. I'm quite happy. I've got Bella. We're
getting married at the end of this month.'

'H'm, well, I have, I think, the ear of the Prince. Now,
come and meet my Duchess. You know, Jock,' as they
moved away from the crowd when Jenny had been
tenderly taken away by two footmen and a lady's maid, 'I
don't think I'll stand much of this life. I think I'll go back
to Canada, some day. Come with me?'

Rob shook his head, smiling.

'Ah well, that's how it goes.'

Jenny was silent when they went back to the hotel. She
did some shopping next day, and went quietly with Rob
to the train to take them home.

Jenny had no love: but Jenny, perhaps, had some kind
of – courage?

XXXII

Sometimes Bella woke up in the middle of the night cold with fear, missing most of all the comfort of Joe's arms, rather than the passion and delight of Willie's embraces. And it seemed that this fear and indecision would remain with her for ever.

What a mess she had made of her life! Was she always to be put off with second-best? If only she could have really loved Joe, if he had lived, if Willie had not married Jenny – and she grew hot with hate at the sheer vandalism of Jenny's travesty of marriage. If – if – if . . . ! The nights dragged – and the days were spent in planning the furnishing of a house that she had always wanted, to live in with a man she didn't even know. And yet – she had known him . . . She remembered the joy she had felt as a child, riding on his back as he turned and twisted round the floor with her, with his muffler for reins and her heels spurring him on, round the table, over to the fire, and, with a heave, into her father's arms.

She looked at Joe's babies, and remembered the hungry days, the cold, biting days of washing on the lines, the spits and jeers of angry women, the torture of a bruised and beaten body, and then at the terrible, recurring nightmare, the picture of small bare feet struggling over broken ice. And she knew she must take what the gods offered. She was very lucky to have the chance of such a good man to care for her. Thousands of women envied her, even this second-best.

She must see Willie once more, one night more, before she left this wee place where she had known peace and tranquillity. Then she would be true and faithful to Rob; she would be respected and respectable.

Rob and Jenny were expected home on the 24th, in time for Christmas. Willie helped her pack up her few treasures, some books that had belonged to Joe, pictures, newspaper cuttings, so much that reminded her of him.

'What are we going to do, Bella?'

'Do? I'm getting married, Willie.'

'I know. Does that mean we can't . . . ?'

'Yes. I won't cheat on Rob. I don't love him, but he loves me, and so did Joe. What a mix-up! But I can't, I *can't*. Oh God, Willie! I *can't* give you up! I can't live without you. I can't *be* without you. Take me away somewhere, just the two of us. I *can't* give you up!'

'Hush now, Bella, don't cry. *I* can't cheat my brother, either. This has got to end. I know it too, and I don't want it to end, either.'

'What will you do? Who will . . . ?'

'Who will love me, eh? Somebody, I expect . . . '

She shuddered. 'I'll settle the babies for the night. This will be our last night, Willie. Make some tea, while I get the bairns' milk.'

The night passed all too quickly. Never had her love been so fierce, so possessive, nor he so demanding . . . nor consequences so summarily dismissed.

He left her asleep, and went out into the dark morning, to cold, deserted, slushy streets.

*

Two years later, the summons came from Her Majesty, the first Victoria, to attend Her Majesty, and receive the accolade of the sword on the shoulder, and arise, Our True and Faithful Knight, Sir William Munro.

And His Lady.

XXXIII

Rob took a two-room flat in South street, while the house was being built. On the day after New Year 1883 they were married in Willie's house, and by the end of September, when her son was born, they were just ready to move in. Rob was almost delirious with joy. He grabbed Willie's arm. 'I thought I was useless after my accident. Mother, you've got a grandson at last. Isn't he braw? We'll call him John for Bella's father. Are you all right, Bella my love?'

She smiled faintly. Yes, she was all right. She had the best of everything. Life would be good, now, and always.

When she got up, after the birth, she walked out and stood to look at the beauty all round her. This, after all, was what it was all about. She thought she would never have got over the day of wonder and joy – the first day Rob had brought her up here to see the house, not yet papered or painted. It was almost too much to bear. This should be the reward of virtue, not a gift to a woman who had not always kept the Commandments she had been brought up to respect. But she was *here:* it was actually *true:* she was to live in a house on the hill. This almost unearthly grandeur made a mockery of all the petty struttings of puny humans defying destiny, or plunging into careless rapture with no thought of time or retribution.

Whatever, then had been, or still was, between her and Willie, it had no place here.

Whatever, then, had been, could be no more. This was
the meaning of her life. It was as if, just by opening her
arms, wide, she could encompass the whole world of
these glories.

It was a long steep hill, up to the summit. Rob said, 'I'll
get you a horseless carriage, Bella.'

XXXIV

The children were too young to remember the removal
from the flat in South Street to the grand new house. The
house seemed to grow round them in the years that came
on. It was hushed when Millie died in her sleep, and it
boomed with laughter and shouting as the children grew
up, and the McGarvie children came to play, and grow,
and fall in love.

Andy's three children David, Elizabeth, inevitably
called Bessie, and young delicate Hugh, gazed in awe at
the rich carpets, the gas lights, and the bathroom. Young
Joe, now adopted and brought up as Munro, with his
sister Florrie, accepted their adoration as naturally as
they adored their mother. Joe was quick and eager, and
clever, snatching at bright life with both hands, helping
his sister build castles with bricks, and picking her up
when she fell: and she remained solemn, quiet and shy.
That they were Joe Mulligan's children could easily be
seen. The new baby, Jack, was everybody's favourite.

Bella found her hours and days filled to overflowing.
The big house to be kept clean, three children to be cared
for, but hard work had never bothered her, and she was

well and happy. She had a garden and a good wash-house, and she was sure she could manage.

Willie called to see them often, but since that night of tempestuous memory, she had never been alone with him. If her heart ached for her lost love, she never showed it. Rob helped her in small ways around the house, but he was slow, and sometimes she became impatient with him, and then was sorry afterwards. He was so good, kind and warm, thoughtful and willing, and he lavished his love on the twins equally with the little one, Jackie.

It was a day early in March when they had been in the house about six months. There was a knock at the door, and Bella went, drying her hands on her apron, from her wash-tub. A woman stood there, with a young girl by her side.

'Bella? Hello Bella.'

'Oh it's Maggie! Maggie, oh lassie, come away in. My goodness, you've climbed all the way up here. Come in. This is . . . it's Annie, isn't it?'

'Aye.' Maggie followed Bella into the sitting-room, and looked round her appreciatively. 'Aye, it's Annie. She's seventeen now, and she doesn't like working in the shop, where she's been. I'm thinking she should go into service, and I wondered . . . Well, Eddie and I wondered if you would know of anybody who . . . ?'

'Maggie, do you know, Rob just said to me this morning that he would get me a girl. This is really too much for me . . . after all, I'm nearly forty! Maggie, would Annie come to me?'

Maggie grinned. 'That's what we came for!' she said happily.

'Well, that's splendid, Annie. I'll teach you to keep house nicely, and wash and iron. And then when you want to get another place, or go and get married, you'll be more experienced. Would you like that, Annie?'

Annie was heard to mumble into her mother's sleeve that 'she didn't want to go anywhere else'.

So Annie's father brought her tin box, and Annie

stayed till she was carried out, in a flower-covered coffin, when she was seventy.

Bella made a lot of improvements to the house. She loved any kind of new inventions, and as soon as telephones were available for private houses, she had one put in.

So the years rolled on, and the world rolled on, to crisis and tragedy. And the children grew, and the golden-haired Florrie, who was Joe Mulligan's daughter, loved young David McGarvie as soon as she realised that he was quite different from her brother Joe. That was when she was twelve, and David about fifteen.

*

The Conservative and Unionist Party put up Mr George Heathley as candidate in the General Election of 1895. As sitting member, it seemed probable that Willie would retain the seat. The Tory Party, under Balfour, was divided and exhausted, and their integrity largely discredited.

With Bella supporting him, and the lovely Jenny canvassing so charmingly, the result was not unexpected. Bella spoke at meetings, and organised gatherings in her home. The fundamental policies were not altogether to her liking: she had learned so much from Joe. She had seen so many hungry children, had seen, and could still see, the flashing razor of despair in the brilliant sunshine. And she herself had suffered at the hands of Mrs Heathley.

She felt herself drawn more and more to the Church, so, although the church she had known as a child was no longer within the realms of the Scottish Presbyterian Church, she joined another one, nearer to the house on the hill.

'Joe used to say that the church was just a pan – pan – '

'Panacea?' said Willie.

They were sitting in her well-furnished sitting-room,

over tea. Rob and Willie were at the table, and Bella sat in a deep armchair, animated, content and happy in her surroundings and her company. She had grown a little plump – after all, she was over 47! Rob loved to sit and listen to Willie and Bella. They had achieved that almost impossible relationship that comes between a man and a woman after a devouring love affair.

'That's right . . . a panacea for all ills, like a cup of tea,' Bella answered.

'Yes, he was an extreme socialist.'

'And a good man!' Bella snapped.

'Yes, a good man, Bella, but the world isn't ready for his kind yet.'

'Will it ever be?'

'Some day,' said Rob. 'But it's got a long way to go. It'll be another hundred years or more.'

'There were hungry children *fifty* years ago. Do you mean to tell me there will *still* be hungry children in *another* hundred years?' Bella was furious.

Will looked thoughtfully at Rob.

'I want to see a healthy economy with Lloyd George. He stands against the taxing of food, which the Unionist Party wants to do.'

'Women ought to have a vote,' Bella chimed in again.

'They will, they will, but not yet. I must think of something . . . Bella, are you sure Joe didn't have anything else he was working on? After the King Charles thing?'

Rob sat up.

'What King Charles?' he demanded.

So they had to tell him about the events, and about the paper that Bella had taken from the library . . .

'Where is it now, Bella?' Willie asked.

'Back in the library.'

'Back in . . . What do you mean, Bella? How did you–?'
She twinkled.

'I took them in openly to Mr Westfield, he was the head librarian, if you remember. He was absolutely flabbergasted! I said I had borrowed them, because Mr

Mulligan had wanted to see them, and I thought I'd better show him where to put the envelope back!'

'Bella, you are the limit,' Will said.

'Well, I didn't tell any lies. But all the papers had been shifted and we couldn't find the place I had taken them from. So he said he'd get them bound properly, and put them among the very special papers in the archives. So you see, that's that. But I have got something else . . . and I don't know what to do about it.'

Bella hesitated.

'I'll leave it for a day or two. I have to think about it first. But I don't think you'll need anything more, Willie. You've proved yourself a good MP. I think you'll win anyway.'

Sir William Munro, MP, was returned as Liberal candidate with a large majority.

Jenny was rather happy.

XXXV

A feeling of dreadful expectancy hung over everything all that long hot summer when Florrie Munro and David McGarvie fell in love. Church was still the favourite place for young people to meet, the Bible class, and socials, and although they lived at opposite ends of the town, David came often to see the family – and Florrie.

There was a war, in faraway places – there was the death of a Queen and a country in mourning – and some of Mrs Foster's ten sons did not come home . . .

Florrie and David lay on the hill in a little hollow with whin and mulberry bushes hiding them, the setting sun giving a golden glow over the purple hills, stars coming lazily into view like diamonds on black velvet, and distant trees making a pattern of black lace against the sky.

> He came for me in the twilight,
> With laughing lips and eyes.
> He took me away to a woodland glade,
>   Where shadowy stardust lies.
>
> On top of the gleaming pathway,
> We watched the moon arise,
> And there in the stillness I gave my heart
>   For a glance from his laughing eyes.
>
> He went from me in the twilight,
> There was never a hint of pain
> In my answering smile to his gay farewell,
>   'Until we meet again' . . .

'You'll have to go, Davie? To the war?'

'Aye, love. Florrie, oh Florrie, I don't want to leave you. What have *I* got to do with people in South Africa? I feel I'll never see you again. Tell me again you love me?'

'I love you, Davie. I love you always, all my life. I'll keep myself for you.' This was a whisper into his waistcoat buttons.

'Florrie! Florrie love, I can't stand it. I've got to go. Kiss me, hold me.'

'Davie love, I want only you. Hold me, love me, love me.'

David marched away, swinging his kilt, marched away with his braw young countrymen. The Jocks are always there, in every battle . . .

He loved the house on the hill too, and in the hot desert ditches of bloody war, he remembered the green lawn in his last moments, when he could still feel the searing agony of pain in his legs – although they were not there at all.

But he will not come with the sunset,
He will not come with the dawn.
I have lost the path to the woodland glade,
Where the shadowy stardust shone.

For my love, my love lies bleeding,
And his heart is cold as stone.
Life's love and laughter are fled from me now,
And the glory for ever gone.

XXXVI

The rain lashed with savage fury at the windows,
bounced in little cascades off the pavements and made
little pools of mud in the grass and gravel paths round the
garden. A miserable, dull day in a dark, dreary, cold
February.

Annie came in and put some letters at Rob's place at
the breakfast table. He looked casually at them, and then
gave a kind of whoop. 'Bella! A letter from Jimmy. Wait a
minute. Oh gosh! they're coming over for a holiday! It
will be grand to see them again. I wonder how Martha is
. . .'

He broke off and looked at Bella.

She would probably not have noticed if he had not
stopped what he was saying. She looked up from her
plate. Florrie got up and started clearing the table, to
help Annie. Joe had his eyes on a book, while he gulped
tea and gave an occasional glance at the clock.

'Martha? Who's Martha?'

'Oh.' Rob looked embarrassed. 'A girl in America,
friend of Jimmy and Louise. Jack, have you finished?

Right, off you go to work. You going to be in time for your train, Joe?'

'Yes, just off. Ta-ta.'

'Joe seems to be enjoying being at the University. Did you like school, Rob?'

'*No*, Bella, I didn't! That's why I had to go to the Mechanics' Institute . . . to learn something while I was waiting for you to grow up!'

'Well, I think Jack takes after you. He never seemed to care whether he went to school or not. Who's Martha?'

'Bella, I never meant that there would be anybody in my life but you. But Martha was . . . She was a nice girl. I needed somebody. When you're young, you know, it seems different. More sort of necessary.'

'Were you married?'

'*No!*' He was vehement. 'I swore I'd marry only one girl, and that was you, Bella. But she came to live with me. She was very good to me.'

'Just like Joe was with me,' said Bella, with a soft, reminiscent sigh, as she looked out far beyond the rain streaming down the windows.

'Yes. We've both been guilty of – what is it – adultery?'

'Not you. *I* was. You weren't married, or promised. I was. But they were good years, Rob.'

'So were mine with Martha. But she knew I loved you.'

'Anyway, your letter. Jimmy and Louise are coming?'

'They're leaving New York on the 28th February. They'll be here two weeks after that. My, it only takes two weeks now.'

'That gives me time to get their room ready. Will they stay here all the time?'

'He says they want to get about. Here's the letter – you read it. I'll go and write a reply.'

'". . . want to go and see London and maybe Paris. . . " oh Rob! My goodness – all that, and there's still so many poor people. It's all wrong, Robbie!'

'Now, now, Bella, you promised you wouldn't fret so

much over the affairs of the world; and I'm glad I've been able to give *you* all you need. It will all come right, some day. And *you've* had your share of being poor, *and* done your share to help people. Now, I think I'll go and write to Jimmy. A letter will just get to him before he sails.'

Bella read right through Jimmy's letter, mostly written by Louise. Jimmy was never a writer!

. . . thought you'd like to know that Martha Hallam that was, married the minister of the wee church. We all thought she was for staying an old maid, because she's not so young now . . . she must be fifty-six or fifty-seven, but they seem quite happy, and she always did a lot of work for the church. I told her we were thinking of visiting the Old Country soon, and she said to give you her very kindest wishes. She hopes you're very happy. Well, old chum, hope to see you real soon.

Love from Jimmy and Louise.

'Bella! What year is it?'

'Oh, Rob – really! It's 1904 – You are the limit!'

'I might ask you the same thing tomorrow; I can't remember these things!'

The great day came at last – a day of bitter wind and sun, a day of hard brightness that tore at papers and hats and swept them away.

The big steamer dropped anchor at Princes Pier, and all the family were down on the pier to meet the tender. Such talk and reminiscing – such memories over the re-union of two old friends.

' . . . and when he walked in that day I can tell you, Bella – I thought I was sent for!'

'It was the same with me – when I walked down the stairs and found him standing in my front hall,' Willie had to chime in.

'Tell them, Jimmy, how it happened.'

'Aye, lass. Well, you see, I'd just got one of these new-fangled telephones. Anyway, it seems Rob here went into the hotel, and asked for a room. Then, he asked the manager if Mr Miller still lived in the town. Well, I did, but we'd moved to a bigger hoose, ye ken. So the manager says, "I'll telephone Mr Miller and see if he's in." So he did, and our young George answered it.

'And he says, "Pa, there's a Mr Munro waiting for you at the hotel." Well, you know, my heart missed a beat – and then I thought – you daft sod, it's very likely Willie here from Scotland. So I shouted to Louise that we might have a visitor – Rob's brother – and I got into my buggy and went down to the hotel. Well, as I said, I thought St Peter had sent for me. My! That was a day!'

'Have another drink, Jimmy; thirsty work, talking.' Willie held his hand out for Jimmy's glass.

'But I don't understand,' he said, as he poured from the decanter, 'how it happened that he could be alive after all, and we didn't know.'

'*I* puzzled about that too. You see how it was; I went straight back to New York and straight home. Old Benny – I beg his pardon – the Duke! – said he would be going to Dawson City as soon as the floods stopped. It seems the thaw lasted a few weeks and caused flooding, so that he had to wait till it was all cleared away. Meantime he'd worked on Rob, and got him alive again – thank God! – and wrote to me and posted it in Dawson. But I never got it. It may be lying at the bottom of a post-office sack or something – but it's just one of the funny things that can happen. But when I saw him, man, I tell you – I got a fright . . . Here's your bonnie wee health, Bella and Rob and all the family!'

Jimmy and Louise stayed for the summer – then went to London, and across to Paris and to Monte Carlo, and came back fit and well; glad – and a little bit sorry – to be going home.

And then they were gone – leaving a glow, a serenity that only the timeless bonds of true friendship can hold.

*

Rob pottered about the garden, walked along the hill
road, slowly, or went with Bella in their horseless
carriage, into town, or church, and down into Gourock
and Ashton.

At seventy-one, he was beginning to feel a little bit
tired, forgetful. The only things he remembered clearly,
of his old life, were strangely the years with Benny in the
snows of Canada which were clear and complete in his
mind, except for *when* it was! And he remembered
vividly, Bella, as a baby, and the little cot he had made
for her.

'Where is it, Bella?'

'Where's what, Rob?'

'The wee crib I made for you.'

'I told you, Rob. Andy had it for his children, and
then I got it back. It's out in the wash-house.'

'Aye, so you did.'

And without warning, Rob sat down in his chair one
day, and died. Cerebral haemorrhage, the doctor said.
Perhaps he had had some news that worried or upset
him? Yes, just the day before, they had got the news that
his old friend, the Duke of Peterbridge, had died in
Canada, in the offices of the Hudson Bay Company. He
had left his duchess, and a son of eighteen, now the duke,
who was studying at Oxford.

And in another house, a fashionable meeting place for
the élite of the town, when Lady Munro heard of the
death of the duke, she shut the windows of her elegant
bedroom, turned on the gas fire, and forgot to light it . . .

She had met him, and spoken to him, only once in her
life, and she had lived all these years in the loneliness of
an empty title. Her 'm'lady' was empty, empty.

XXXVII

Florrie withered in the years after the Boer War, but she said no word to anyone about her night of loving and giving.

Willie came to see Bella some time after Jenny's death.

'Bella, I think I'll have a trip to America. See Jimmy and Louise again. I wondered . . . ' He broke off, and looked rather sheepish.

'What? What is it, Willie?'

'I just thought, now Rob's gone, Jenny's gone, we could . . . we could be together, if you would marry me . . . '

He broke off again, and looked away from her. 'It would be companionship. We're both older now, but I'd take care of you, Bella, and we wouldn't be lonely any more.'

Bella smiled, and gave a soft little laugh.

'You didn't like me once, Willie,' she said.

'I thought I didn't. Well, will you come with me to America?'

'No, Willie.'

'Are you sure?'

'Quite sure. I said I'd never leave here, and please God, I never will.' She hesitated. 'Willie, tell me, was Rob very rich?'

'Very, very rich,' he assured her solemnly.

'Oh.'

'You'll never want again, Bella, as long as you live. You'll never have to leave the bairns and come to me for help.'

'Don't! Don't, Willie. I didn't know where to turn.'

'I'm glad you did come to me that night. You gave me a lot more than I gave you. Happiness, and my self-respect. Bella . . . ' He hesitated again. 'Tell me: Jack. Rob's gone, Jenny's gone. Is he . . . I'd like to know, Bella. Is he Rob's son, or mine?'

She turned away, just for a moment. Then she turned and faced him, straight and serious.

'Jack is a Munro. That's all I have to say, Willie.'

'Ah well, I suppose that's the way it has to be. You know best. So, I'll take a trip to see Jimmy, and when I come back, Bella, will you . . . could you . . . ?'

'No, lad. The storm has passed. But there's no reason why you shouldn't come and live here. The boys would like a man in the house, and you know Florrie and Annie adore you! Off you go, and come back to all of us.'

He was thoughtful for a moment.

'Do you remember that first election I fought, when you had the papers from the library?'

'Yes?' She looked at him with a reminiscent smile.

'Well, there *was* something else I should have told you – don't look so frightened, Bella! I thought of the three wee laddies – you know, when they stowed away on Morrison's ship?' (She closed her eyes.) 'Then there was the Merchant Navy Shipping Act in 1894 – but I thought, you can't stop boys wanting to go to sea – especially Greenock boys! So I thought it would be a good thing to be able to teach them something about sea-going. I've given my house, Bella, for an extension of the Nautical Training School in Glasgow. That's the best I can do, love.'

He looked at her rather apologetically.

She jumped up and hugged him, resting her head contentedly on his chest, and said, 'I love you, Willie!'

'I'm awful fond of you, Bella.'

She sighed.

'Och! Get away with you, lad. But – it seems it might be confession time.'

'What do you mean, lass?'

'You remember I said there was something else I wanted to do, apart from the papers?' He nodded. 'And you remember that day I went to the Parish – and what I said to Mrs Heathley?'

'Good God! What have you done now, girl?'

'Not what I've done – what I intend to do.'

'All right – go on.' He sat on an armchair and stretched his legs out in front, in great comfort, and lit his pipe.

'I found out, about two years ago, that she had stolen ten pounds from the church bazaar funds.'

He stopped with a match half-way to his pipe.

'Never!'

'I had to deputise for her, one bazaar day – she had had a slight accident. You know she was treasurer – she was in *everything* – I counted up the money we had taken, and put a slip in the cash box for the minister. It was £168.16.4½d. When the minister read it out in church the following Sunday, he said it was £158.16.6d.'

'You're sure about this, Bella?'

'Quite sure.'

'What are you going to do?'

'I said I'd see her in Hell – and now I think I can. For the way she's treated the poor people of this town for years.'

'Be careful, love. She's got a lot of friends.'

'So have I!' she laughed. 'I'll deal with her. Now get away to America, lad, and come back to us, and be with the family. There's only us two left now, of the old ones. We all love you . . . '

Mrs Heathley was surprised to have a telephone call from the matriarchal Mrs Munro. She had never given another thought to the shabby woman who told her twenty-odd years before that she would 'see her in Hell first', because there were so many who wished her the very same fate.

'Yes, Mrs Heathley would be delighted to come to tea with Mrs Munro; delighted.'

A new horseless carriage brought her, resplendent in fox fur, to the front door.

Annie opened the door, proud in her cap and apron. Proud she was, and happy. This was a bad woman, and *they* would show her . . .

So she announced Mrs Heathley, formally, with a very tongue-in-cheek look at Bella.

Florrie got up from the sofa near the fire.

'I'll make the tea, mother.'

'Yes, Florrie, that would be nice. You'll take a cup of tea, Mrs Heathley?'

'Oh yes, thank you, Mrs Munro. So kind of you.'

I hear there are some distressing cases coming before the Board these days. Can I help? A donation, or something?'

'Not at all, Mrs Munro, thank you. Such lovely china. There's so much malingering.'

'Surely not. The whole country is in the same state. Something wrong, surely, after a dreadful war? It's not easy for people to come and ask for help.'

'Nonsense! That class . . . no sense of independence, or looking for work.'

'So you send some of them to the workhouse?'

'Yes, of course.'

'What are you going to do when the workhouse is full?'

Mrs Heathley's face crimsoned.

'Do you remember telling *me*, Mrs Heathley, that you would send me to the workhouse, when I had two little babies, and no money? And you would have taken my babies from me too? And do you remember what I said to you that day? Do have some more tea, Mrs Heathley. I can afford it now.'

Her tone was bitter, sarcastic, and murderous. She contained herself with difficulty. After all these years, this woman was just the same; had no regrets or humanity.

Agnes Heathley stuttered and spluttered.

'Oh! I didn't know it was you. That you would . . . '

'That I would become a rich woman, and also, become the treasurer of the Churchwomen's Guild?'

'I was only doing my duty.'

'Your duty? Well now, it was your duty, was it not, to be the treasurer of *your* women's guild for bazaars and other functions?'

There was a wary look in Agnes Heathley's face now. She didn't answer. Florrie came in with a fresh pot of tea.

'Florrie?'

'Yes, mother?'

'Before you go out, will you bring me that wee brown box beside my bed – the little wooden box with a brass handle on top.'

'Yes, mother.'

Mrs Heathley hurriedly drank some more tea.

Bella opened the box. 'Thank you, Florrie.

'I replaced you at one bazaar when you had a slight accident, and I counted the takings. They came to £168.16.4½d. But the amount given in the newspaper gave *your* church's contribution as £158.16.6d. Did you give them the three-ha'pence to ease your conscience?'

Mrs Heathley was speechless. She thought quickly.

'It was a sudden impulse. I needed the money.'

'*You* needed the money? Ten pounds? I've seen your husband's ships come into the docks. I've seen the poor devils of Malays, and Chinese, the crews he got to work the ships for a handful of rice a day. *That's* how your family made its money, and God help us, you're not the only ones. I know other shipping lines . . . and then you have the *audacity*, the *impertinence*, to turn on people who can't answer back, and you give somebody the odd half-crown, and you have told at least *one* good woman to sell her wedding-ring. Well, you're going to stop it *now*, Mrs Heathley. You are going to resign. And you will pay this money back to the church. You can do it anonymously if you like, but pay it you will!'

'All of it?'

'*All* of it? Ten pounds? You mean there was more?'

The other woman bit her lip. She had made a false move. She was caught.

'Well! That's too much for *me!* We'd better consult the Town Clerk.'

'No! Oh no! It would kill my husband. Don't, please, Mrs Munro. I'll pay it all back.'

'All right. I said I'd see you in Hell, and I think you are pretty near it now. Right, when I see your resignation announced in the paper – from *all* your Offices! – and when I see an anonymous gift of – say – £200 – to the town for the relief of the poor, then I'll destroy this note. Better still, I'll send it to you. Goodbye, Mrs Heathley. Florrie, ask Annie to take Mrs Heathley to her motor.'

When the woman had gone, Bella walked out to the garden, and breathed the sharp, cold air.

She felt clean again: as though something monstrous had gone out of her life. She had achieved a small victory over one woman; she had been true to Joe's teaching. But had the long battle, begun so long ago, over a System, indeed been won? Not yet . . .

*

Willie stayed about two years in America, seeing all the projects that had made up the wealth of the brother he had loved so much. And he came back, to live in the house on the hill, where he was totally spoilt by Florrie and Annie, and of course, Bella.

XXXVIII

The German Bands seemed to be disappearing from the seaside towns: it seemed, also, that the only cure for the ills of poor people, and the spread of unemployment, was to take arms against somebody, anybody. Slump or war. It seems almost time to end this silly system.

But the system was still there, and there was poverty and injustice all round. And Mrs Heathley was replaced by a Mrs Hannah, who was, if anything, worse than her predecessor.

On an April day, a great ship, unsinkable, was sunk, with the loss of over a thousand lives. And a country, greedy for land and possessions, gathered its young men, and soon, millions of young men were left hanging on barbed wire, or sunk in Flanders mud.

But this time none of it touched the family on the hill. Andy McGarvie was too old; little Hughie was too delicate, and Joe Munro was exempt because of a slight cast in his left eye. Jack had an essential job in his uncle's coal firm. And peace came again, to the land fit for heroes.

They were sitting in the garden on a day of warm, bright sunshine. 'I think I'll go for a wee walk,' said Willie. 'Coming, Florrie?'

'Yes, Uncle Will. I'll get my hat.'

They walked slowly, and not very far, for Willie was now nearly 80, and felt his years.

They came back and had tea, then he and Bella sat and looked at the river, watching the sun set.

He reminisced absently, his thoughts far away.

'Jenny, a bonnie lass she was, but I never really knew her.' His voice trailed off.

He dozed a little, and then he said he would go and have a bath, and go to bed. He felt tired. Jack found him in the bath, when he broke the lock open.

Bella thought she could not live another day; she felt, still, all the love she had had for this man, ever since she was conscious of him at all, since she was eight – over sixty years! The storm had passed . . . but oh! the glory of its thunder, the splendour of its lightning – and the serenity of its passing.

Now she was really alone; the last one left of the old days – the last one, to remember how it used to be.

Now she watched them put the coffin down, deep in its narrow grave. She knew then, that some day they would meet again. When she had said his name softly to him as he lay shrouded in his coffin in the darkened room, he didn't answer.

'Willie,' she said, and again, 'Willie, my love.'

But he didn't answer.

She went out of the back door and stood a little while looking at the scene below.

'You must sit down, ma.' Florrie fussed with a light basket chair.

'I've lived a long time, Florrie, love.'

'You'll live a lot more, mother.'

'Aye, I have a feeling I will. But at least, I won't live to see another war. They said *that* was the war to end wars.'

*

She watched the 1924 election with some nostalgia, remembering Willie's first attempt, and her first words in public. The crowds in George's Square and Nelson Street that December night jostled and shoved . . . would the Socialist Party really get in? Oh! Joe Mulligan should be alive to see this day! At last – at last! Justice for all, fair shares for all! The men who *built* the ships, would be able to *travel* on the ships.

Not the Church now, but Socialism, was the panacea for all ills. And Ramsay MacDonald told them they would go up and up and they went off the Gold Standard whatever that meant and people laughed to see newspaper pictures of elderly, bearded Jewish men scrubbing pavements in Berlin and families had to separate because there was too much money coming into one household to qualify for the charity of Parish relief. ('You know,' said Bella, 'I think they've never forgiven Victoria for dying'.) Lovers found bliss, even on the dole; and politicians dared not defy the Balance of Power that shuddered at every frontier; long lines of unemployed men walked four hundred miles to London to ask for work; and men committed suicide rather than submit to the Means Test. (They were looked on as a separate species.)

Bessie McGarvie, Andrew's daughter, married Richard Carson, a gardener who worked in one of the big houses on the Argyllshire side of the river. She had two sons and a baby girl who died when only a few months old. The eldest boy, Matthew, eventually married Alice, the daughter of a river steamer Captain. Matt served his apprenticeship in the shipyard from 1918, when he was fourteen, till 1923. He, like the old member of the family, Robbie Munro, was a carpenter, and the yards were still, if somewhat precariously, building ships. Fewer and fewer.

Bella kept every member of the family, no matter how distant, within the circle of the house on the hill. Big buses ran up there now, and so many people had motor cars. It had all seemed so prosperous – when the war was on.

Matt and Alice had only one child, a boy. And the yards grew empty. A launch meant another empty basin. Repair work came in, small things, but the gradual dribble went on, and soon there were more men on the dole than there were working. Bella was angry. But in this case, helpless.

Then Mrs Heathley rode again in her successor, Mrs Hannah.

Matt held his wife in his arms while sobs shook her, and her hysterical moaning lessened.

'Hush, lassie, she's away. It's all right. I'll see to her.'

'Oh Matt! She's horrible, with her wee nose-specs, and her swanky costume – and such rings! She looked at the pan on the stove and opened the press. And you know my granny's silver wedding presents? She said we didn't need that, and the wee rug at the fire that we made last winter. Oh, Matt! What's to become of us?'

Matt carried her over to the bed, and laid her gently in it and covered her with a quilt. The sobbing subsided into broken weeping, and he found a tiny spot of whisky in a bottle at the back of a cupboard. (Heaven help them if Mrs Hannah had found *that!*) He poured it into a glass and added a drop of water.

'Come on, lass, drink this, and tell me what happened. What made her come here? I haven't asked for Assistance?'

'No, I know. But somebody must have told her I had new clothes, that coat Auntie Bella gave me. And I got shoes for Bobbie with the money she gave me, since you've been on the dole, all these years. Oh Matt! Is it never going to end?'

She started weeping again, tears of heavy quietness, unutterably sad and hopeless.

'I'll knock her bloody brains out so I will. I'd like to choke the life out of her. There there, Alice love. It must end soon. Go on, tell me what she said.'

'She looked in the soup pan, and then she said they'd likely cut your dole money if we kept on getting gifts from friends. And if we needed any more, I could . . . could sell my wedding ring.'

Matt's face went grey; the knuckles of his clenched fist were white with the agony of clutching at something, anything, to stave off the blackness that surrounded him. He said through his teeth, 'Christ! They're still saying *that!* They told somebody else that years ago, Auntie Bella told me.' But he went on. 'I'll swing for that bloody woman yet, so help me. I'm going on the march, to London. It's time the working people got together and showed them how strong we are. Hush noo, lassie. I'll make you a wee cup of tea. She'll no' come and say these things to you again. *I'll* sort her. You're right, it's been too long like this. Since after the war. Damn it to hell!' His anger boiled up again.

'Is this what my Uncle Davie died for . . . and millions like him?'

'Will you *have* to go on the march, Matt?'

'Aye, lass, I'll need to go. But I'll make sure that woman doesn't worry you any more.'

'What are you going to do, Matt?'

'Nothing very drastic,' he smiled. 'Only take you to stay with Auntie Bella till I get back. I remember how your dad and mother helped her, when she needed it, before Uncle Joe and Auntie Florrie were born. And now, when she would do anything to help *us,* they won't let her. What a daft world! I'll go and see her tonight, on my way to the meeting. We're meeting at the Mid Kirk to arrange the time for the march.'

'Oh Matt! It's terrible!'

'Aye lass, it's terrible, right enough. But we won't forget it. I'll away now; just be easy, lass, till I come back.'

Bella just said, 'Oh, she did, did she?' and prepared to take Alice and little Bobbie under her wing.

She remembered Mrs Heathley. She had no doubt she would get the chance to deal with her acolyte, in good time.

As always, when she needed comfort – or celebration – she went out to the garden and looked at the river.

She raised her head to the mountains across – and tried to remember only the love she had had all her life.

Even the dark shadow born on the day of Joe's death

was less frightening: Joe, seeing her in his last moments, had looked and thought he saw the face of a sister he had not seen for over forty years. No, carrying it alone, this dark secret now seemed less grim, or possible. No, she thought; there's nothing wrong with Florrie; she had mourned for her lost love, but she had kept silent. And Joe, her twin, now at Glasgow University: there was no insidious illness or peculiarity in either of them.

'Ma? Are you all right?'

Florrie came out and put her arm round Bella's shoulder. 'Come in, Ma. It's getting cold.'

'I feel, suddenly, that I'm going to live for a long time yet, Florrie.'

'I'm sure you will Ma. You'll see us all out! Only come in now. Alice and Bobbie will be here soon.'

Slowly, she went into the front hall and looked in the mirror. Lines across her brow; eyes not so large, or deep-lashed as they were once – she was nearly ninety.

Yes, Alice – and the lady with the wee nose specs, the 'Mrs Heathleys' would pass: they *must*.

She looked through the window, rain-streaked with an occasional shaft of sunlight. The landscapes may change, a little. But the calm beauty of the lochs, the swift bouncing streams from the hills – they would stay. But it seemed that there were people in the world who cared nothing for calm beauty.

Strident voices from across the Channel; the cacophony of mankind's 'progress' in weaponry, since the bow and arrow, and soon, it was inevitable. Prosperity came again; factories needed workers to make torpedoes, bullets, tanks, guns, mines; for it seemed that only by killing, could the world look for peace. Surely there must be a silver lining, somewhere?

She watched Florrie put some coal on the fire. The late August evening, in that year of 1939, was chilly. Now she was ninety-one, and she had seen three wars.

'They're saying there's going to be another war, Ma. Do you think so?'

'It looks like it, Florrie love.'

'What for?'

What for, indeed.

On the Sunday, they listened to a very tired man telling the world that we were now at war with Germany.

Bella said, to no one in particular, angrily gazing over the river below: 'Oh! Will they *never* learn!'

EPILOGUE

On 19th January 1946, a cold day with the first winter snow, several hundred people gathered at the peak of the Lyle Hill to watch the unveiling of a monument. A cross: not the Cross of Calvary, but the Cross of Lorraine, in homage to men who had been no less crucified in the stupidity of total war. The inscription, on one side in English, and opposite in French, reads:

> This monument is dedicated to the memory of the sailors of the Free French Naval Forces who sailed from Greenock in the years 1940–1945 and who gave their lives in the Battle of the Atlantic for the liberation of France and the success of the Allied cause.

Bella, now 98, sat in a wheelchair, wrapped in blankets and a fur coat. The man who stood at the back of the chair, holding it, was her son Joe: Joe Mulligan's son.

'Education,' the first Joe Mulligan had said . . . *'that's the thing'*. And his son had gained a degree in history at the ancient University of Glasgow, and was now a professor there. The girl who stood beside the wheelchair, with her arm lovingly across Bella's shoulder, was Jenny, Joe's daughter; the lively, brilliant girl of 18 who was 'going to be an actress.' She had spent much of her schooldays with Bella and adored her.

'Not too cold, Grandma?'

'No, my love, just sad.'

Wartime memories, such as the children torpedoed on

the *City of Benares*, for children at sea always recalled the children on the ice of Newfoundland, would never leave her.

After the unveiling, privileged guests were given lunch at the Lorne in West Blackhall Street (McKay's tearooms). The Provost came to Bella at the end of the lunch.

'Bella, I must come and see you. Something very important has come up for next year.'

'Next year? God knows where *I'll* be next year!'

'Still with us, I think. I'll come tomorrow, about tea-time.'

His visit was short, but compelling, and his news was surprising. The centenary of one of the yards in the river had been in 1944, but there was no possibility of celebration during the war. Next year, the first *civilian* ship would be ready for launching, so they would combine the two events. One of the royal family had agreed to perform the ceremony. And the Provost personally invited Bella to be on the platform.

'Me? With the royal family? You're daft!'

June 1947

Bella was 99 now. Still upright, a little slower, but wise and dignified as always. The doorbell rang about 7 o'clock and Florrie let in the Provost, agitated, almost incoherent, and soaked. A telegram . . . the royal personage was indisposed; she suggested Mrs Munro perform the ceremony. And Bella said the same thing she had said a year ago. 'Me? You're daft!'

Launch day broke bright and sunny, a perfect June day. The big official car took Bella, Joe and Jenny to the shipyard. The bands in the shipyard at Charing Cross were playing 'Eternal Father Strong to Save', 'The Green Oak Tree', 'Scotland the Brave', and lastly 'The King'. Launches in plenty this river had seen, but never one like this, and never enough of them.

The great ship stood, held safe in the stocks, until the touch of a button should release her. The old men, the old riveters, platers, carpenters and engineers, watched the preparation with some misgivings. The lean years were dimmed; only the old remembered them – and surely they would never come again? Surely, Bella thought, as the car drew up at the covered entrance to the platform, surely her countrymen had more spunk than to *let* them come again? With loving hands helping her, Bella climbed the steps to the platform, red carpeted and curtained. Across, there was a boom with a camera and other cameras and microphones in odd places. Charlie Kingston, the Provost, led Bella to the window that looked straight on to the bridge.

'Just here, Bella.'

The TV producer asked: 'Just touch the button lightly after you've spoken. You know what to say?'

'Oh yes,' said Bella. 'I *know* what to say.' The last notes of the anthem died away. Hesitantly, at first, she went on, 'It is my great privilege and honour to name this ship *PSS Lancaster*.'

She said the time-honoured blessing – but, to the astonishment of the throng, she added a few special words of her own. She saw a great ship take the water, Clyde-built, slowly, almost contemptuously, to become a living thing as she met her natural element.

Waiting for Bella at the foot of the steps was her first son, Sandy, home from Australia, with stories to tell.

*

On a warm soft day in June 1950, Jenny pushed Bella's wheelchair into the garden – where she could see this shining corner that had been her whole world – the dancing river and the proud mountains.

'So you made it, you old Grandma?'

'Made what, child?'

'100 – 101 – now 102! Fantastic!'

'I think I'll have a wee sleep now, Jenny. There was another Jenny once. You should have been Jenny Mulligan.'

'I like that . . . I might use it . . . my next play is about an Irishman.'

'What's it called?'

'*Death has no tact.*'

Across three-quarters of a century, Bella looked at the lovely face and smiled: 'Neither has Life, come to that!' she said. And then, as she had done when first Flora McGarvie had taken her to her bosom, on that dark November morning a century ago, she sighed, and smiled, and slept . . .